Saltwater Joys

Dianna Brown

Published by Modern Betty Press, 2018.

This is a work of fiction. Similarities to real people, places, or events are entirely coincidental.

SALTWATER JOYS

First edition. May 4, 2018.

Copyright © 2018 Dianna Brown.

Written by Dianna Brown.

Dedication

This book is dedicated to my parents, Dennis and Nellie, for giving me roots in Newfoundland and Labrador. Thank you for reversing our families 'outmigration' during my childhood. No matter where I live, Newfoundland will always be considered my home. And to my Mom, who has been my dedicated reader over the years as Saltwater Joys was motivated by your love of reading. Thank you for your encouragement and multiple reads of my manuscript. It is said that writers write with a reader in mind, and for me that person is you. And to my Dad, thank you for your stories, facts and recounting our family history in Newfoundland. This book is also dedicated to Chris, Austin and Owen. Chris, thank you for giving me the opportunity to write and for always supporting me. For my two boys, I also dedicate this book to you, in hopes that it will inspire you to learn about and explore Newfoundland. It is a part of you and I hope I have instilled within you a feeling of home when you think of Newfoundland.

Acknowledgements: Thank you to a dear friend, Tammy Bailey, who was also a devoted reader of my first manuscript of Saltwater Joys. I am thankful for your feedback. Serendipity led me to author, Anne Sorbie, who helped me navigate the world of publishing, gave me direction and edited my beginning chapters, your insight was more than I could have ever asked for - thank you for your guidance. Thank you to my brilliant editors, Wendy Lukasiewics, Owl Editing, and Brandi Dickman. I am blessed to have crossed paths with each of you, and I am grateful for your attention to detail as well as the overall investment in helping me develop and fine tune the characters and plot. Thank you to Robyn Curdie, RLC Photography, for your photo of Ireland's Eye which was artistically rendered by the ever-talented Brandi Dickman, who is also a graphic designer. I am in awe of the cover of my novel as it has exceeded my expectation. It is a work of art. I also wanted to say thank you to author, Katherine Dell, for your mentorship leading up to the days before the release of this novel.

Saltwater Joys
Just to wake up in the morning,
To the quiet of the cove
And to hear Aunt Bessie talking to herself.
And to hear poor Uncle John,
Mumbling wishes to old Nell
It made me feel that everything was fine.
I was born down by the water,
It's here I'm gonna stay
I've searched for all the reasons
Why I should go away.
But I haven't got the thirst
For all those modern day toys
So I'll just take my chances
With those saltwater joys.
—Wayne Chaulk, *Saltwater Joys*

I am delighted to have the permission of Wayne Chaulk, from Buddy Wasisname and the Other Fellers www.buddywasisname.com to use his beloved song title as the title of my novel. Saltwater Joys is a song near and dear to my heart, and a song my Dad would strum on guitar while my sister, Crystal, and I sang— always for our Mom. It is also a song sang to my Nan Brown in the hospital as she prepared to transition to the distance shore of heaven. Thank you to my grandparents, Roy and Ruth Powell, for the many stories you've told me over the years and all of the fun times we've had together in Newfoundland, as well as my heavenly grandparents, John and Betty Brown. I feel blessed to have experienced saltwater joys during my visits to Happy Adventure and Sandy Cove, in Eastport, NL. These memories are ones I will remember forever.

Last but not least, for everyone that's contributed to my novel in meaningful ways: words of encouragement, helping me navigate the publishing world, assisting with research, discussions over coffee, reviews of my work, giving me honest opinions, and for helping me believe in myself.

> **But we loved with a love that was more than love—I and my Annabel Lee . . .**
>
> —Edgar Allen Poe, *Annabel Lee*

IF YOU EXPLORE ANY outport along Newfoundland's twenty-nine thousand kilometres of rocky coastline, you will step back in time and experience the fun-loving spirit of Newfoundland and Labrador. The settlement of Newfoundland began in the late 1500s, when Europeans claimed fishing rights over Newfoundland's cod-abundant waters. Money-hungry captains abandoned their seasonal workers so they could make room for more fish on their boats during the return trip across the Atlantic. These stranded souls had no choice but to make Newfoundland, in all her beauty and harshness, their home.

Fast forward four hundred years to the 1900s, when outport communities flourished with self-sufficient, honest, resourceful people capable of surviving Newfoundland's fickle weather and isolated geography. Their lilting voices and colourful language reflected their merry spirits, which built a breakwater within their hearts to protect them against the changing seasons and sometimes vindictive ocean. Despite the many hardships they endured—with no electricity, running water, plumbing, health care or roads to other communities—the fishing communities survived. That all changed when Newfoundlanders witnessed the largest forced mass migration brought about by a political shift—Newfoundland's confederation with Canada.

On March 31, 1949, one minute before midnight, on the eve of April Fool's Day, Joseph Smallwood, Newfoundland's Liberal premier, surrendered Newfoundland's independence and made Newfoundland the newest Canadian province. Joey Smallwood was thought both an angel and a devil for bringing social welfare benefits to Newfoundlanders and for tearing a unique people from its deeply rooted culture. In 1954, the provincial government began a formalized social and economic plan, the Centralization Program. Their ultimate goal was to funnel people into larger communities with social services, health care and education—basic services deemed too expensive to provide to hundreds of small outports. Families volunteered to resettle and relocate their homes to receive government assistance.

Many were of the mindset that they should resettle while resettlement paid. After the move, many regretted their decision and felt manipulated by the government's insidious plan. While some families were able to tow their houses over the water, others had to disassemble them and rebuild. It was a time of desperation as these older homes often could not withstand such a move, and families could not afford to buy a new house with the money provided by the government. A feeling of betrayal consumed many Newfoundlanders as they sold their boats and fishing gear, abandoned the homes they had built with their own hands, and gave up a way of life handed down over generations. By 1959, twenty-nine communities had voted in favour of resettlement.

In 1965, the federal government made another self-serving attempt to concentrate outport families in "growth centres" designated by the Fisheries Household Resettlement Program. These larger settlements were equipped with fish plants, infrastructure, schools, hospitals, water and sewer. At least 90 percent of the families had to resettle to receive government assistance. By 1972, twenty-seven thousand people had relocated from two hundred and twenty communities. By 1975, two hundred and fifty outports were abandoned, and 40 percent of Newfoundland's population had been resettled.

When families resettled their homes to the larger growth centres, they soon discovered these new communities lacked enough jobs to employ everyone. Local fishermen had seniority over the fishing grounds around the growth centres, so men who had fished their entire lives were forced to work in fish plants or were unemployed. The cost of relocation for an average family was much greater than what the family had received. For most, it took twenty years or so to replace the money lost during resettlement.

There was no pride in accepting the government's assistance, only a sense of displacement. In hindsight, these Newfoundlanders realized they had traded their very identities for the promise of modernization. They had given up a life they would long for evermore. Many felt cheated out of their heritage, and some felt as though they'd robbed their children of a better, less-complicated way of life. Returning to their birthplace was an impossible dream, and an unbearable sadness and grief swelled in their hearts. The emotional impact divided friends and families, further antagonizing the already heart-wrenching move. Resettlement cultivated a sense of loss that was passed down to the generations that followed, as children listened to romanticized stories of outport living from parents or grandparents. As the spirit of the abandoned outports dissipated, the communities along Newfoundland's coastline became ghost towns.

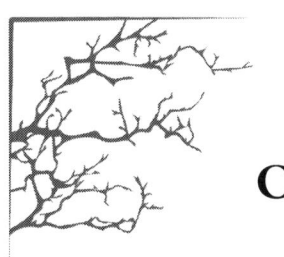

Chapter 1

October 12, 1965

THE INCESSANT SURF of the Atlantic Ocean crashed against the craggy shoreline of Newfoundland's Smith Sound, where a young seagull soared across the thoroughfare tickle, a narrow passage between the islands of Random Island and Ireland's Eye. The gull passed many small coves until it turned a corner to enter a horseshoe-shaped harbour with a tapered inlet. The harbour held the same name as the island: Ireland's Eye. Marsh and low-lying shrubs, plump with wild berries, ascended from the rocky shoreline to summits of grey rock that jutted and eventually blended into rolling, grassy hills on each side of the entry to the harbour. Cold-hardy black spruce, fir and yellow-leafed birch trees lined the high hills above.

All along the harbor, hoary sheds dotted the shoreline fixed to rickety wharves jutting out from the water's edge. Reminiscent of their once bright-red ochre colour, the faded stages were used by fishermen to split and salt codfish. Retired nets, tied by fishermen's hands, lay torn and useless on the ground. Dozens of empty wharves were held up by countless skinny sticks meticulously tied together, each stick speckled with patches of white barnacles that marked the water level at high tide. The tiny crustaceans permanently attached themselves, adapting to the rising and falling tide by sliding little plates across their delicate bodies for protection. At high tide, the barnacles' feathery legs beat rhythmically with the rocking waves to draw in plankton.

The entire harbour was peppered with empty fish flakes—hundreds of tight rows of chopped trees with barren branches, spread out like a conveyer belt in an assembly line over the foreshore. Once used to dry and bleach salted codfish, the flakes allowed air to circulate under the fish while preventing the fish from burning on the wooden planks or the rocky ground in hot weather. Wooden boats, also home to legions of barnacles, were hauled up on the grassy banks and overturned, like a memorial of Newfoundland's lost cultural heritage. These barnacles, abandoned to the elements, were left to dry up and starve to death.

In the distance, on the highest hill at the plateau of the harbour, stood a large white church. It overlooked weather-beaten saltbox houses, built two-storeys high with steep saddle roofs, nestled along the cliffs on both sides of the harbour. All the front windows faced the sea. The uneven terrain was covered with large boulders surrounded by grass and bushes. There were no roads and no vehicles on the small island since everything was within walking distance. Narrow cowpaths led around the shoreline meadows, from house to house and down to a small creek to the right of the harbour. It was the only source of fresh water, and each day families carried the heavy buckets they filled from the creek to their homes.

As they had for generations, the community survived with no electricity, running water or sewer. While they secretly longed for the conveniences of centralized living, they saw no need to change what they were used to living without. The general store and the post office had been their connection to the rest of the world, but Confederation took these services away. There was now no hope for a road lined with electrical power from the sound to the thoroughfare, with a causeway across the tickle.

On the shore, twenty empty houses sat perched in defiance, deemed unfit to withstand the force of the ocean or unworthy of being dismantled and rebuilt in a new location. Many of the houses challenged the boards that leaned against them, soon to be nailed over doors and windows, a homeowner's desperate attempt to protect wistful memories of days gone by. Smoke had stopped rising from the chimneys, and flickering candlelight no longer glowed from the windows at night. The houses stood bold, but as still as gravestones, left to crumble under the blows of strong northwestern winds. For now, they resisted both wind and sea, watching over the bay, yearning for the longliners to come back for them. But they couldn't escape their fate: they were soon-to-be relics of forgotten traditions, triumphs and hardships once taken in stride.

The spring of 1959 had brought news of the government's plan for Ireland's Eye. In anticipation, ninety-two residents had gathered with crossed arms and anxious faces around the government wharf. Women shushed their children and shooed them behind their long skirts. A government official stood before the community with a long letter scroll. He cleared his throat and pulled his glasses from his shirt pocket, positioning them on the tip of his nose.

"The Canadian government will resettle the community into promising growth centres," he said in a voice devoid of inflection, "with necessities and services that Ireland's Eye will forever lack."

The residents were not surprised by the offer that followed. They knew that providing services to each outport would be too expensive. The official then offered the residents a monetary amount to move to the growth centres, dependent on the size of their family.

"Every person over the age of eighteen is required to vote," the official added. He handed a pile of papers to one of the fishermen standing beside him and passed the store owner a locked box to collect the votes.

"What do we do with these?" the fisherman asked, his face pink as his illiterate eyes stared blankly at the first page.

"They'll answer any questions you might have," the official said, putting his glasses back in his front pocket. "I'll be back next week, as long as the weather holds up, to collect the ballots."

"Oh yes, oh yes," the store owner said, holding tight to the locked box. He offered a pretentious smile.

The official waved his hand dismissively at the sight of all the downcast eyes. "I knows it's an awful shock, but I believes it's for your own good. Lots of the other outports have resettled, and you must've known it was coming." A half grin curled on one side of his face.

A sharp voice abruptly rang out from the silent crowd. "I hears tell from the fellas in Trinity that they wished they never left."

"In that case, you all better be of the same mind," the official said, a little too quickly. He tipped his hat to the crowd and boarded his boat.

Since some of the residents of Ireland's Eye were illiterate, votes were cast inside the schoolhouse, with volunteer readers to help those who couldn't read. It was no secret even before everyone cast their ballots that the majority would agree to leave. The money was a motivator to get going and a hope for a brighter future for the children. Families were given subsidies and a promise of employment, and no one wanted to miss out on a once-in-a-lifetime opportunity. Many figured their kids would leave eventually, so they might as well follow them now.

Over the ensuing years, many of Ireland's Eye's homes were towed to the New Bonaventure area, as families vanished like the early morning fog after sunrise. They left with sadness, but to keep their pride they plastered false bravado on their faces, convincing themselves they had made the right choice.

When the population of Ireland's Eye had fallen to sixteen in 1964, each person became fierce with independence. Since the tasks of daily life were no longer a community effort, each individual had to master each job. The men spent most of their time hauling boatloads of fish from the cod traps to the stages to split the fish. The women worked around the clock, curing and drying the fish, cooking, washing clothes and dishes, ironing, sewing, cleaning, and carrying buckets of fresh water from the creek to their homes. Many mornings were spent on hands and knees scrubbing floors. Oak panels lining the walls of the homes were polished and the kitchen table was always covered in freshly ironed white linen. They took pride in the little they had accumulated over their lifetimes, and they worked hard to keep everything just so. Still, even with everyone pitching in, life was difficult. There were no small children left on the island, and the absence of shrieks, laughter and the chatter of little voices left an unexpected stillness in the harbour.

Although the downsized community believed the others had been wrong to resettle, in the winter of 1965 their capabilities were found to be overestimated. The Coopers' youngest son fell sick with a life-threatening fever, and the nearest doctor was a boat ride away. Despite an incoming storm, the Cooper family boarded their boat and rowed for New Bonaventure.

Days passed with no sight of the Coopers, until Mrs. Cooper and her son returned in an unfamiliar boat. With them came the news that Mr. Cooper hadn't stayed in New Bonaventure but had returned to Ireland's Eye that night. The others couldn't hide their shock and horror. Mr. Cooper was missing, and when night fell, despair swelled in each heart. A couple of days later, his body was found in the waters near the harbour. Mrs. Cooper's, and the remaining families' grief, coupled with the lack of services, led the community to accept the government's offer and say goodbye to Ireland's Eye. There was nothing left to prove, hold onto or fight for. They had fought a losing battle for as long as they could, and now it seemed any further efforts, half-hearted at best, would leave them defeated anyway. The government had won.

OCTOBER 12, 1965, MARKED a monumental juncture for Ireland's Eye. It was moving day for the remaining residents of the harbour. Although the weather was cool, John's back was soaked with sweat. He didn't flinch as dry slivers of rope penetrated his calloused hands. John joined in the chorus of men's gruff voices as they hollered the shanty "Johnny Boker," progressively quickening with each consecutive repetition.

"Oh! Do, my Johnny Boker, come rock and roll me over. Do, my Johnny Boker, *do*!"

They shouted the last word of each line, a cue to heave the ropes in unison. John listened to his father-in-law, Bill, lead the song, the loudest voice among them. Bill was also the foreman of the summer-house hauling operation. Half a century of fishing and backbreaking labour had crippled his body with arthritis, so he couldn't physically help haul the homes.

A dozen men, including John's closest childhood friend, Charlie Hodder, had returned to Ireland's Eye to help haul the last livable houses out of the harbour. The wives of the men came along to keep the men fed. They also came to reminisce and gossip and to search for any forgotten belongings in the homes they left behind.

John's foot slipped on the rough gravel trail of the steep slope of the hauling path. The men thrust each weather-beaten clapboard house onto a bed of skid logs and pulled each one down to the shore over a long path of peeled logs coated in a slippery concoction of cod blubber. John clenched his fists around the rope and took a deep breath, giving one more massive effort to pull this house a few more feet.

This particular house being hauled was John's. It had belonged to his father, Ned Lee, who died of some unknown ailment at age forty-nine. That was in 1958, when John was just nineteen. As Ned's only son, the house was handed down to him. Ned had been a crucial contributor to the survival of the small community, and before he passed, John had realized he needed to know his father's secrets. In Ned's dark, musty bedroom, John had listened intently as his father whispered about the particular way to manoeuvre his finicky boat, the specific place he'd hidden his possessions, the details of family traditions long forgotten. John regretted not asking his father more, regretted he hadn't listened longer and paid better attention when he was younger. But he had thought his father invincible. John knew that the knowledge Ned shared—like the tip of an iceberg—was miniscule compared to what he held inside his head. It was too much for mere words. Moments before he inhaled his last breath, Ned made specific requests for his funeral.

A makeshift casket had been placed in the middle of the living room floor the night Ned died. All the curtains had been pulled together. Upstairs, John lifted his father and hoisted him over his shoulder. He carried him down the stairs, not alone, but with friends following in a solemn procession. In front of the casket, John braced his father's stiff back with one hand, using the other to support his head. John's muscles quivered under the weight of his father's body. Charlie sprang forward to help, but John dropped Ned into the casket with a clobbering bang. Everyone gasped, and watched in silence, expecting Ned to sit up, jolted awake. When he didn't stir, John put pennies on his eyes, tied his big toes together, and pushed the coffin until Ned's toes pointed to the east. He then wrapped a bandage around his head to keep his jaw in position.

Tears blurred John's vision as he scoured the room for the picture of his mother, Marylou, that his father loved so much. He placed it on his father's chest and promised to pay his respects each Sunday, and to hold fast to the life his father had worked so hard to preserve. The casket remained in place for three days, until there was no chance Ned would miraculously wake up. John dug a grave that day. The next morning, he buried his father beside his mother, with the community gathered around him.

John could have left to resettle after his father's death. He stayed to help the dwindling community survive. He had taken over his father's boat and small crew, and for six years he fished the waters around Ireland's Eye. He had considerable debt to pay to the shrewd and stingy merchant from St. John's. As with everyone else in Ireland's Eye, John both dreaded and anticipated Thomas Slade's visits to the community each fall, when he picked up the dried codfish in exchange for food and necessities. The residents survived on a barter system. Cash was a rare sight. A bad season meant the debt carried over to the next year, and John's father had seen many bad seasons. Not even death excused debt, so Ned's years of debt had transferred over to John's tab. John felt trapped, yet he vowed to cherish his time in the harbour with the love of his life, Annabel. The two had announced their engagement in December 1964, so it had come as no surprise when Annabel had yet another announcement in the new year: she was expecting John's baby. A wedding was held in the spring, with friends and family packing the church until they were overflowing out the doors. Everyone welcomed the reason to return home.

Now, Annabel was due any day. She and John were staying with her parents, Bill and Lillian Toope. Bill and Lillian's house would soon be abandoned too, as it was too old to withstand the calmest of waves. Ruth, the community's midwife, had agreed to return to Ireland's Eye to deliver the baby. Ruth wouldn't hear of taking Annabel out on the water this late in her pregnancy; it was too risky. So, she and her husband Ed had made plans to stay after the house haul. For John, Annabel and the Toopes, it was a valuable excuse to remain a little longer in the harbour, and savour the extra time together.

John's muscles ached with heaviness. As the house inched forward, he could hear the clatter of cupboard doors and the clank of cutlery from inside. The men only stopped when the shanty ended and the house was down to the shore ready for the big float, a large wooden raft built on top of steel fuel barrels to prevent it from tipping on its journey as it bobbed through fourteen kilometres of tidal currents. Once the men secured long logs around the perimeter of the house to hold it in position on the raft, they marched in hip waders into the freezing rush of the tide and began to ease the house into the water. John held his breath when the house completely left the land and took its first plunge into the sea. At any time, the tide could set the raft off balance and tip the house to crash on the shoreline. When the raft steadied, the men whooped and hollered. They prepared for the last leg of the journey by lacing the ends of the ropes to a couple of punts, twenty-foot round-bottom boats, that would tow the house through the shallow water to a longliner, a larger-decked fishing boat, that waited farther out in the harbour.

As John looked at his floating house, he wondered if all the work was worth it. He could be happy anywhere with Annabel, but he longed to stay in the only place he'd ever known as home. He cursed Confederation and everything it had taken from him. He couldn't imagine any other life besides the one he led in Ireland's Eye. Here, he had dreamed of building a future with his wife and child.

"Take a break now, b'ys!" Bill said.

Many of the men sat down to ease their backs or darted to the last standing outhouse. A few walked up the path to the small creek, where they slurped cold water from their cupped hands.

John thought his floating house looked as awkward as the sight of a fish flopping around on land. It was something out of place—something unnatural. He secretly wished the house would sink. The impending death of the house brought him a sense of pleasure in misfortune. In his mind, he smashed the house to end his demise. Despite his violent thoughts, the house stayed afloat and was set for its tow across the Smith Sound.

Bill sat down on a large beach rock beside John and offered him a cigarette. John lit up and puffed with haste, his attention now focused on the nets he had set with Charlie early in the morning. He'd need Charlie's help to empty the cod traps and haul the fish to shore that evening, but he also knew Charlie needed to head back to New Bonaventure with his wife Sarah, who had returned to the harbour to visit Annabel. Charlie and Sarah needed to get back to their five-year-old son, James, whom they'd left in New Bonaventure in the care of Charlie's oldest brother's wife.

John had considered selling his father's punt and fishing gear to a man in Trinity to help pay off his accumulated debt, but it wouldn't have been enough, not even with the fish John cured over the summer and an old gold coin he had in his possession. He decided to make a secret deal with Thomas Slade: John would have a fresh load of cod ready for the merchant's return trip to St. John's. Although fishermen were often warned of the dangers of guaranteeing a fresh haul of codfish on a particular date—setting yourself up for crucifixion, his father had said—John dreamed of a clean financial slate, a life free of the clutches of debt that tied him to the merchant. With a fresh catch, all debt would be cleared, so John spent his spare time mending old nets left behind by resettled fishermen. Thomas called it a favour; John called it an opportunity. Thomas was coming in the morning, leaving John no choice but to haul in the fish that evening.

John called to the men to head back to the floating house after the short break, anxious to tow it to its new destination.

"Keep an eye out for those fellows," Bill said, eyeing Charlie and his two brothers. "Charlie might be your buddy, but that's yours and Annabel's future on the water. The harbour is as safe as being in God's pocket, sheltered from the winds and all, but as soon as you turns the corner out the harbour, you're at the mercy of the sea." He cracked his gnarled knuckles and massaged his left hand.

"I'll do me best, Skipper." John took a long draw of his cigarette, and a brisk gust of wind made him shiver. He wondered if he was mistaking his sudden anxiety for anticipated freedom. It was hard to decipher which one was which.

"When she's being towed, make sure she's not being pulled too hard on one side." Bill's eyes narrowed, directly gazing at the house. "Use that fog horn if you needs to get their attention." He jutted his chin toward the longliner. "Ruth says Annabel's ready any day now, so you'd best hurry back."

"Yes, sir."

"I'll fire a couple of shots if the baby starts coming, just in case you're close enough to hear." Bill gave John a pat on the back. "That way you knows to hurry home to be here when the baby's born."

"Yes, sir," John said. "I'll make sure the b'ys gets the house safe across the sound."

"Fair winds to you and hurry back." Bill gave John another firm pat on the back before standing up and heading back to his house.

John turned around to find himself in Annabel's firm embrace. Once he had his arms wrapped around her, she kissed him square on the lips. The bulge of her belly moved between them.

John caught sight of Sarah, as she ran down to the boat to meet Charlie.

"She wants to stay a little longer," Annabel said, "just in case I has the baby before you gets back."

The entire harbour got an earful of Charlie and Sarah arguing. Charlie wanted Sarah to go with him that moment, but she had her mind made up to stay with Annabel until John returned.

"Will you be back for supper?" Annabel asked.

"I'll be back before too long. We got one last haul of cod to bring in on our way back."

"What are you talking about?"

"It's a bit of extra money to get us through, is all. So we can start fresh." John tried to soothe away her doubts, but his voice was full of impatience to get going.

Annabel looked down at her belly. "Just be careful then."

"I will."

Sarah approached the couple triumphantly as she walked away from Charlie and hooked arms with Annabel. "Charlie said we can stay the extra night."

A lone crow cried out over the harbour from the calm copper weathervane anchored to the top of the church steeple. It caught John's attention as he boarded his punt and pulled out of the harbour.

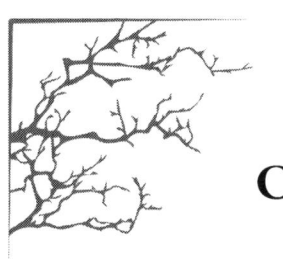

Chapter 2

JOHN HAD FALLEN IN love with Annabel when they were both sixteen. Living in an outport really limited the chances of falling in love at first sight since everyone was a stone's throw from each other. Fences didn't exist between homes. Instead, they lined the meadows to prevent goats from eating turnips, cabbage, carrots and berries in private gardens. Doors were always unlocked, and a knock on the door was usually troublesome news. Everyone knew everyone, and what one person knew, everyone knew within hours.

John and Annabel had been friends since childhood, when John often got in trouble for chasing her around the schoolyard. Too young to help on the flakes back then, they kept themselves busy playing hide-and-seek with the other children, teasing the tide, picking gooseberries, gathering wood in their arms, catching bugs in the meadow by the shoreline, or popping myrrh bladders with twigs and collecting the sap—commonly used around the harbour to heal wounds—in small glass jars. Together they sought mischief and adventure.

Her small and feminine features notwithstanding, Annabel tried hard to be the son her father never had, and she always kept up with the boys. John admired Annabel's courage as Bill taught his daughter from a young age how to fish from his boat anchored in the harbour. She was the only child after her mother's many miscarriages. Although a girl's role in the outports was to mind the flakes, prepare meals, mend clothes, cook, clean, and care for the children, Annabel would often sneak away from the flakes to help her father carry loads of codfish from the wharf to the stage, where John, the appointed cutthroat, would catch her peering over his shoulder as he'd wield his stubby knife to slit the throat and slice open the white belly of a codfish. The sound of a snapping fish head, mixed with the screech of hungry gulls, would send typical girls into hysterics when they occasionally visited the fishing stage to bring water or sandwiches for the men. Annabel never flinched. Every now and then, John would give Annabel the knife. She was never bothered by the stink of the fish or the sliminess of a fish eye when she jabbed her thumb through it. With a quick stroke of her blade, Annabel didn't seem to mind when the head and guts of the fish fell through the hole in the stage floor between her feet into the lapping ocean below. Like her father, she was careful to collect the livers of the fish and would drop them in a bucket beside the table.

As they got older, John would go fishing while Annabel stayed on the shore to wash the salted fish in a metal fishing tub. She would often tell John she'd rather be out on the ocean than left on the shore with the women. When she turned fifteen, Annabel talked Bill into letting her fish alongside him. John would be in his own father's boat, directly across from them, and he would admire Annabel's mass of loosely tied brown curls as they all reeled in nets brimming with codfish. After a day on the water, John found himself tickling Annabel's side each time he passed by. Their childhood bond gave them a special connection, and John couldn't hide his adoration for Annabel.

JOHN'S MEMORY OFTEN wandered back to the community garden party of 1959—the last of its kind in Ireland's Eye. He remembered how that night had set in him an acute desire. He and Annabel were no longer kids, and he needed to make a move to prove to Annabel how serious he was about her, before resettlement changed everything.

He mourned the end of such parties, where women's lips would gossip as they prepared salads, fresh buns, moose stew, and heaps of fish and brewis with plenty of desserts; where races and games were played through the day and a driftwood bonfire blazed on the beach at night. He loved how the shadows of the crowd danced on the white exterior of the church, and how the air bustled with dense melodies of guitars, accordions and fiddles, as a chorus of voices kept the night alive for young and old alike. In John's memory, he could hear the popular folk song "Mussels in the Corner" echoing around the harbour. He had plucked the strings of his guitar, stomped his foot to the upbeat tempo, and stolen the odd glance at Annabel dancing with her friends. When he caught her eye, she motioned him over to dance with her. He shrugged his shoulders and did a little jig with his legs from where he sat. She shooed away his foolishness with her hand.

Eventually, the music slowed as Oscar, the oldest resident in the harbour, played the "Newfoundland Waltz" on his accordion.

John's heart beat like a kick drum on the inside of his chest as he put his guitar down and walked toward Annabel. She stood alongside the church, tired from all the dancing.

"You want to dance?" John held out his hand. There was something about Annabel that made him eager to be near her. When she gave him her hand without a second thought, he couldn't wipe the smile off his face. They stood for a moment, looking awkwardly at one another, until Annabel put her arm on John's shoulder and stepped on his foot. She smiled up at him. He pulled her a little closer, his gut flip-flopping, and they began waltzing with clumsy feet and clasped hands.

"We'd make good dancers, Johnny, if it weren't for a couple of things," Annabel remarked, looking down.

"What's that?"

"Our feet," she teased, her face beaming with delight.

John had a hard time keeping his hands off her, so he placed her leading hand on his shoulder, and rested both of his hands on the small curve of her back. He could smell a touch of perfume on her neck. The crowd turned into a blur around them.

When the song ended, John lowered his head to kiss her lips. He knew she'd never kissed any of the boys in the harbour before, so he closed his eyes, expecting to feel the sting of her palm across his cheek or Bill yanking him away by his collar. John's eyes opened wide when her lips gently swept against his cheek.

SALTWATER JOYS

"Let's get outta here," she said, a glimmer in her eyes. She grabbed his hand and led him down to the shore, toward the dying fire in the distance.

They sat on a flat rock on the beach, the salty wind tangling Annabel's long locks about her face. The rising moon was a pearl in the black sky, shining bright among the blinking stars. John wanted to kiss her again, but Charlie and Sarah came running and nearly tripped over them in the dark.

"What are you guys up to?" Sarah asked.

"Probably the same thing as you guys," John said with a wink.

The four of them moved to sit beside the fire, but they weren't alone. Across the smouldering embers sat old Skipper Ray, smoking a cigarette. Charlie flashed John a half smile and nuzzled his face into Sarah's strawberry-blonde hair. Ray held a long stick and poked it into the dying fire. A burst of flankers, like tiny fireworks, exploded in front of him, giving off just enough light to illuminate the strange look in his eye.

"You fellas ever heard about Pirate Peter Easton?" he asked. His words slurred together in a sombre voice. An empty bottle of moonshine clanked against the rocks at his feet.

"We've heard it a dozen times, b'y," John said. He pulled Annabel closer to his chest when he felt her sit a little straighter.

The old man cleared his voice. "Not this one, you ain't."

With the embers reflecting in his eyes, he pointed out to the harbour. "The ghost ship still makes her rounds. I hears tell that not too long ago, a few skippers in Trinity saw the ghost ship come up alongside their boat then disappear in a puff of smoke. If you asks me, it was Easton looking for more unfortunate souls that died at sea." Smoke slipped through his lips.

"You expects us to believe that?" Charlie chuckled.

"You know, he buried three chests of gold at Money Point," Ray continued. He turned his head and pointed a long, crooked finger toward the lookout, past the church and behind the graveyard. "He shot one of his own crew and buried him with the gold to protect it for eternity." Ray lowered his finger, his eyes squeezed tight. "Rumour has it that three men tried to dig it up a while back. They moved the rocks all night long." He opened his eyes, and with a flick of his wrist sent his glowing cigarette butt into the ocean. "When they went back in the morning, the hole was all filled up again with the rocks. Some says it was the ghost of the dead pirate putting them back. The chests are still up there, you know. Long as I heard, no one's ever gotten them."

"Lord tunderin'!"

Annabel and Sarah squealed at the booming voice behind them. It was Beatrice, Ray's wife, a lady who resembled rising bread dough overflowing the rim of a bowl.

"They don't need to hear them kind of stories, you old fool. Come on now, give 'em all nightmares, you will." She grabbed his arm and marched the drunken man home.

"You wanna go see for ourselves?" John whispered in Annabel's ear. She shoved herself into his chest, nodded and looked toward Money Point.

John and Charlie glanced at each other, said they'd be right back, and ran to John's house to grab an oil lantern, a pocketful of matches and a shovel. Money Point was about a mile south, past the graveyard. The garden party showed no signs of slowing down, so they hoped no one would notice they were missing for a couple of hours.

The teenagers were careful not to get spotted entering the woods together. Many courting couples had occasionally been reported missing around the harbour, often by a younger sibling or a jealous friend who saw the pair go into the woods together. Sam and Bev were one couple who had been forever humiliated. Billy goats on the island were kept for milk and meat, and while they were very tame and could be caught easily, they were notorious clothes eaters. When Sam and Bev engaged in premarital courtship, a roaming goat found their pile of clothing and chewed it to pieces. In their unfortunate predicament, they planned to curl up together in the woods until night and wait for darkness to sneak home. The community thought the worst—that they had perished at sea—so everyone set out in all directions to search the beach and then moved inland before nightfall. The missing young lovers were found stark naked just before dusk.

The snickers eventually faded, but for years after, when Sam, Bev or their families stepped foot in the church, a suppressed belly laugh would turn into a snort that spread like wildfire through the congregation. When the minister demanded answers to this growing nuisance, he lost his composure as someone took a laughing fit. Many churchgoers would have to leave their pews to grab some fresh air, take a few deep breaths, and do their best to return as serious as when they first arrived.

The adults could never be too careful. With no medical facility, and the nearest doctor a boat ride to New Bonaventure, the threat of tuberculosis, Spanish flu, scarlet fever, whooping cough or diphtheria was challenge enough without the constant worry of their children slipping and drowning. The beauty of the outport masked the danger of the turbulent crashing tides, with an undertow that pulled, drowned and claimed young lives for its own. Though Sam's and Bev's parents had been bothered by their teenagers' illicit behaviour, they were quietly relieved their son and daughter were safe.

John and Charlie made their way back to the beach to meet the girls. John pulled out a match from his pocket, flicked it against his trousers and lit the lantern. The girls led the way, shoulder to shoulder, giggling nervously. They stayed within the circle of light, rarely crossing the threshold of darkness ahead.

"This is even better, John, me boy," Charlie said under his breath as he rubbed his hands together. "I thought the ghost ship would be enough to get them into the woods."

"Yes, b'y, is that all that's ever on your mind?" John elbowed him in the arm.

"Hell, ya!" Charlie said without hesitation. "You'd be lying if you told me otherwise."

Once they passed the graveyard and headed deep into the woods, the moon shone higher in the sky and helped light their way. Just when they doubted their trail, they turned a corner and found the distinct pile of rocks at Money Point. A dense fog had made its way inland, disguising the precipice of a cliff that shot straight down to the ocean. The tide beat a distant, slow rhythm on the shore beneath them, breaking the sinister sound of silence and warning them not to venture any further.

Before John knew it, Sarah and Charlie were pressed up against a tree with absolutely no interest in anything but each other.

"Charlie, stay outta them woods, you hear?" John's voice was stern.

Charlie gave him the middle finger and, within minutes, disappeared into the edge of darkness with Sarah.

Annabel grabbed John's hand. "Come on, Johnny. You're not scared, are you?" She pulled him toward the rock pile near the edge of the cliff.

"I don't trust the two of them, is all."

"They're fine. How far down do you think it is?" Annabel circled the pile of rocks.

"Frig, Annabel, I don't know." John looked toward the woods. "That fog's going to be moving in, and I don't think there's time to move that many rocks. Let's get the b'ys and get outta here."

"Johnny, we came all this way. Help me dig." She began plucking at the rocks, like digging up turnips in the garden. "Come on!" A devilish smile grew wide on her face.

John set aside the lantern, and a half hour later they had dug a hole in a corner of the rock pile down into the ground. John stood up straight and turned his back to see if he could spot Charlie and Sarah, when Annabel grabbed his arm.

"Holy moly, Johnny! Is that what I thinks it is?"

John grabbed the lantern, holding it high over his head and saw a flash of gold glisten from between a section of shale rocks. "It can't be. That old bugger must've planted a bit of fool's gold, knowing we'd be stunned enough to come down here."

Annabel wriggled one tiny hand through the small crevice and pulled from the rocks a gold coin. Her eyes were wide. "But it's heavy. It must be worth a fortune."

John tipped the coin from her hand into his. The coolness and weight proved to him it was legit, but he put it between his teeth anyway.

"Is it real?" Annabel asked.

John stood dumbfounded.

"Johnny, the story must be true!" She started grabbing more rocks. "Let's keep digging until we finds the treasure. Can you imagine how much it'd all be worth?"

"Come on, Annabel. I don't have a good feeling about this. That old skipper said the pirate ghosts filled the hole back in to protect the treasure. What if it buries us alive?"

"That can't happen 'cause there's no such thing as ghosts." She tossed a rock in his direction. "Besides, we must be awful close if we found one piece of gold already."

"Annabel, I hears something!" John grabbed her hand and pulled. She moved with him, but resisted when they heard low voices and the crunch of dead leaves.

"Don't be foolish." Annabel smiled. "Sarah told me Charlie used that one on her a while back."

The low voices turned to moans. John's eyes darted to where Charlie and Sarah had disappeared into the woods. He walked over with the lantern.

"They're gone."

"You're not fooling me, Johnny. Tell those two to come out." Annabel walked past him and peered into the trees. "Touch me, and I'll send you to kingdom come."

"No, Annabel, I'm not pulling anything." He held the lantern up to cast light down the path from which they came. "Look, the fog is rolling in again, and it's gonna be hard to find our way home."

"You'd like that, wouldn't you?"

"Yes. No. I don't know. I just wants to get the hell outta here."

Branches cracked and the moans got louder.

John shook his head. "Sarah! Charlie! Come on, we're leaving!"

From behind them, a towering figure cloaked in shadows approached. John dropped the lantern, tossed Annabel over his shoulder, and ran toward the path.

"Johnny!" Annabel pounded his back. "Fire!"

John stopped and turned around. The lantern had burst into flames, lighting the dry brush around it. The dark figure unveiled itself as Sarah clumsily climbed off Charlie's shoulders.

"What the hell!" John set Annabel on her feet, and they both ran back toward the fire.

John and Charlie hauled off their sweaters in one quick motion and started beating the growing flames. Annabel grabbed the shovel and hastily threw dirt in the direction of the fire. Sarah stomped the flames with her boots. Since the fire was surrounded by rocky ground, there was nowhere for it to go.

"I'm going to kill you, Charlie!" John clobbered him in the chest, knocking both of them to the ground.

"Sorry, b'y!" Charlie wriggled under John's weight. "We were just trying to have a bit of fun. With you so afraid of ghosts and all."

Annabel grinned. "Is that so, Johnny?"

John stood and said nothing.

With no lantern, the couples walked home in the moonlight, now hazy under a thick blanket of fog. John held tight to Annabel's hand, guiding her around large rocks and bulging roots that might trip her. Charlie and Sarah followed close behind, but no one spoke. When they reached the perimeter of the woods, they saw women scooting children into houses and men carrying away the chairs and tables from the day's events.

"Goodnight, you two," Charlie said as he winked at John. "I got to get this pretty girl home so her father don't shoot me."

Sarah gave Annabel a hug. "I'll tell Lillian you'll be home the once . . . , if you want to, you know . . . ." She pulled away and spoke louder. "You swat him if he tries to pull anything on you."

John and Annabel were silent as Sarah and Charlie disappeared into the haze of fog that curled all around them. John had no idea what time it was, and he didn't care. He could feel Annabel's desire to linger a little longer, so they took a walk down to her father's wharf. He realized he was still holding her hand. The wind picked up and brought a chill that sent Annabel's body into tiny convulsions. John took off his sweater, dirty and full of holes from the fire, and offered it to her.

"I don't know how warm it'll keep you." He helped her pull it over her shoulders.

They sat on the wharf, peaceful and quiet, listening to the ripple of the tide and the onset of plinking raindrops. John pulled the coin from his pocket.

"What do you think it's worth?" he asked.

"I don't know, but I think you should hold on to it in case my mudder or fadder finds it. They'd keep it. Better for you to have it and put it toward the future."

John put it back in his pocket and glanced toward the woods to see if anything might have followed them out.

"Johnny, we better go." She put her hands over her head to shield herself from the rain.

"Yes, we should." He wrapped his arm around her shoulder. "It's really coming down now."

Annabel nestled her head into his chest. Neither of them moved until, in a burst, a downpour of cold rain soaked them. Annabel jumped up and sucked in a deep breath of air. John was at her side, teeth chattering as cold water streamed down his back. He felt no hesitation from Annabel when he grabbed her hand and ran up the slick wharf to the door of Bill's stage. He swallowed hard as he unlatched the hook. They snuck inside, still holding hands. The rain pounded the rind-cladded roof.

"They won't blame us for coming in here until the rain stops." Annabel was practically shouting.

John latched the door and pulled out a match from his trouser pocket. He flicked it with his thumbnail, and a fragile flame danced. The blackness lifted, and he saw her face, drenched like morning dew speckled upon flower petals. The match burnt out. No others would light, so they stood awkwardly in the dark, until the flash from a lightning bolt lit the room around them. A loud clap of thunder followed, rattling the shed.

Annabel grabbed John's arm.

"We could make a run for it," John said, pulling her shivering body closer. He hoped she couldn't hear the throb of his heart that banged loudly in his ears, louder than the thunder that boomed all around them.

John looked down the same moment Annabel looked up, and he tasted the sting of salt on her lips. They stayed like that for a moment, neither knowing what to do next, until John leaned in and pressed a little harder. When he felt her kiss him back, he lifted his musty sweater over her shoulders, and she struggled out of its wet confines. His next brazen attempt to lift her shirt was met with a slap on his hand, but it never slowed their kiss.

John could have stood there with Annabel forever, but the thunder of her father's voice broke their trance. The shed was quiet, and John hadn't noticed that the rain stopped.

Annabel let go of him and fumbled to unlatch the door. "In here!" she called. "We got outta the storm!"

John pulled her back for one more kiss.

"Johnny, we gotta go, for sure this time," she said, pulling him to follow her. "Come on, before you drowns me in love out here."

John wished with all his might that he could follow her up to her bedroom and fall asleep beside her. At that moment, he knew that he had met his match. She was the girl he was going to marry.

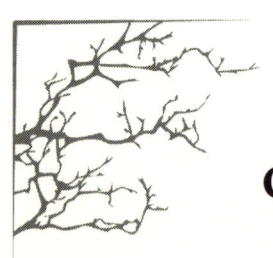

Chapter 3

DURING THE SPRING AND summer months of 1964, John and Annabel spent all of their free time together. They cherished the fleeting moments when they could sneak away, despite the chill of the wind, to curl up on the gaze overlooking the ocean, delighted by the very presence of each other.

After one successful sunny day on the ocean, John brought a boatload of fish to the wharf, where eager hands loaded it into wheelbarrows then onto the splitting table, to immediately start the curing process. Once all the fish were hauled off the boat, John felt a rumble in his stomach. The provisions Annabel had provided for the day had lasted just as long as it took to leave the harbour. She had met him at the wharf that morning with a brown-bagged lunch and a mason jar of cold water. No sooner had he pulled away from the wharf than he unrolled the crunchy twist of the bag, and the warmth and aroma of freshly baked bread rushed out. He fetched the thickly sliced, buttered-bread sandwich piled with fresh lettuce, thin slices of ripe tomato and a sprinkle of salt and pepper. He tried to take only a couple of bites, intending to save the rest till hunger struck, but he could only find satisfaction when the sandwich was finished.

The grumble in his gut now unbearable, John made his way from the wharf to the beach. Clouds gathered furiously overhead with the scent of impending rain, and a rising fog bank stretched along the horizon, past the mouth of the harbour. To John it resembled an incoming tidal wave, approaching at an alarming pace. Newfoundland's weather, an uncontrollable variable in the production of the salt fishery, was ever-changing.

John saw Bill's head tilted toward the sky, his forecasting eyes keeping a careful watch on the weather, ready to salvage the fish on a moment's notice. Because of Bill's physical condition, he became the shore skipper, overseeing the drying process. With meticulous skill he built up weather-resistant piles of fish covered with rinds, that resembled haystacks scattered around the harbour. He knew how fish needed to be handled in all weather conditions, throughout the different stages of the drying process. This allowed him to make any necessary adjustments to produce the high-quality salt fish demanded by the merchant. Rain reduced the value of the fish, meaning each pile had to be immediately sheltered when clouds threatened any amount of precipitation.

Bill soon joined the women on shore, quickly transporting the partially dried fish to the shed. To his delight, John spotted Annabel, her arms full of layers of fish.

"Johnny!" Annabel said as he approached her. "Go tell the b'ys to get out here with some tarpaulins before the clouds lets go!" Before she ran past him, she stopped momentarily to steal a kiss.

"You smells some good, m'lovey." The stench of fish met his nostrils, and he could feel the heat on her breath that came from her dry lips.

"Go on, you ain't no better. Now hurry up and tell 'em to grab some rinds too, in case there's not enough time to get it out of the rain." She ran with the fish to the shed and piled it high inside.

The men were already on their way with tarps and rinds, the air thick with the imminent rainstorm. The flakes were lined with dehydrated codfish, their white flesh split down the middle and laid in alternating triangles—patterns of heads and tails. Not one could afford to be lost. The communal spirit of the outport remained as alive as ever. The survival of a few was just as important as the livelihood of many, so every person worked with great intensity to get the job done. Once the tarps and rinds ran out, the women piled the men's arms as high and heavy with dried fish as they could manage. The men then sprinted to the shed. John ran to Annabel, and she gave him the pile she had collected.

"Come on, now, you can pile faster than that." John grinned.

Her eyes widened as she accepted his challenge and stacked until she could no longer reach. "Don't you go dropping any and getting too big for your boots." She patted his rear as he took off, swaying a bit as he struggled to keep his balance.

The fog bank rolled into the harbour just as the last few armloads of fish were put into the shed. John was the last to come out and found Annabel waiting outside the shed door. As soon as he stepped out, she closed the door and latched it. Drops of rain pecked their faces. John grabbed her hand, and they joined Bill and Lillian to return to their house to wait out the downpour.

"Wait," John said, letting go of Annabel's hand and shielding his eyes from the rain. "I gotta grab my stuff outta the boat so it don't get soaked. I'll meet you back at your parents' house." The rain beat down harder.

"I'll help you. The rain will help wash the stink off of me." She ran past him, her face to the sky, ignoring the sting of the pelting rain.

When they reached the wharf, John jumped aboard his boat and grabbed his soaked clothes and supplies. The fog had settled itself like the whiteout of a blizzard, and they were clear out of sight of the houses.

"You wanna do something real crazy?"

Before John could answer, Annabel stripped down to her underwear and leapt into the water. John stared in disbelief. He stepped out of his boat and stripped off his clothes too, tossing them on top of Annabel's. He yelped when the cold water hit his body.

"Refreshing, ain't it?" Annabel said when John resurfaced. Her teeth clacked together harder than a northern flicker woodpecker drumming its beak against the trunk of a tree. She wrapped her shivering body around John's as he treaded water. Plummeting raindrops broke the surface tension of the water and splashed back up at their faces, causing them to blow air from their mouths like the playful harbour porpoises that migrated to Newfoundland shores during the summer months.

Sudden panic spread across Annabel's face. Her voice was unable to carry past the noise of the rain and the sudden shift of the wind, so she furiously kicked her legs and turned John's body around. He saw the merchant's ship pulling into the mouth of the harbour. Not wanting to get caught, John motioned for Annabel to follow him, and they swam toward the wharf. He quickly kissed her before lifting her onto the ladder. He followed close behind and felt the air embrace him like a warm blanket, until a breeze pricked his whole body with goosebumps. They were both giddy at the thought of getting caught skinny dipping, moving in almost comical slow motion as they fumbled to pull on their wet clothes.

John grabbed Annabel's hand and yelled over the pounding rain. "Come on! We got to get back before Slade sees us."

They headed back to Bill and Lillian's to warm up, dry off and to warn the others of Thomas Slade's impending arrival. Inside they found friends and neighbours gathered, with Lillian cooking up her own storm. In a bath of butter, she fried fresh cod fillets tossed in flour and eggs, boiled potatoes, and roasted carrots and turnips, to be served up with a tray of her homemade buns. Although the government had shut down the store and luxuries were scarce, every household offered boundless hospitality to their neighbours. The aromas from the fish and vegetables and the burning logs in the stove ignited John's appetite.

With news of the merchant's surprise visit, John was relieved no one had questioned his and Annabel's whereabouts as Annabel grabbed two dry towels hung on a clothesline over the pot-belly stove in the living room. It didn't take long until a firm knock interrupted the conversation, and a hush fell over the crowd. They were all conditioned to dread such a knock; it signalled that Thomas Slade meant business. The door creaked open, and the merchant's wife, Millie, stuck her flaming red-haired head into the kitchen. She smiled wide at the sight of the kitchen party.

"You don't mind if we stops in for a cup of tea, do you?" She laughed jovially. "We were on our way back to St. John's, and I talked Tommy into a quick rest stop till this downpour blows over." She stood aside while Thomas and their teenage daughter, Helen, entered the small kitchen.

Lillian stepped away from the frying fish, and took Millie's coat. "Come in and have a seat," she said. She gathered their three damp coats and passed them to Annabel, who hung them to dry on the clothesline. Lillian scurried to add three more place settings to the table, then motioned for Bill and John to give up their chairs.

"We don't want to put you out, now." Millie sat down and gave a stern look to Thomas, who hesitantly joined her.

"We insist," Lillian said as she returned to her cooking, directing John to get three more stools and Annabel to fill the table with the platters of steaming food.

John couldn't help but notice how attractive the Slades' daughter was as she walked by him. Helen had often come to the harbour as a child to play with them, oblivious of the role her father played in the community. As she got older her visits became less frequent, likely the result of a dawning realization of the class division that separated her from the others in the community. She was all grown up now, and John flushed when she slipped out of her sweater and caught him sizing her up. She smiled timidly as she took what had been Annabel's place beside him at the table, draping her sweater over the back of the chair.

Annabel gave John a sharp jab in his rib with a serving fork. "Stop it," she whispered in jest as she pulled up a stool on the other side of him.

John smirked at Annabel's display of jealousy. "She's got nothing on you," he whispered back. He grazed his lips on hers when no one was looking.

After the meal, the women cleared the dishes while the men pulled out their cigars and cigarettes. Lillian tried to excuse Millie from the clean-up, but the merchant's wife pulled up her sleeves and plunged her hands into the sink brimming with bubbles. The women laughed and carried on with their tasks.

Thomas didn't engage with the others throughout the meal or after. He kept his chin pointed toward the window, watching for the moment the rain stopped. He silently announced their departure when he gathered their coats and stood at the door without so much as a nod to anyone.

Millie thanked Bill and Lillian for their hospitality.

"I'll be back next week," Thomas said to the crowd.

Millie slapped him on the back of the head. "What Tommy means to say is that we appreciates all the hard work you puts into making the highest-quality fish in all of Newfoundland. This is as much our livelihood as it is yours, and you all plays a key role in keeping the industry alive." Millie extended her arms to Lillian and gave her a kiss on the cheek. "I hope to see you again, before too long."

As Thomas helped Millie put on her warmed coat, Helen reached for the sweater she had forgotten on the back of the chair. John handed it to her, and she leaned in close.

"See you around, Johnny."

John was relieved to see Annabel busily filling cups of hot water to pass around to the crowd.

The moment the door closed behind the Slades, John called to Bill. "Skipper! Get that fiddle of yours out here."

Despite his flared arthritis, Bill started playing a lively tune. Lillian threw a deck of cards on the table. The clouds were still spitting, and although it required much patience to wait out a storm, it was sometimes a great excuse to enjoy a kitchen party. It was no trouble finding entertainment when everyone was together. Mugs of hot toddies amplified the quick stomping songs that told tall tales of days gone by.

John drank from a flask and sat down beside Oscar. His withered body weighed down by the more than seventy years he had accumulated, Oscar's blue eyes still smiled. John knew him well during the days when he had been Bill's right-hand man. He was a silly but respected and well-liked man in Ireland's Eye—the kindest person anyone knew; a man who would give anything he owned to help someone out, including the trinkets he collected over his lifetime. Most were worthless but rich with meaning, and Oscar never forgot the intricate stories attached to each piece. If he saw someone eyeing one up in his cluttered home, he'd tell the story and immediately gift it. Oscar took great joy in others' pleasure.

Although he was generally quiet, he was quick to retell stories of the poverty-stricken grandeur that encapsulated his childhood. His voice, low with old age, brought a slur of Newfoundland dialect that would be hard for the common ear to understand. He often punctuated his own stories repeatedly with one word—Jeepers; then he'd pause to puff his pipe when the emotion became too strong, the memory too alive in his mind.

John loved it when Oscar told the story about the shirt of many colours his mother had made for him from burlap potato sacks. John asked him about it now. Tears formed in Oscar's eyes as he began the tale, and everyone listened in like it was the first time. He recalled how his father had died at a young age, and how his mother had done the best she could with the scarce resources she had.

"My brothers and I took turns going to school in the winter months," he said. "We only had one pair of warm boots between the lot of us. There was no extra money to buy everyone their own pair."

When it was his turn to go to school, Oscar recalled the shirt his mother made and how ugly it was. His bottom lip trembled, the sagging skin on his face rippling like the ocean waves.

"I kept my coat zipped right up to my chin to hide that burlap shirt." He brought his pipe to his lips. "But my friends still gave me a hard time. I always wore it though, 'cause I knew it was my mudder's love that stopped those bitter winds." He puffed on his pipe.

Music, dancing and chatter, and the usual cloud of cigarette smoke, filled the house into the wee hours of the morning. As folks trickled back to their own homes for the night, John found Annabel sound asleep on the chesterfield in the living room. He covered her with a blanket, kissed her forehead, still salty with brine, and headed home.

AS RED, ORANGE AND yellow seeped into the green leaves of the harbour's deciduous trees, more houses disappeared from the shoreline. A cold tempest from the Atlantic compelled the branches to throw the last of their leaves in a final surrender to winter's arrival. With the population down to sixteen residents, the winter of 1964 seemed to last forever for the remaining fishermen and their families. No matter how tiring or gruelling the lifestyle, living off the ocean became an involuntary response, like a heartbeat that pumped salt water through their veins. Fishing was their lifeblood—they fished to live, but they also lived to fish. The intense labour always brought vitality and a great feeling of satisfaction into their lives. To survive the winter months, the group displayed remarkable endurance. Men worked with zealous ambition chopping wood, mending fishing equipment, snaring rabbits, hunting moose and partridge. The women bottled the meat to preserve it while still busy with the cooking and inside chores. They all prayed it was enough to get them through another winter.

John lived alone then, in his deceased father's house, and at the end of many exhausting days he and Annabel would often lay on John's bed and fall asleep. Besides playing a game of cards, or Annabel reading a book out loud to him, he didn't have energy for much else. Some days were so tiring that their evening naps would turn into sleepovers. On those nights, John would wake up startled to find Lillian holding a lantern in the bedroom doorway. He'd pretend to sleep until Lillian's determination to bring her daughter home faded, once she realized they were fully clothed. Since the women who fed on gossip had already resettled, Bill and Lillian overlooked the sleepovers as they became more frequent.

In the evenings, only five houses, lit up like pumpkins, chugged a steady stream of smoke from each chimney. As easterly winds howled through John's house during the first snowstorm of the season, John and Annabel curled under a blanket on the chesterfield next to the wood stove. A lantern was set on the coffee table as they listened to the fury of the storm outside.

"You better walk me home, Johnny," Annabel said. "My parents will be worried to death that I'm stuck out in the cold, or get suspicious if I'm staying over all the time."

"You think they'll blame you for not walking home in this?" John pulled her a little closer, but she wriggled free. He watched as she walked over to the window and pulled the curtain to the side.

"Look at the snow piling up on the windowsill." She sounded worried. "I see the lantern still burning in their kitchen. I knows they're waiting up for me."

"All right, come on then," John said, mustering a gruff tone. He stood up and wrapped a blanket around her shoulders. "You wants to leave me all by myself in this winter storm? I get it. Go ahead, get your coat and boots on." His brazen charm brought a smile to her face.

From the window, John saw shadows moving in the glow of Bill and Lillian's kitchen. John grabbed his lantern and stood in front of the window and waved. He knew it caught their attention when they waved back. When Annabel waved

SALTWATER JOYS

her arms, they waved once again. They watched as Bill and Lillian's lantern moved from the kitchen through the house, until it extinguished upstairs in her parents' bedroom.

"Well, I guess that's that!" John looked back to see Annabel smiling in disbelief.

"I suppose you're right." She peered out the window to the blackness that encased them.

"Well, come upstairs then. I got something I wants to talk to you about." He carried the lantern in one hand, leading Annabel up the stairs with the other.

As she lit the candles on the dresser, the wintry breeze from the window made the flames dance and flicker, casting shadows around the room. Annabel pulled out a sweater she had hung in John's closet and put it on. Just as she was about to climb into bed, John stopped her. His lips were tight and his breath quick and shallow. He knelt on one knee and reached for Annabel's hand. He slipped a ring on her finger and, without looking up, asked her to marry him.

"Oh, Johnny!" Annabel examined the sparkle of a small diamond on a thin gold band. The ring was a few sizes too big for her slender finger, so she locked her fingers in a fist to keep it in place. "But what about my father?" She didn't take her eyes off the ring.

"I got his blessing."

"I dare say you did," Annabel's unblinking gaze turned and focused on John. "That's probably why they shut out the lights? They must have thought you already proposed." She smiled coyly.

"Well now, what do you say?" John grinned.

She gave him a jaw-dropped wide smile, the answer clear in her red-rimmed eyes. "How on earth can you afford this, Johnny?"

"I wants to marry you, Annabel, and that's all you needs to know."

"I knows you don't have extra money kicking around. None of us do." She looked at him, a little disheartened "You owes enough to Mr. Slade."

"I'm going to work it off this summer, m'lovey. It'll be a good season, I knows it," he said, choosing not to tell her that he'd used the gold coin as a down payment for the ring. He knew it would upset her as she wanted it to go toward their future. John thought it a fair trade to ensure she'd be in his future.

"Don't be making deals with the devil, Johnny. Sure, you knows I would have married you without a ring." She pushed him onto the down-filled mattress.

The air was cool, so they wrapped up tight in the blankets. Neither one could sleep that night. They talked about their wedding plans, about babies, about what their future would hold. John voiced his concern over having to move someday, because there would be nothing on the island for their children.

"Don't be so sad." Annabel tried to soothe him. "Just think of all the things that's happened and how different it is here now. I'm a little excited to think about all the ways things would be easier. I'll miss it here, there's no doubt, but maybe it'd be worth it in the long run, especially if we has a few youngsters. A bit of running water and heat would sure feel nice."

IN THE MORNING, JOHN watched Annabel wake and take a look at her ringless finger. She flushed red, not realizing the ring had slipped off in the night. John reassured her that the proposal wasn't a dream, fetched it from underneath the pillow and put it back on her finger. With each exhale of breath, an icy-white vapour filled the air, a nagging reminder to John that he'd let the fire die out through the night. Each corner of the blanket was rolled under them to keep their warmth from escaping. John basked in the glow of Annabel's warm spirit, but even that and the blankets weren't enough. John lifted the blanket on his side and slipped out, trying not to let too much cold rush in underneath.

"Don't go, Johnny. We can just stay here all day long and keep each other warm." The tip of her nose blushed pink from the bitter nip of the air.

He already had his coat on and was grabbing a hat from the floor. "I'll get the fire going so we don't freeze more than we are now."

"Hurry!" Annabel laughed. She pretended to get sucked in by the pile of blankets on top of her. "I'm not coming out until you comes back."

"I'll have this place as hot as hell in a minute."

John went down the narrow stairs to the living room and saw that the harbour was tucked under a heavy blanket of snow. He grabbed a couple of junks of wood piled high beside the wood stove. The cast-iron hinges squeaked as he opened the small black door, shoved in the wood, and squirted a little kerosene to light it faster. A fragrant cloud of smoke circled overhead as the fire cracked and spread through the kindling he'd built around the logs like a teepee. He ran into the kitchen, rubbing his freezing hands together, and tossed some more logs into the kitchen stove. The cook stove served double-duty, heating the house along with the food. Once the fires roared, he picked up the kettle and found the water inside frozen. He put it on the open hole of the stove, above the licking flames. He bolted up the stairs, dropped his coat and hat to the floor, and jumped back into bed with Annabel. John's hands wriggled under her layers of clothes, grazing her bare back.

"Your hands are freezing!" Annabel yelped, but didn't push him away.

They stayed huddled together for a long time, not saying a word, until the soft whistle of the kettle called John from Annabel's arms. By then, the heat from both stoves had risen upstairs. Annabel dressed and smoothed her hair with her fingers. John went downstairs so she could use the salt-beef bucket, a makeshift toilet.

John took the kettle off the stove, added more wood, then poked the glowing embers. He lit a cigarette from his dwindling pack. He sliced up some of the homemade bread Lillian had made for him and set the slices to toast on a bent metal coat hanger over the stove. He opened a bottle of partridgeberry jam, still frozen but thawed just enough around the edges to smooth over the toast. The table was set with cups of steaming tea and lightly blackened toast when Annabel came downstairs with a roll of scotch tape.

She proudly displayed how the ring fit snugly on her finger, with tape rolled around the band under her finger.

"I won't lose it now." She beamed.

"Good morning, m'lovey." He gave her a kiss and pulled out a chair.

"I could get used to this, Johnny."

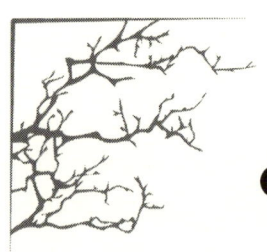

Chapter 4

OCTOBER 12TH, 1965, was eerily calm. John's house had been successfully moved from Ireland's Eye and set on a piece of property in New Bonaventure earlier that afternoon, but he was forced to stay longer than planned as the main floor had flooded in transit. The house needed to be drained of knee-high-deep water. It also had a slant from dragging it out of the water. Fearing it might collapse on itself, he and Charlie hammered boards over the cracks that zigzagged down the walls.

By the time John and Charlie were back in the water, on their way to haul up nets, the air had thickened with humidity. The putt-putt-putt from the engine of John's punt slowed as he approached a line of bright orange buoys. Charlie's boat heaved on the waters a couple of metres away, and John guided himself parallel to Charlie. He turned around and threw the kellick, a long stone wrapped in flexible sticks used as an anchor, over the bow, then took a long draw from his cigarette. John knew it was past six o'clock in the evening, when the sun made its descent into a glowing horizon swollen with towering cumulus clouds. Sea smoke steamed from the ocean as cold air circulated over the warmer water. The small spiralling columns impeded visibility as they grew higher than the boats.

"Skipper, you ready to haul 'er aboard?" John's cigarette bounced between his lips as he yelled over his shoulder to Charlie. He looked down, and just under the surface of the water, he was thrilled to see a massive swarm of codfish enclosed in the net between the boats. Their glistening red bellies reflected the glow of the sunset.

Charlie gave John a silent nod the second he lit and secured his lantern. They both knew the dark came fast. As John contemplated the endless Atlantic opposite Ireland's Eye, he felt a slight wind pick up and heard the steady slap of water on the side of the boats. The sound was a beacon for the hungry gulls that swooped and scavenged any surfaced fish. John grabbed handfuls of knitted twine, and together he and Charlie, facing one another, hauled up the cod-laden nets with their freezing hands.

With the sun's descent, Charlie stopped and pointed past John to something on the other side of John's boat. "What in the livin' name of God is that?"

Through spitting rain, John turned to see a boat coming toward them. He took the cigarette out of his mouth and squinted his eyes. A yellow apparition materialized through the eerie platoons of fog, wearing a pair of oversized oilskins. The boat banged into John's, and tiny hands clenched the front of a yellow sou'wester, the long brim at the back of the hat thrashing in a sudden gust of wind. Familiar brown eyes blinked fiercely through the cold rain.

"Annabel, what in God's name are you doing?" John flicked his cigarette butt into the salt water that splashed around the bottom of the boat. "You shouldn't be here!"

Charlie shook his head in disbelief. "Throw her the rope," he said. "She might as well stay, now she's here."

John threw her a rope, and as soon as Annabel let go of the yellow hat to grab it, the wind propelled the hat like a kite into the overcast sky. Her long hair whipped around her face until the moisture weighed it down and stuck it across her cheek. John couldn't make out what she was saying over the sudden roar of the whitecaps.

"Give me your hand and I'll help you climb in my boat! I'll tow that one home with us!" John guided one of her bulky rubber boots into his boat and took her weight on his shoulder to get the other boot in.

"Storm's comin', Johnny! Hurry up, and let me help so you can get home safe," Annabel yelled in his ear. A strong wave slammed over the side of the boat and sloshed more salt water around and inside their rubber boots.

"What are you talking about? This is nothing, b'y!" Then he noticed that the white puffy cloud formation on the horizon had spawned leaden clouds, now brewing closer. As the wind picked up it cleared the fog, and John spotted a series of long waves in the distance. He knew they'd soon intensify around them. Hundreds of seagulls swarmed in a vortex that spiralled upward till they were so high they looked like a horde of black flies in the dim sky. The clouds spewed a heavier rain.

"Shit," John whispered in quiet defeat. He jutted his chin to Charlie to continue to pull in the nets. Charlie worked faster.

A rogue wave smashed against the boat, knocking Annabel into John's shoulder. She screamed in spite of herself. "Fadder said he wouldn't send his worst enemy out in this! It's the worst one yet." A look of terror swept across her face as a clap of thunder boomed high above the boat.

"He don't know what he's talking about!" He joined Charlie pulling the nets. "This is the last one. Won't take long."

"Let me help! I knows what to do."

John hesitated before he gave her a long-handled dip net. He stood close to her as he and Charlie finished pulling up the nets, exposing hundreds of swarming codfish. Annabel's silence amplified the tempo of the rhythmic beat of the crashing waves on the boat. They all filled their dip nets full of codfish, to add to the huge pile already collected in the boats. John noticed Annabel's arms quiver as she filled then dumped the dip net. He wondered if it was from the weight of the fish, or fear.

Without warning, the thunderclouds joined forces with conflicting fronts of opposing temperatures, and collided with violence. A heavy rain poured down. Although he was only a few metres away, John could barely see Charlie's boat through the thickening fog. Distant sea winds moaned, taunting John about the accuracy of Annabel's warning. John scooped and dumped his dip net from the cod trap, alive with thrashing fish tails.

"Throw 'em overboard, b'y," Charlie said. "It's not worth it!"

John inched the net, hand over fist, progressing to the back of the net to get more cod to surface. Ignoring the sting of the salt water on his torn and bloody hands, he continued to wrestle with the heavy twine. He expected Annabel to yell at him, agreeing with Charlie, but instead she helped him haul in the fish until the net was almost empty.

"Good enough," John said. "I'll come back tomorrow for the nets. Let's go!"

Just as John freed the net from his boat, the mounting sea shrieked, then an eerie quiet filled his ears. Another rogue wave curled high above them, threatening to capsize the two boats.

"Hold on!" Charlie yelled right before it hit.

The impact flooded the vessels with salt water. John slammed into the bow, codfish flying around him in all directions. Annabel screamed.

John lunged for her, but she was gone.

"John!" Charlie yelled from his boat. "She's overboard!"

John jumped feet first into the water, the frigid current nearly paralyzing him. He resurfaced to see Charlie leaning dangerously over the side of his boat, holding out the flickering lantern as far as he could.

"Over there!" Charlie pointed just behind John.

He spun in the water and saw Annabel's yellow jacket. She was on her back, bobbing on the frantic waves.

John's rubber boots suctioned to his feet, weighing him down like anchors. He swam hard against the swells to reach her. He grabbed her outstretched arm and turned her over. Her eyes were closed. He didn't know if she was breathing.

"Hold on!" John pulled her rigid body to his and tried to swim back to Charlie's boat. Hypothermia found its way into their bodies as the waves and rain lashed at them in the foggy darkness. The continuous thunder made it hard for John to hear Charlie's directions, but he saw him throw a rope.

John glanced at Annabel, her hair fanned around her face in the icy water, eyes open, her lips as blue as the ocean. Relief flooded John's heart that she was alive.

"Johnny," Annabel sputtered as a wave crashed over them.

He pulled her close, and Charlie revved the engine nearby. She tried to speak, but he couldn't make out what she was saying.

"The baby. Evelyn."

John felt his heart sink at the thought of his child, freezing in Annabel's womb. "Stay with me, m'lovey."

The salt water choked his lungs, and the numbing temperatures made it hard to suck in air. The wind and pelting rain whipped his face like sprung tree branches, but he never took his eyes off Annabel. He tried to make out what she was so desperately trying to tell him, but Charlie's boat pulled up next to them, and the noise of the engine was too loud in John's ears.

"Come on, b'y! Grab the rope!" Charlie called out as he killed the engine.

Using every ounce of strength, John kicked his frozen legs and slapped his free arm as hard as he could against the waves and lashing wind. His other arm was numb, but he was sure it was fastened around Annabel.

"Come on! Grab the rope! I'll pull her in!" Charlie's voice was harsh and urgent through sheets of rain. John grabbed the rope just as another wave crested above them. It crashed down, sending John under water and tearing Annabel from his grasp. John opened his eyes under the surface of shimmering blackness. Annabel's yellow oilskin was nowhere around him. His rubber boots caught the net that hung from Charlie's boat, preventing him from being pulled by the strong current that carried Annabel away from the boat. John surfaced, took another deep breath, and plunged downward. The net twisted around his legs and came with him as he swam in all directions, arms cutting a wide swathe, hoping he might snag Annabel. Feeling as helpless as a tangled codfish, he thrashed around. Just as he came up for a breath of air, a wave crashed down and forced him under once more. He felt a sudden jerk of his body as Charlie pulled the net aboard. Charlie struggled to pull John's slippery lower half into his boat, but he eventually hoisted him up, feet first. John had managed to kick one boot off, and it hung, entangled in the net. Wanting to jump back in the water, John tore apart the net that ensnared the other boot, his hands bloody. He pulled the boot off his foot and chucked it into the seething ocean. John felt Charlie grip his shoulders, preventing John from jumping back into the ocean.

"Let me go, Charlie! I got to find Annabel." John's voice was thick with heavy sobs. The wind had subsided as quick as its onset, and the boat was once again sheathed in fog.

"We'd be better off spotting her from the boat in this fog, in case she drifted away." Charlie started the engine and cast the net away from his boat.

John looked toward his boat and the one anchored to it. He wondered if she could be hidden between them. John pointed in their direction.

Charlie manoeuvred to search around the two abandoned boats, careful not to snag the floating net in the boat's engine. They searched in a growing spiral around the boats, but with every breaking wave, the hull crested and slammed hard against the water. John held on to both sides of the slender bow that came together at a raised point. He bashed his head against the wooden bow, again and again, to kill the torment that clutched his chest. The bloody gashes on his face burned from the sea spray. He gnashed his teeth and braced for another self-inflicted blow.

Charlie grabbed his shoulders. "Damn it, John! We'll find her, b'y."

No sooner were the words out of Charlie's mouth than they spied the bright yellow oilskin rising and falling with the rapid motion of the waves. Charlie left John's side to steer the boat in that direction. He revved the engine, a reverberating growl that dared to compete with the booming thunder overhead. John leaned over the side of the boat and grabbed at the jacket with useless arms. He didn't have enough strength to pull her in.

Charlie cut the engine and hurried over in a panic to help John haul Annabel inside the boat.

A white flash of lightning revealed an empty oilskin. John leaned over the boat, as still as death. He closed his eyes and let out a violent wail against the storm that hissed all around them. His cry echoed through the fog. Tears of rage fell from his eyes as he tried to comprehend the unimaginable.

Somewhere in the two-hundred-billion-year-old intricately spaced universe, the galaxies had teamed up to cast a minute ripple that swelled with time to produce a chaotic twist of fate. Like a supernova, John's world went out with a catastrophic bang. His heart pressurized and collapsed into a black hole, as endless as the ocean beneath, when he realized Annabel had slipped out of the oilskin.

Charlie started the engine and sped through the storm until he reached the calm embrace of the harbour.

"What do I do? What do I do?" John repeated until his mouth went dry.

"We'll get help," Charlie said.

John lay slumped in the boat, dead fish swirling around him. His forehead throbbed as a deafening silence overtook his mind and his eardrums. Just before he fell unconscious, John wondered what Annabel had tried to tell him.

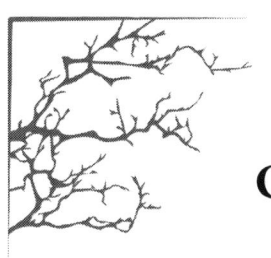

Chapter 5

ANNABEL HAD GONE INTO labour merely one hour after John had left the harbour with his house in tow. When Bill climbed to the highest point of the harbour, he fired a couple of shots into the air, then scanned the horizon with his binoculars. The billowing clouds along the ocean's horizon foretold the onset of a terrible storm. When Bill couldn't see any trace of the floating house or John's boat, he returned to the house, figuring John must have reached New Bonaventure already.

With the news of the impending weather, Annabel worried that John would encounter the storm's wrath on his way to haul in his nets. At first sign of labour, Annabel prayed the baby would wait for John, but her contractions progressed quickly. When there was no sign of him, she was determined to push to get the baby out before dark, then get out on the water to warn John. Annabel gave birth to a healthy baby girl just after three o'clock in the afternoon. Annabel told everyone she was worried about John. Sarah, just as worried about Charlie, echoed her sentiment. However, Ruth ordered Annabel to stay put in bed—she was at risk of hemorrhaging.

The wind picked up and lashed at the windows around six-thirty, at the same time Annabel's newborn started to cry for milk. Lillian brought the baby into Annabel's room, stopping cold when she saw the empty bed. She called to Bill and, sure enough, Bill noticed Ed's boat missing from the wharf. There were no boats left in the harbour, so Bill, Lillian, Ed, Ruth, and Sarah were left helpless, confined to the shore when the storm hit hard at seven o'clock.

Since any light reflecting off the windows would make it difficult to spot a sign of John, Charlie or Annabel, the lantern glowed from behind the closed door of the porch. It waited there to be snatched at any hint of the trio, to guide the way down to the shoreline. They all sat in terror in the growing darkness, as the baby cried for her mother. It was after seven-thirty when the roar of an engine was heard, and the group darted as one from the house toward the wharf, leaving the baby in the bassinet. Lillian held the lantern as she ran, the light swinging erratically. Bill's arthritis made him fall behind, but he was moving faster than he had in years. At the wharf, they watched Charlie's boat emerge from the fog.

Ed helped Charlie lift John from the boat, and Ruth examined the gashes on John's forehead and checked his pulse. Sarah ran and held fast to Charlie as soon as he let go of John.

"Where's Annabel?" Lillian asked Charlie apprehensively. Her eyes cast past the boat to the impenetrable fog. "Did she find you?" She turned back toward the house when the baby started crying from inside.

Charlie nodded, but stood speechless.

"Where is she then?" Lillian's voice quaked. She took off, nearly running into the water.

Charlie stepped away from Sarah to put his arm out to stop Lillian from getting her feet soaked, even though Bill was right behind her. "She helped us haul in some nets, but she got knocked outta John's boat," Charlie's voice choked into a sob. "She got pulled down."

Lillian stumbled backward. Bill caught her before she fell.

"She's gone. We tried to find her," Charlie said as he shook his head again, "but we couldn't. We needs help."

Despair pressed in on Bill's chest, and his knees buckled.

Ed and Ruth called out to help move John into the house.

"I wanted to go with her. I should have gone too!" Sarah's eyes squeezed together as she turned her pained stare from the ocean to Charlie. She wept into Charlie's chest as he tightened his arms around her.

"Don't say that, Sarah. That would have been no good. Not for any of us. I wouldn't be able to pick up James without you." Charlie rested his chin on the top of her head. "He'd never forgive me if I didn't bring you home."

"I'm so thankful you're all right, Charlie." Sarah let go of him to wipe her eyes with her sleeve. She waved for him to help Ed carry John's unconscious body into Bill and Lillian's house. Bill wrapped Lillian in his arms. Her face had lost all colour, and Bill looked no better.

Ed and Charlie carried John up the stairs to Annabel's bedroom, where the women stripped him of his icy attire. Sarah wrapped herself around his hypothermic body. Lillian gathered her strength and every blanket she could find in the house and tucked them around John and Sarah. When his convulsions diminished to a constant shiver, Sarah slipped out of the bed and helped Lillian wrap dry towels, warmed over the wood stove, over his head and chest. Throughout the night, the baby would cry from downstairs. Lillian did her best to soothe her granddaughter with some warmed tin milk.

Ed, Charlie and Bill left the house immediately. With the light from two lanterns, they climbed into Charlie's boat to head back out. Hours later, they returned to the harbour with Ed's and John's boats in tow. Charlie and Ed dragged John's boat up onto the shore, where it hit the rocks and tipped over, spilling dead fish all over the rocky shoreline.

In the morning, the fog had dissipated enough to see the horizon, so Charlie and Bill boarded Charlie's boat again, ready to search. Ed and Ruth headed home in Ed's boat to share the tragic news, and get more men out on the water searching. Ruth urged Lillian to come with them and bring the baby to New Bonaventure, but Lillian refused. She couldn't leave without her daughter, and Ruth didn't have the heart to take the baby from her.

Sprawled across the foot of the bed where John slept, Sarah woke when the kettle whistled from the kitchen stove downstairs. She removed the towels from John's shivering body and sponged a little water on his lips. She covered his body with blankets and put her hands on his chest. His breath was rapid and light.

The kettle continued to whistle, so Sarah slung the cool towels over her shoulder and was about to head downstairs, when she looked out the window and noticed the merchant's vessel tied up at the wharf. She didn't see Charlie's boat.

Downstairs, a salty aroma filled the house from a large pot on the stove boiling with salt beef and vegetables. Lillian was preparing a salt-beef dinner, not only to keep the men energized for their search for Annabel, but also to keep her hands busy as she waited for news. Sarah slipped on an oven mitt to lift the high-strung kettle off the stove and place it on a trivet. She removed the warm towels hanging from the clothesline over the wood stove in the living room, set them down, and quickly pinned the cold ones to the line. Before she headed back upstairs with the warm towels, Sarah caught a glimpse of a familiar receding hairline and thick grey sideburns. Thomas Slade entered the house with Lillian, who was swaddling the crying baby girl in her arms. Sarah rushed up the stairs, out of sight of Lillian and Thomas but within earshot of their conversation.

"So you're telling me I'm not getting paid in full?" Thomas wore a three-piece suit, blanched by sun and salt water. "You knows that bit of fish out there ain't enough to square up what John owes me for the wedding ring." He smirked.

"What are you talking about? John worked like a dog all summer, and he should have plenty enough to pay his debt. My daughter's missing! Don't you have any sympathy at all?" Lillian spoke in as stern a voice as she could muster.

"I was doing him a favour."

"The fish is out in the boat if you wants it bad enough."

"Annabel's blood's on that fish." His eyes darted around the room for anything of value. He stopped at the child. "Whose is that?"

The newborn cried louder as Lillian cradled her to her chest.

Thomas stepped closer and towered over her. "Whose is it?"

"John and Annabel's." Lillian repositioned the baby, rocking her body at the hip. "Annabel gave birth before she took off last night." Lillian turned her head toward the harbour and stifled her own cry. She kissed the top of the child's head.

"Who's going to feed her?"

"When we gets to New Bonaventure, there's a nursing mother there. The midwife says she'll make enough for both."

"Until then?"

"Well, we feeds her the bit of tin milk we got." The last tin of milk sat empty on the kitchen table.

Thomas paced the room and scratched his chin. "I tell you what . . . ." He pulled up a chair. "How about a fair trade, Lillian? I'll write off your debt completely. I bet when you gets to New Bonaventure, you'll make only enough to survive."

Lillian's face flushed. "No, Mr. Slade. You wait to do business with my husband when he gets back."

John moaned from the bedroom, and Sarah left the stairway, the towels considerably cooler now.

"I got to get to the other harbours, you know," Thomas said. "We can work this out between ourselves."

"What do you want?"

"Let's just say, Millie and I will provide a good home for that there youngster."

Lillian's bottom lip drooped and trembled. "No, Mr. Slade. John don't even know she's been born."

"He doesn't need to know."

"Why do you want her?" Lillian went to the window, where there was no sign of her husband.

"Millie's always wanted another child. After Helen, she couldn't get pregnant again." He walked over to where Lillian stood. "She'd make a good mother for this baby. She's out there in the boat."

"How do I know you're not just saying all this, Mr. Slade?" Lillian looked at the merchant with undisguised loathing. "You're a sneaky bugger, ripping us all off all these years. Robbing us blind. You don't know the work that has to be done to get the bit of stuff you provides."

"We all got to make a living, Lillian. But I'm willing to offer you a clean slate. I'll even pardon John's remaining debt." He cleared his throat. "On my way out, I'll notify the coastguard that Annabel is missing. You never know, she might have washed up on shore somewhere."

Sarah stood at the top of the stairs again. She needed the warm towels; the ones she had brought up weren't keeping John warm. As she descended, she looked at Lillian, but Lillian had her head bowed, eyes closed, her lips pressed against the baby's forehead. Sarah's heart raced fast as she entered the living room. She ignored the merchant, silently unpinned the warmed towels from the line, replacing them with the cooled ones, then went back upstairs. She quickly placed the towels on John's chest and feet, and exited the room, returning to her previous spot to catch the rest of the conversation.

"Her name's Evelyn." Lillian sobbed. "You must call her Evelyn."

"You're making the right choice, Lillian. Evelyn will be in good hands."

When the front door closed, Sarah moved to the window at the top of the stairs and saw the merchant rushing to his vessel, carrying what Sarah could only presume to be the baby coddled in a blanket. She put her hand to the window and banged on the glass, as though she could stop the merchant from getting on his boat. The merchant motioned for the crew to stop what they were doing and get aboard. Sarah couldn't tear herself away from the window. When Sarah saw Millie come up from below the deck of the boat, she opened the window.

"You can't just take their baby, Tommy!" Millie's voice echoed around the harbour.

Thomas stood in her way when she tried to get off the boat. He placed the baby gently in her arms. His voice was low and soothing.

Sarah couldn't hear what he was saying.

Within minutes, the ship was on its way out of the harbour.

Sarah ran downstairs to find Lillian staring out the living room window at the ship.

"Evelyn," Lillian whispered. Her knees buckled, and she fell to the floor. Sarah ran to her side and pulled her head to her lap, raking her hair with her fingers.

"I had to do it, Sarah," Lillian whispered. "I had to do it. There's no milk. A baby can't survive on water, and I can't leave the harbour."

"I know, my love." Sarah stroked Lillian's short, tightly woven grey curls.

"This shouldn't have been my decision to make. Oh Lord, forgive me." She made the sign of the cross and touched her wrinkled hand to her mouth. "What have I done?"

Sarah did her best to soothe her best friend's mother. "Just think of it as she's being taken care of until we finds Annabel and gets settled away." She helped Lillian sit up and hugged her.

"You think they'll find her?" Lillian asked.

"I hope so." Sarah held Lillian in a stronger embrace until they heard Charlie's boat pull into the harbour.

Sarah brought Lillian to her feet and helped her walk outside. Charlie and Bill were coming in slow. The colour drained from Lillian's face when Bill shook his head from the boat. Lillian ran toward them, her hurried footsteps loud on the rocky shore, and waded into the piercing tide. She sobbed uncontrollably and held onto the boat. Bill jumped out and let Lillian pound his chest with weak fists. When she stopped, Bill led her from the water, back to Sarah.

"What about Annabel?" Lillian's eyes squeezed together, preparing herself for his response, her body shaking with cold.

"It's too late, my dear. By now she's filled up with salt water." Bill cried in coughing sobs.

Sarah's mouth opened wide to cry, but nothing came out.

Charlie hopped out of the boat and ran to Sarah. "We looked everywhere, but we couldn't find her. There's no sign of her." He trembled as he held Sarah tighter than he had ever held her before. "I can't help but think what I would have done if you'd have gone out with her," he whispered in her ear.

Sarah moaned as she grabbed fists of Charlie's jacket and pulled at it. The pain was heavy, and she couldn't escape it. "If

I did go, maybe she'd still be here." The sudden shock made her entire face bunch up until she couldn't see. She turned her head into Charlie's chest to hide her cries.

Charlie rubbed Sarah's back and lifted her chin with his finger until she looked at him. "Come on, now. We needs to pull ourselves together. There's no good in us getting all upset. It won't bring her back." But even as he spoke, he couldn't convince himself enough to keep his composure. "We needs to be strong for John."

"Oh, dear Lord!" Lillian's face twisted into a horrific stare. "Oh, my good Lord! I gave him the baby!"

Charlie gasped and met Sarah's puffy eyes.

"What are you talking about, Lill?" Bill asked. He looked to Sarah.

Sarah nodded, squeezed her eyes shut, then lowered her head back to Charlie's chest and sobbed.

"He cleared all our debt." Lillian held her face in her hands. "Go after him, Bill. I made a mistake. I don't know what I was thinking." Her knees buckled again, and Bill propped her arm over his shoulder, helping her walk up the path to the house.

"That son of a bitch, Slade." Bill clenched his fists but released them when Lillian stumbled.

Charlie and Sarah followed Bill and Lillian to the house. "Are we gonna tell John about the baby?" Sarah asked. She looked up to Annabel's room and saw the curtain was drawn to the side. Her eyes remained fixated on the window until the curtain closed.

Bill turned back to face them. "It's best for everyone if we lets him believe the baby drowned in her womb, for now," he said. He grabbed his handkerchief from inside his coat pocket and blew his nose. "He'll find out soon enough, once we gets to New Bonaventure. Till then, we aren't stopping until we finds Annabel.

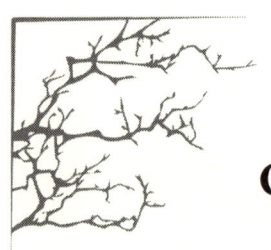

Chapter 6

A CRACK OF MORNING sunlight broke through the closed curtains, making its way across the room to John's tightened eyes and twitching face. Random jolts shook his naked body from the frigid cold of the salt water that had penetrated deep into his bones. He was buried under a heap of down-filled patchwork quilts, and beside his feet was a large beach rock wrapped in warm towels. Sarah kept one rock near the stove, then switched them every hour to help keep him warm and prevent pneumonia. John's wet clothes were still in a pile on the floor. The stench of stale salt water filled the room.

In a haze of semi-consciousness, John struggled with a phantom weight that pressed down on his chest, trapping him inside a nightmare. He was awake and could hear the bedroom door creak, but his body was paralyzed. His eyes darted from one side of the room to the other. He caught a glimpse of a woman's silhouette entering the room, the hallway behind her lit with a bright ray of sunshine.

"How long you been up?" Sarah walked over to the bed and stood still when she noticed his rapid eye movements. Sarah took a quick look around the room. "John, were you up looking out the window?" She lifted the blankets and placed more warm towels on his chest. When there was no response,

Sarah rubbed the towels against his body, hoping the extra friction would warm him up. She placed the blankets back over his chest.

"Annabel!" John leapt forward from the clutches of his dream. He grabbed Sarah's arm. His body ached with every movement, and he was forced to lie back down.

"Good God, John!" Sarah wrenched her arm, but John didn't let go.

"Annabel, I had the worst nightmare." He pulled Sarah closer and felt her body go rigid under his hands. "I dreamt that damned Pirate Easton had me good." He coughed and sputtered, the inside of his throat feeling like it was ripped and bleeding. A ravenous thirst overcame him. "Wanted his gold coin back."

"John, my dear, I'm not Annabel," Sarah said in a soft voice. She pulled herself away from him to open the closed curtains.

John squinted through the sudden burst of sunlight that blurred Sarah into the intricate patterns of flowers and vines that lined the walls of Annabel's soon-to-be-abandoned bedroom. The ceiling suddenly spun, and he tried to focus his eyes on the crucifix above the bed. He closed his eyes when the spinning didn't stop. Sarah sat down beside him and propped herself up on his pillow.

"Where is she?" John asked. He clenched his jaw, the salty grit of sand grinding between his molars.

"They're gone out again looking for her." Sarah wiped her runny nose with her sleeve. "They're not giving up. They're going to find her."

John put his head to her chest, and she held him as a mother would a child. The heat from Sarah's body tamed his convulsions but unleashed memories of the night before. John turned his head into her sweater to muffle the sound of his heavy sobs.

"Come on, John. There's still hope." Sarah stroked his matted hair.

"I gotta find her." John propped himself up on his elbow to look out the window. He swung his legs to the side of the bed, wincing at the sudden movement, but he had to get to Annabel. He stood up and stepped onto his sodden clothes. The immediate chill sent him to the wooden floor with a sickening thump. When he opened his eyes, a woodlouse scurried past his face and disappeared under the bedroom door. At the same moment, Lillian opened the door and crushed it under her shoe. John winced. The crunch of the bug sent a jitter through his nerves.

"You all right in here, Sarah?" Lillian's face flushed at the sight of John's naked body lying across the floor. Sarah draped a blanket over him and helped him back onto the bed.

"Oh, my son, you're not feeling well enough to go out and help search, are you?" Lillian's question hung somewhere between demand and defeat. Her voice trailed off as she turned to go back downstairs. "What have I done? What have I done?" She leaned on the wall. "The baby, my baby. She's gone. They're gone."

"Come on, Lillian." Sarah rushed over. "No need getting all upset until we knows for sure. Someone might have been out and rescued her, you never know."

Lillian leaned on Sarah, and wept. Sarah led her out of the room and walked beside her down the stairs.

From Annabel's bedroom, John had a clear view of the beach and harbour. A low fog wrapped around his upturned boat. John was sure it was his. Beside it, he recognized the yellow oilskin. His body went into convulsions, and he clutched his chest.

"Goddamn it!" He reached for the clothes on the floor. He beat himself from the inside out at the thought of Annabel and their unborn child lost to sea while he slept in her bed. He cursed himself for sleeping.

"How you feeling, John?" Sarah asked when she came back into the room, holding a pile of dry clothes.

He shook his head.

"Put these on." Sarah handed him a pair of underwear and turned her back. She busied herself untangling a pair of inside-out long johns. John put the underwear on and sat back down on the bed. He felt like a child as Sarah lifted his legs to inch the long underwear up. She slipped a pair of wool socks over his feet, followed by a pair of slacks.

"Put your arms straight up," she said.

He struggled to lift his arms as high as he could. She pulled a long-sleeved shirt over his head and helped him wrestle his arms through the armholes. "Bill has another pair of rubber boots you can wear. I warmed one of his coats. It's draped on a chair by the stove for when you goes out."

John rubbed a flicking twitch from his eyelid. "How in God's name am I supposed to find her?" He made his way to the bedroom door. "I'm thinking this must be a goddamn dream. She's all I got. Her and the baby is all I got."

Sarah shook her head and reached for him. "I wants it to be a dream too." She pulled him back into the room and closed the door. "I wasn't going to tell you this, but I can't keep it in. I hope you don't hate me for telling you." With her back to the door and hands clasped in front of her chest, Sarah struggled to find her words.

"Tell me!" He grabbed Sarah's shoulders.

"I saw her, John. I saw Annabel. From outside the window this morning. Or at least I think it was her. Someone pulled the curtain to the side when I looked up."

"Come on, Sarah. What are you trying to tell me?" John shook her without even realizing what he was doing. "Is Annabel still alive?"

Sarah unclasped her hands. "I saw her last night too. She came to the door once we brought you into the house. I thought it was just the wind at first, but when I opened the door, she stood right in front of me, soaking wet. She told me she loved you so much, then some force pulled her backwards into the fog. I didn't want to frighten Lillian, so I ran out barefoot and screamed at her to wait as I ran to the shore, but it took her fast. I couldn't find her."

"I got to get out there." John moved her away from the door. "Maybe she's out along the shore somewhere."

"I thinks it was her token."

"What?"

"Her ghost." Sarah sucked in a shaky breath.

"What did you say?" He couldn't control the rage that began to simmer in his chest. He grabbed Sarah by the shoulders again.

"She came later in the night too," Sarah whispered. "Nearly scared me half to death when I saw her head peek up from outside the window."

John frowned and opened his mouth to say something.

"I knows it sounds foolish, John. I ran downstairs to let her in, but she wasn't there. I ran out the front door, and there was no ladder propped up at the window. When I ran back upstairs, the window was open, and you were in convulsions. I wrestled the window closed and got you warmed up again." Sarah looked to the window. "I suppose she might have been checking on you."

"Could it have been a dream, Sarah?" John asked, nearly nose-to-nose with her. "Could you have been sleeping and dreamt it up?" John's face pleaded, his eyes hungry to find a glitch in her story, to make it a false recollection.

"Maybe, but I knows what I saw," she said. "I shouldn't have told you, but I can't explain it."

John let go of Sarah and headed downstairs. His head spun, and his bones still ached with cold. Sarah followed him down and immediately went to Lillian, who was crying in the doorway of the kitchen.

"Don't worry, my dear. They're going to find her," Sarah whispered in a soft voice.

The screen door creaked open as John stepped outside, Lillian's cries following him even after the door slammed as it latched closed. Sarah ran after him and put the warmed coat over his shoulders and a tarnished silver flask into his hand. A swig of moonshine helped to silence the constant shiver of his body.

John walked to the shore, trying not to look at the swarm of seagulls, crows and flies attracted to the fish spilled from his boat. He scanned the shoreline. There was no sign of the yellow oilskin. Bill and Charlie soon pulled into the harbour, once again with defeated faces. Bill stood soaked and shivering, his lips tinged with blue.

"Still no sign of her, b'y," Charlie said. His eyes were bloodshot and, by the look of him, he had a touch of hypothermia. He accepted the flask that John held out to him and tipped it to his lips. "We been looking all morning. Some of the others are out walking the beaches along the island, and there's talk that the coastguard is searching the deeper water, where she could have been dragged out to." He handed the flask back to John. "I'm sorry, John, b'y. I got to get some rest, then I'll be out again."

Bill remained silent while John and Charlie pulled the boat ashore. John offered his hand to Bill to help him out, then put one of Bill's arms around his neck and bore the weight of his limp body to the house. Sarah and Lillian were at the kitchen table when John opened the door, trudged through the kitchen, and put Bill on the chesterfield.

Without a word, John ran out to his boat, stomping the pile of dead fish that spilled on the rocky shoreline. He tipped the boat upright, pushed it into the tide and hopped in. One codfish laid motionless at his feet. His pulse pounded as he started the engine and the pungent smell of gasoline hit his nostrils. He revved it to its max and sped out into the vast Atlantic toward New Bonaventure to see if anyone else was on their way to help search.

SALTWATER JOYS

John soon spotted the merchant's ship in the distance. Within minutes, he sped dangerously close and hollered at Thomas, who was pacing the deck. John thought he registered fear in Thomas's eyes. A gentle cry came from below the deck. John turned his ear toward the sound.

"John!" Thomas shouted. "I heard the bad news." He placed his hand on his chest. "I'm heading out to meet with the coastguard to make sure they're taking every measure to find Annabel."

John scowled. Thomas's sincerity was about as solid as a sudden gust of wind.

Thomas reached into his trouser pocket and pulled out an envelope. "Your receipt for a cleared debt. I suppose I should have left it with Lillian, but the poor thing didn't have any sense left in her."

"I don't want it." John said.

"I don't want your fish anymore. It ain't worth the time it would take to collect their scattered corpses off the shore."

John's chest heaved.

Thomas tossed the envelope, where it fluttered near John's boat and landed in the water. Then he threw a small velvet bag. "Take this too." It landed beside John's boot. "It's cursed!"

"The devil himself!" John picked up the bag and hurled it into the water. He had recognized it immediately—it was the velvet bag he had given Thomas with the gold coin inside. John manoeuvred his boat at a sharp right angle till the lip of the vessel was level to the surface of the water, then he headed in the opposite direction.

He settled his rampant heart with another mouthful of moonshine and began in earnest to search for Annabel. The dying codfish on the bottom of the boat suddenly flipped and jerked, attempting to draw in the last bit of oxygen from the scant amount of seawater sloshing around it. The tingling of alcohol in John's veins set his blood afire. He cursed when the splashing water and the codfish's slick, speckled scales brought desperate images of Annabel in her oilskin to his irrational mind. Releasing an anguished roar, John grabbed the tail and smashed the fish on the side of the boat. It thrashed in his hands, its bulging eyes taunting him. John opened his mouth wide and ripped the head off. When a stream of blood and guts spewed over his tongue, John swallowed hard then immediately lunged for the side of the boat, heaving fish dregs and alcohol into the calm waters below. The headless fish floated away.

Another swig of alcohol killed the bitter taste in his mouth but added to the delirious thoughts in his head. His ears filled with sudden screams as he imagined Annabel calling from her sea grave. He took another swig, emptying the flask this time. As he stood to see where the screams were coming from, a hand shot out of the water and clung to the side of the boat. Without thinking twice, he grabbed for the hand, Annabel's hand, the wedding band clearly visible on her finger. But before he could reach her, she let go and vanished into the blue below. John fell backward, bewildered by the thought of Annabel haunting him.

"Haunt me, Annabel! Haunt me!"

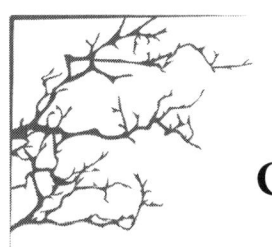

Chapter 7

AFTER ENDLESS HOURS of rowing and searching, John pulled his boat up onto the shore, defeated. His heart pounded through his shirt, resounding in his eardrums, a reminder he was still alive. Lines of familiar boats came into the harbour like a funeral procession, docking at the wharves to unload passengers. He knew that word spread quickly when someone was lost to sea, but he stared in disbelief when he saw Charlie's brothers hauling a wooden cross along the path toward the graveyard. Lillian ran down to the shore with her arms stretched wide.

"My son, there's no sign of her," she said with a drunken slur. "That storm was too much for her to survive, they tells me."

Lillian was dressed in black with a shawl draped over her head, her grey curls, looser than usual, poking out in all directions from the crocheted holes. She reminded John of a black pirate mast, her hair a dancing skeleton in the middle of the flag.

Lillian folded her hands in a prayer position. "Folks caught wind of her death, and they headed back here with the minister to mourn her soul in some kinda funeral ceremony."

Bill walked over and held Lillian.

John cursed under his breath, watching as the men disappeared into the woods toward the graveyard. "There's no body to put in the ground!" he yelled at Bill, now standing beside Lillian. "Giving up's not gonna bring her back. She's still out there, for frig's sake!"

"I know, but we got no choice. It's awful kind of everyone to come and lend a hand, you know?" Bill bowed his head to the minister who'd walked over to join them. The wise old man looked like he hadn't bathed in weeks. His shirt and trousers were stained and wrinkled. He resembled a scarecrow, travelling from outport to outport preaching the gospel.

"What if she's washed up on the shore somewhere? What if she's fighting to live, thinking someone's out looking for her?" John massaged his forehead as he paced before Bill, Lillian and the minister.

"It's very unlikely, John," the minister said gently, "after all this time."

"I killed my child too," John mourned.

Lillian's pale face flushed a deep pink. "It's such a shame they aren't out still looking," she said. "They came and filled me full of liquor and told me it's for the best. What am I supposed to do?" Lillian looked out over the water. "Oh, dear Lord, what do I do? There's nothing I can do to save my baby!"

Bill put his arms around her and guided her back to the house. John and the minister watched as Bill struggled under her drunken weight. The two men caught up with the couple, and John nodded to Bill to let him take over.

"I knows you'll find her, John." Lillian rested her head on his shoulder and closed her eyes. John picked her up and carried her inside the house. A room full of blank stares greeted him solemnly, and Skipper Ray and his wife moved out of his way. John could smell the stink of alcohol on Ray's breath as he passed by and headed upstairs to Lillian's bedroom. He heard Ray begin an impromptu, and drunken, eulogy.

John couldn't hide his rage. The food, the racket of children, the mourning crowd, Skipper Ray—it was all too much for him. He bounded down the stairs. "What? That's it? Not even one day, and you're all giving up on her?" Spit flew from his foaming mouth.

The crowd looked at him like he was a complete stranger. Oscar puffed on his pipe at his usual corner of the kitchen table. Sarah's parents sat next to him, holding Charlie and Sarah's son, James, who was fidgeting to get down. Their looks of pity were no match for the guilt that festered in John's conscience.

"We got to accept it, John," Bill said.

The minister pulled a chair between John and the crowd. He stood on it and pulled a small, leather-bound bible from his pocket. Gripping it over his head, he cleared his throat. "Let us now make our way to the church for prayer and to begin Annabel's service. I hear there's another violent storm coming, and by the looks of those black clouds out there, we don't have much time." He stayed where he was, standing guard as the crowd trickled out the door.

Bill placed his hat over his chest and bowed his head. He offered his hand to help the minister off the chair.

"Son, let this be a lesson." The minister's eyes were on John as he took Bill's hand and stepped down. "Let this tragedy be a test to you. Your faith is shattered. Take this opportunity to make it right with the Lord and have faith that you will redeem yourself and find salvation. I have no doubt Annabel has been embraced by Heaven and is now a beautiful angel on some distant shore. Keep her alive. A part of her lives on."

Bill looked away.

"She's still alive, and she's got to be somewhere out there. Until there's proof that she drowned, with all respect, I believes she could still be here." John took the empty flask from his pocket and filled it with the bottle of moonshine left on the table. His lip trembled when he let himself think that Annabel could be gone forever. He chugged the remaining mouthful of alcohol in the bottle before throwing it against the wall. Shards of glass littered the floor.

"She will always be alive in our hearts and in our memories," the minister said. He looked John straight in the eyes, his warm blue eyes shining through his wrinkled face. "Faith is believing in what you cannot see."

"I can see what everyone else believes. She's gone, and they thinks I did it," John said. "I shouldn't have pulled in the nets last night. I'd have a wife and child still."

The minister put his hand on John's shoulder. "You didn't kill them, John. You have to believe that. It was beyond your power and knowledge. It was Annabel's time to go home to the Lord."

"I'll prove you wrong once I finds them," John said. "Until that day, I'll live on this island to serve my time for what I did."

"John, you can't survive here all alone. We barely survived the winters when everyone was here," Bill said.

John turned away and looked out the window.

Bill put his arm on John's shoulder. He shook his head and covered his pinched lips with his hand.

"Skipper, with all due respect to you, I can't leave." John sat on the chair the minister had stood on. Fatigue washed over him. "What I did is unforgivable." He pointed his finger at the minister. "Not you or anyone can save me from this."

"She's gone, John," Bill said through sharp breaths. "You knows as well as I do that they would have found her by now." He started to walk up the stairs. "I've got to wake Lillian. Let's all say goodbye while everyone's here, and it's done proper by the minister."

John put the flask in his coat pocket and pulled out a cigarette from a pack left on the countertop. He opened the door of the wood stove and knelt down to the smouldering ashes to light it. He walked outside and stood out on the front step for just a moment before he turned to go down to the shore.

"John! Wait!" Sarah ran past some of the stragglers who were still on their way to the church. She was flushed and breathless when she reached him. "I heard someone yelling over there in the woods. I thought it was one of the youngsters, so I ran in, thinking someone was lost," she hesitated, "but it was some sort of a scream that came from the direction of Money Point."

John shook his head. "Probably a kid playing a prank on you." He looked up to the woods. "Watch, any minute one of them will run out."

"You don't believe me?" Sarah pulled his hand. "Remember the night we were up there looking for that treasure?"

"For frig's sakes, Sarah, what are you talking about?"

"Follow me."

They ran through the woods, branches flicking their faces as they tripped over roots and stones, never slowing down until they reached Money Point. The large pile of rocks taunted John as he and Sarah stood still and listened. The wind rustled through the leaves and heavy waves lapped on the rocks below. A scream rang out.

"The cliff!" Sarah kept a safe distance from the edge and pushed John ahead. "What are you waiting for? Go look!"

John crouched by the cliff that plummeted forty feet to the ocean. He almost lost his balance when he saw the oilskin washed up on the rocks. He looked back at Sarah. His bloodshot eyes were livid.

Shrieks grew louder from below the cliff.

"I think we should get outta here." Before the words left her mouth, Sarah was running back through the woods.

John took one more look over the cliff. He held his breath as his eyes scanned the shoreline. The oilskin was gone. He waited a moment to see if it might have gotten tangled up with the undertow, a strong current that was inescapable if you got caught in it. After a few minutes, it didn't reappear.

John took off and caught up to Sarah, motioning for her to follow him to his boat when they got back to the harbour.

They pushed the boat into the water. Gulls bawled overhead, circling like vultures. Sarah was knee deep in the water before she jumped aboard. John peeled off his jacket and put it over her shaking legs. With no words, they took off toward the bottom of Money Point. The clang of the church bells rang out over the harbour. John's heart sank deep in his chest.

Even though the engine revved at full power, it seemed to take forever until they reached the bottom of the cliff. There was no sign of the yellow oilskin. The telltale sign of swirling ripples allowed John to carefully manoeuvre the boat around jagged rocks that jutted from the ocean floor, hidden just beneath the water's surface. If he struck one, it would puncture the hull of the boat and sink it. With no shore nearby, they would be in a terrible predicament. Without warning, the same scream echoed all around the boat. John's eyes met Sarah's.

"Where's it coming from?" Sarah stood up.

John pulled Sarah down, stalled the engine and listened. There was no low-lying ground for miles, and the sound was not coming from above. It seemed to radiate from millions of tiny air bubbles that surfaced around the boat. Sarah pointed to a constant stream of bubbles that grew larger by the bow.

John dug through his storage box and dropped a jigger overboard. He let the weight fall steadily as the rope slid through his hands. It stopped when it hit the ocean floor. With a few flicks of his experienced wrist, he made the jigger dance. John's body stiffened when the line met resistance.

"I bet it's the jacket stuck down there," John said. The lapping waves quieted as the wind died down. The bubbles stopped, and all he could hear was his own heavy breathing.

He gave a few good hauls. "I got it stuck on something." It took every ounce of John's strength to pull the jigger through the water with the heavy weight attached.

Sarah sat frozen, except for her twitching eyes that darted from John to the tiny circle of ripples spreading out from the jigging line.

"What the hell?" He looked up at Sarah as his muscles strained under the weight.

"You think it's her?" Her voice trailed to a whisper.

John stopped and almost let go of the rope. He didn't know if he was prepared to see Annabel's drowned body. He hadn't considered what he would do if he hauled her up. They had no bag or blanket to cover her with, and hauling her on shore would surely be a disturbing sight for everyone. He wondered what she'd look like, whether she would be swollen up like Mr. Cooper. He wondered if her eyes would be open or shut.

"Look away," he said.

Maybe they'd make it back in time for a proper burial, he thought. He looked at Sarah and hauled the rope, hand over fist, until he knew the end of the jigger was about to surface.

"Oh God! Oh God! John, are you sure about this?" Sarah was in tears as she clutched the opposite side of the boat.

John gave a mighty haul, and the jigger came loose. Something solid flew over the side of the boat and crashed between his and Sarah's feet.

Sarah shrieked. "It's a head!" She buried her face in her hands.

John scrambled to wipe away the mounds of green seaweed, secretly hoping to see Annabel's face one last time, no matter how gruesome. A hollow feeling crept into his soul when he discovered a chunk of coral reef.

"It's not a head," John said. He wiped his brow, then lifted the coral high up over his head and fired it back into the ocean.

"What's that?" Sarah pointed toward the bow, her eyes transfixed on another steady stream of tiny bubbles rising to the surface of the water.

John stripped down to his underpants.

"Stop it, John." Sarah's voice was high and frightened. "I wants to go home now. Let's head back."

The cold sting of water muffled Sarah's words as he dove into the ocean. The feeling brought him back to the night prior, when he lost Annabel. He followed the stream of bubbles until the pressure on his chest was too much, and the bubbles disappeared into the darkness below. He struggled to make it to the surface. When he broke through, he sucked his lungs full of air and lifted his convulsing body into the boat.

Sarah handed him his clothes, and he quickly dressed. Although shivering ferociously, he refused to go back to the harbour. He and Sarah searched the area until another clang of bells signalled the end of the phantom funeral.

It was late afternoon, and the fog that had dissipated rolled back in with the next approaching storm, brewing massive clouds far along the horizon. In the distance, John spotted Charlie's boat. Tiny cracks of thunder rumbled louder with each passing minute.

"What the hell you guys doing out here?" Charlie yelled as soon as he was close enough for them to hear. "We were all out searching for you. Sarah, you had me worried sick." Charlie helped Sarah board his boat. "Geez. Sorry, John. I . . . ."

John shook his head.

"Listen, John, follow us to New Bonaventure and get a good night's sleep. Come back tomorrow and get a few of the b'ys to come back with you."

"I've got to keep looking for her," John said.

"Then, as long as the storm holds back, we'll stay and help, b'y."

The two boats spread out to increase the chance of spotting any sign of Annabel. When the storm threatened to move closer, they made their way back. Boats of mourners were leaving the harbour. Everyone kept to the sides, looking out, as if still watching for Annabel over the vast blue spread around them.

John couldn't bear the solemn eyes that met his. The looks were nothing more than heartfelt sympathy, but the alcohol that lingered in his veins tricked him, making him see faces full of bitterness and hate. The group's silence screamed, "Murderer!" Their shaking heads and tears howled, "Monster!"

When John entered Bill and Lillian's house, he was surprised to find the place empty of its former charm. Only the eclectic furniture remained—covered with ghostly white sheets—and the kitchen table and chairs. He took a seat. He assumed that the friends who had come to mourn Annabel had helped the Toopes pack and transport their remaining belongings. What was left was a dreary sight. Despair washed over him. He felt as deserted as his surroundings.

Charlie and Sarah followed him into the house.

"We got to get back home now," Charlie said.

"Charlie, I thinks we should tell him," Sarah said from the doorway. "I'd want to know."

John stood up and headed toward the stairs.

"Slade has her," Sarah blurted, then blushed profusely.

John stopped and turned around. "Annabel?"

"No, Annabel had the baby yesterday. A baby girl. Lillian gave her to Thomas this morning." Sarah sat down at the table and pressed her cheeks into her hands, waiting for John's response.

John gave a quick, disgusted snort.

"It's true," Charlie said.

"That's the most ridiculous thing I've ever heard. You want me outta here, so you're using my unborn child as bait. Unbelievable!" John could feel his blood pressure spike and his temperature rise.

"Just come with us," Sarah said. "You'll see."

John stumbled back a step. "I'm gonna stay here and find her, and you can't change my mind, no matter what lies you tells me." He cracked his neck from side to side, looking like he wanted to punch the wall.

"It's the truth, John." Just as Sarah was about to approach John, Charlie grabbed her hand.

"We have to get back before dark," he said, pulling Sarah out the door. "We'll deal with this later."

A dozen bottles of homemade beer sat on the kitchen table, left over from the wake. John sat and drank them, one after another, all the while contemplating whether there could be any inkling of truth in Sarah's words. In his drunken stupor, he staggered toward the shore with bottle-fisted hands. He tripped and fell, holding tight to the bottles. With nothing to break the fall, his head struck a boulder. The crack of his skull echoed around the harbour, with the sound of shattering glass following soon after. The violent shock sent John into a temporary unconsciousness. The alcohol in his blood knocked him out, preventing him from waking, as he lay beside Annabel's ocean grave. In the distance, a wild storm raged.

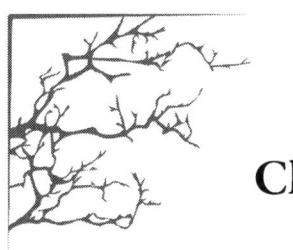

Chapter 8

THE NEXT MORNING, JOHN opened his eyes to his exile, now a strange and ugly place. His head ached. In a retrograde amnesia, he couldn't remember the events that led him to waking on the shoreline with a swollen bloody gash on the side of his forehead. The last thing he could remember were the passersby as they left the harbor. But, looking around, the harbour didn't look anything like it used to. The clear blue sky mocked his cold, beaten body, hung over from the previous night's binge. Empty glass bottles were smashed across the rocky shore; his hands cut and splintered with slivers of glass. The sun shone bright, and its penetrating light burned his eyes. The calmness of the ocean gloated, claiming victory in Annabel's death. The harsh cries of crows replaced the obnoxious screech of seagulls, while the surge of the tide and the roar of the surf assaulted John's ears. He hated every sound. He hated the absurdity of life—that everything he had ever wanted could be taken away in a moment. All the familiar, all the good in his life, transformed into wretchedness in an instant.

With numb hands, he slapped the buzzing black nippers around his head. Each bite took a tiny piece of flesh from behind his ears and along his hairline. He closed his eyes.

Just a bad dream, he convinced himself. Something he'd soon escape.

He opened his eyes again, but the place was the same, the empty wharves a stark reminder that he had been left behind. Everything he had ever loved and had worked hard to earn was gone. Always living for tomorrow, he had relied on time to carry him into the future with Annabel. Now, like a reverse trajectory, he had to bear time without her.

If this wasn't a dream, John considered his predicament a dream within a dream. His mind wrung out endless loopholes to escape this torment, to find his way back to Annabel. He decided to lie there that morning and die. Let the tide pull him out and drown him. Drown his suffering and guilt, into the big black hole where Annabel waited under the sea. Without her, he could not live.

His gut growled, racked with hunger. He didn't have the energy to drag his cold body into the ocean. Desperate, he tried to breathe in the water that pooled about his face. The cruel tide teased his effort as it retracted, forcing him into a coughing fit. Oxygen rushed to his brain, and his pulse quickened. He grabbed a large beach rock beside him, but his hands too had lost their strength. When he let go, small loose grains of sand embedded themselves into the deep cuts that lined his palms. It stung more than the salt water. As the tide came back, the grains left the cuts and returned back to the beach. He dug in the sand, squeezing mounds of it in his fists, trying to prolong the physical pain to obscure the anguish in his heart. The harder he squeezed, the faster the sand slipped away.

Like the sand grains, the tide and each breath, Annabel became more distant to John with each passing second. Her face, a sudden blur in his memory, took different shapes until he no longer remembered what she looked like. He remembered her parts but could not place them together as a whole. He could see her heart-shaped hairline, her tiny hands and brown eyes, but it wasn't her. Pieces of her. He looked out and wondered how much water, in the ever-expanding ocean, was between them.

The wind caught hold of the maggoty stench of rotting codfish. John became aware of the increasing racket of cawing crows. They fought over the fish, tearing them apart until the harbour was strewn with fish guts. A rage filled John's chest at the sight of the massacre. He lunged into the water, determined to drown himself, to end the misery consuming him. He needed to quiet the crows, quiet the crash of the tide, quiet the haunting voice of Annabel warning him to turn around and go home. Surely his guilt was heavy enough to pull him down through the water, fill up his lungs and kill him. To his dismay, he floated in the freezing, zero-gravity void. He bobbed on the surface of the water until every bone ached from the cold. He wanted to die. He dared himself to dunk his head and suck the salt water into his lungs. By the time he worked up the nerve to do it, he came up sputtering as the tide washed him ashore. Romanticized thoughts of suicide clouded his mind—to be with her!—, but a hero doesn't have a coward's heart.

He cursed the ocean and dragged himself from the shore, up the path toward Bill and Lillian's house. The sun radiated just enough warmth to keep him from freezing to death. He stumbled and fell beside a thin shadow of a cross cast by the church steeple. He turned his head to the sky and saw on the cross the silhouette of Jesus, thorns of sunbeams radiating from his head. John's personal judgement day. He would be cast aside and sentenced to hell-fires when a heavenly jury declared him guilty of murder.

John thought of the hours he had spent inside the church praying with clasped hands and believing in things he couldn't see. Now, he pondered asking the overshadowing Jesus for forgiveness. But he didn't. His actions were unforgivable, and forgiveness would not bring Annabel back anyway. In despair, his perspective twisted, convincing him that God was to blame for her tragic death; that God had abandoned them and didn't show up in their moment of need.

John pulled himself up on his elbows and grabbed the biggest rock within reach. He looked up at the stained-glass windows beaming like eyes from the soul of the church. He flung the rock and smashed one of the low-lying windows, adorned with praying hands. He crawled closer to the church and collected a handful of rocks. Raining shards of glass plinked on the hard rocks below as John smashed all fifteen windows, leaving the church to gaze out to the harbour with eyeless sockets.

"What do I do?" John yelled, breaking the silence. "What am I supposed to do?" A stream of salt water trickled down his cheeks. A tangy drop rolled into his mouth, but he couldn't tell if it fell from his eyes or his wet hair.

"Annabel, m'lovey, where are you?" he whispered. "How do I find you?" He repeated this over and over, his mind summersaulting the delusional possibility of rescuing her.

The memory of the oilskin bobbing on the sea and the stream of bubbles kindled a fire deep in his gut. When he remembered his nightmare of Easton wanting his coin back, he imagined Annabel's soul stuck in the ocean's black abyss, with the pirate ghosts holding her hostage. There was no way he could kill himself and risk having Annabel stuck down there with the living dead. They would be separated until the next life, or eternity, if he killed himself. And the next life was too far away.

Adrenaline surged through John's veins, and he trudged into Bill and Lillian's house to warm up. The kitchen table was scattered with food from Annabel's mock service. John ate a raisin tea bun to calm the dull ache in his stomach.

He needed to get his strength back if he was going to find Annabel. He set a fire in the wood stove, listening to it hiss and crack as its flaming tongue licked the junks of wood. Warmth rushed around him as he stripped off his wet clothes and hung them above the stove. The numbness wore off as blood flowed back into his limbs, fingers and toes. He lay down on the chesterfield, covered himself with the white sheet thrown over it, and slept.

JOHN WOKE TO SEE THE full circle of the sun as it lingered on the horizon. His head throbbed with each ruthless heartbeat. His clothes were dry, so he dressed himself and went into the kitchen to finish off what was left of the tea buns and cookies.

"I'm going to find you, wherever you're hidden, Annabel," he vowed, broken-hearted. He searched through every cupboard and drawer in the kitchen, and every nook and cranny around the house, until a small pile of items covered the kitchen table. He took off up the staircase to see if there were any more supplies of use to him. The bedrooms were empty, besides a couple of wooden tables, a salt-beef piss pot, and tin cans used for anything and everything. Annabel's room was left untouched. The bed was still unmade and dishevelled from the morning after her death. Her brush still sat on her bureau. A mirror still hung on the wall. Frayed mats were left on the floor, and empty nails protruded from the wallpapered walls.

Before the light faded completely, John pulled down the ladder in the hallway to the attic. Just as he climbed up, the sun crept a little lower on the horizon, casting a red glow through the attic window. The rays of light illuminated every speck of dust and cobweb that had accumulated over the years. Empty crooked shelves lined the walls. A few glass bottles with screw tops were strewn across the floor. John dug through some boxes and found a pair of piss pumps—old rubber boots cut off at the ankle to wear as slippers around the house on cold days. Other boxes were empty or contained odd socks and rags. He stuffed the socks in his trouser pocket. He found a broken frame with a cross stitch of "God Bless our Home" in blue thread and threw it down. He was surprised to find a rolled up sleeping bag, and tucked it under his arm.

As the sun descended below the horizon, a strange and unnatural feeling spread through the attic. Darkness was nearing, and John realized he didn't have any oil lanterns or fuel. All the provisions that would cost a small fortune to replace had been taken. He set down the sleeping bag to dig through one last box of rags. He found a hard-plastic doll with ratty yellow hair and a scratched, discoloured face. John studied its closed eyes and long, black eyelashes. He picked it up, and the brown eyes opened wide. "Mama," it cried, and John whipped it against the wall, where it landed with a thud and slumped into the corner. Its eyes remained open.

John backed away. His ears filled with sounds of the creaking house and scratching mice scurrying through the walls. He kicked the sleeping bag down the ladder and followed it into the hallway. He took it into the living room and grabbed a junk of wood from the woodpile. He held the end in the glowing embers of the wood stove in hopes of making a torch, but he knew it would blow out so he threw it in and closed the door to let it burn. He grabbed another junk of wood and pulled one of the odd socks from his pocket. He put the wood inside the sock, set it on fire and held a torch in his hand. The entire time, the demon doll never left his mind.

John's throat felt constricted, and with each swallow his neck tightened. A sharp thirst struck him, a kind of itch, a nagging tickle that could only be quenched with a drink. He began sucking at his cheeks and under his tongue for a smattering of saliva. He sat for a moment in the light of the burning sock and decided to walk to the creek for some water. He took a tin can from the pile of odds and ends on the kitchen table and headed for the door.

The brisk wind threatened to blow out his flaming torch the moment John stepped out the door. But he was parched, his need for water greater than his fear of the blackness ahead. He knew the harbour and had walked the path to the creek many times in the pitch dark. Though it was different now. The night was filled with nothing and nobody. John didn't know what the darkness held beyond the dim glow of his burning sock. Everything looked so foreign and made him feel like an outsider, an intruder.

The creek seemed farther than usual, and his thirst was rapidly becoming unbearable. John's pace was slowed by the ascent of the hill and the wind. He worked to protect the flame in front of him. In the distance, a scream echoed through the trees—the terrified cry of a child. He stopped in his tracks. He imagined it was his child, scared and alone, crying out through the darkness. The brown-eyed doll seized his thoughts.

He ran to the creek and filled the tin can in the trickling rapids. He guzzled it, then filled it again and again, all the while looking side to side. He wasn't sure what he was looking for or if he could even see if something was lurking. The vicious wind blew and extinguished his torch. As he made his way through the dark, the piercing cry followed close behind him.

"Haunt me, Annabel, but don't scare the hell outta me!" John sprinted to the house and slammed the door. Inside wasn't any better. The fire had died out, and the air carried a chill. He quickly unrolled the sleeping bag on top of the chesterfield and crawled into it. The demon doll commanded his thoughts, and he was afraid to even look toward the staircase that led to the bedrooms.

John lay in the darkness with his eyes wide open. The dreadful lashing of a branch on the window rattled "ta-tum, ta-tum," and his thumping heart soon quickened to match its pace. When he heard the shriek again, he convinced himself it was only the wind through the trees. Still, he imagined Annabel's tormented soul on the other side of the windowpane, trying to scratch her way inside. Each wail saw him sobbing with his hands over his ears until it stopped. He tiptoed to the windowsill and drew the curtain, expecting to see the translucent apparitions of his wife and child. He let the curtain fall. There was no one there. Like a child, John curled into a fetal position on the floor, rocking himself to the rhythm of the beating branches. As the wind died down, the tapping slowed to the sound of a palpitating heartbeat and lulled John to sleep.

That night, John dreamed of Annabel. Her entire being, as she always was, stood in front of him. The bits and pieces he couldn't put together in his mind were whole once again. She smiled, hands outstretched, calling his name, but her voice was muted by the strong wind. She stood at the brink of the cliff at Money Point, her long curls whipping behind her. With her back to the ocean, she waved. Her smile faded, and she fell backward off the edge. John leapt after her, eyes closed, stomach flipping. He opened his eyes to find Annabel's drowned and lifeless corpse lying beside him. Her eyes were those of the demon doll, her hair tangled around her face like the seaweed attached to the jigged coral. Her arms clutched the now-eyeless doll.

John tossed and turned all night on the cold wooden floor, unable to wake, to escape the nightmare's torment.

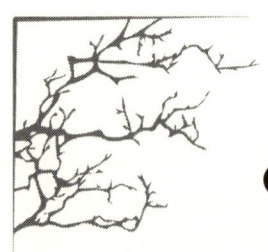

Chapter 9

JOHN WELCOMED THE MORNING light that put an end to the terrors of the night. Disturbed by his dreams, he huddled over the wood stove to collect the last few matches left behind. The house creaked with each frigid gust of wind. He lit a fire, unable to ignore the dwindling pile of wood. He put the tin can of water on the stove top and took it off before it was too hot to touch. The warm water scalded his wind-burned lips. The tasteless concoction made him crave a cup of tea and a slice of homemade toast or a fried touton, with a little melted butter and molasses. John longed for the aromas that used to make this house a home.

The sudden slam of a door upstairs jarred his reverie. John jerked, spilling the water in his cup over the rim and soaking his arm. Daylight brought courage, so he neared the staircase to listen for anything suspicious. He crept up the stairs to the closed door of Annabel's bedroom. A vision of the doll in the attic flashed once more through his mind. He turned the knob, praying the wretched thing wasn't on the other side of the door. He flung the door open, unclenching his jaw only when he was sure the room was empty. He walked in, and the door closed behind him. He stood for a long time, as still as a solid pine tree, until he convinced himself it was nothing out of the ordinary. Strong winds had the ability to shift house frames.

The room still smelled of Annabel. John sat on the bed, laid his head on her pillow and breathed in the all-too-familiar saltwater perfume that had always lingered on her skin. The pillow held long strands of brown hair. John wrapped each one around his finger until he formed a silky layer around his fingertip. He stroked the hair and put it against his cheek. From across the room, he caught his reflection in the mirror. The glass bulged in the middle, distorting his image. He inched himself forward until he was nose to nose with the figure standing in front of him, a shadow of the man he was just days ago. He raised his fist and punched the reflection that stared at him, unblinking and accusing. A solemn reminder of his solitude. The glass sliced his hand, and blood ran down Annabel's hair. He unwound the hair and returned it to the pillow, smudging the pillowcase with blood. From the window, he looked out over the empty harbour and wondered if he'd have enough gasoline in his boat to search for Annabel.

The morning was cold as John headed out to search Bill's abandoned fishing stage for supplies. When he entered, he was hit with Annabel's presence. She was saturated in everything around the harbour. Under each rock and around every corner, her spirit called out for him to remember her, to search for her, to rescue her. He left the stage with his finds—a jigging line, a knife, a blanket and a bucket, dropping the load to the ground when he saw a small boat entering the harbour. He hunched down till it docked at Bill's wharf. When he knew he was out of view, John ran and took shelter in the surrounding trees, skulking like a wild animal stalking its prey. From the corner of his eye, he thought he saw something white dart through the woods, followed by the sound of crunching branches. A fleeting fantasy had John considering whether Annabel might be a fallen angel, trying to lure him into the woods to be with her. He recalled the stories of older generations about the fairy-haunted woods. Little mythical creatures, believed to be fallen angels, wavering between heaven and hell, sent to lure people into the woods. Berry pickers told stories of hearing their name called, only to be found hours or days later, dirty and ragged, with no memory of how they had wandered kilometres away. The fairies made a supernatural lapse of time occur in mere moments. He knew he couldn't trust the fairies; they could pose as Annabel and lead him astray. John was scared of them and knew better than to fall for their shenanigans. He flipped his coat inside out to ward them off and waited at the edge of the woods to see who was in the boat.

Two unfamiliar boys, maybe fifteen or sixteen years old, tied their boat to Bill's wharf. With hammers and empty bags in hand, they ran up the hill toward the church, hollering the whole way.

"Well, b'y, let's go see what kind of treasure's been left behind in these old shacks," the taller of the two boys called out. They went inside the church, their voices muddled by the loud crashes of destruction taking place inside.

John crept from the woods and snuck down to their boat. He grabbed a small but heavy duffle bag, hoping it contained some food. He lifted a pair of binoculars hanging from the bow and draped the leather cord around his neck.

In an instant, he made it back to his safe spot in the woods. He unzipped the duffle bag and found a couple of cans of pop, a bag of salt-and-vinegar chips and beef jerky. Digging a little deeper, he found some cigarettes, lighters and a flashlight. He chewed and drooled over the salt-spiced meat while conspiring a plan to scare the kids from his harbour.

John collected some rocks in his arms and moved through the woods until he was behind the church. He fired the rocks against the outside of the church, and the brazen pair jumped out of a broken window, their chests puffed out like roosters, hammers and bags still in hand. They scanned the area, dropping their weapons and loot when they spotted John's silhouette creeping toward them. John had only been alone in the harbour for a day by himself, yet he looked wild and frightening. His back was hunched, his body severely beaten, his face caked with dried blood. He snarled and growled through clenched teeth, his eyes ablaze with fury.

"What the hell?!" The shorter boy took off like a shot at the sight of John.

"It's a friggin' ghost!" the other yelled.

They both hightailed it to their boat, tripping and spinning dirt from their shoes as they ran down the hill to the wharf.

Within minutes, John heard the full force of the engine turn the corner of the harbour and fade away. The vandals didn't have any time to notice their missing things. Satisfied with his tactic, John collected the duffle bag from the woods, the hammers and bags left behind, then put it all in his boat. Before he pushed his boat off the shore into the water, he realized it was nearly out of gas, John ran back to Bill's fishing stage to grab a set of oars to leave in the boat, in case he got stranded. He cursed under his breath for not syphoning some gas from the vandals' boat before he scared them off. To save the little gas he had left in the engine, he started rowing. His torn shoulder muscles burned as he furiously paddled to the lookout at Money Point, where he last saw the yellow oilskin. His heart ached at the revived thought of Annabel beneath the water.

The ocean was gentle, and there was no sign of Annabel or the oilskin. In his mind, he searched for direction. He needed a map or some kind of psychic ability to create a path to where she was. He spent hours going in circles around the area where the trail of bubbles had surfaced the day before.

He paddled out to the abandoned nets and decided to haul them up, in case Annabel had gotten tangled up in them. Despite the urge to stop, he heaved, pulling in dead fish hung on the twine, attached by their gills. John cursed the sight of them. He cursed the merchant, and he cursed himself. He cursed Annabel for even going out that night to warn him. There had been no need; he would have been just fine. For a moment, he was able to bend his love to hate. She took herself away because she forced him to make the decision that killed her. He winced to think he had chosen the goddamn fish over her.

As he pulled the net, his rubber boot appeared, the one that had held him back from her that night. He untangled it, launched it as far as he could and watched as it glugged full of water and sank. He set the net again, hoping it might catch her.

John docked the boat at Bill's wharf a couple of hours before sunset. The dead fish spread on the shoreline were still covered with black crows. The stench of the rotting flesh was unbearable and served as another solemn reminder of the hell John was sentenced to endure.

He decided to search the other abandoned houses for anything of use before anyone else got to it. He collected knick-knacks in an old burlap potato sack. It was mostly junk, but he thought the odds and ends might come in handy. He headed back to Bill and Lillian's house where, to his surprise, a large box was sitting by the kitchen table with a scrap of paper tucked into the folded flaps. It read:

John,

Surely I knows you ain't dead yet, and I also knows you're too stubborn to leave, so I brought you back some stuff to hold you over for the winter. Lill put in some food, but she says to come to New Bonaventure before you starves to death. The promises made to us were broken already. No place to raise a family because there's no work for the lot of us and it'll be hard to live on nothing. Me and Sarah are going to the mainland. Good luck, me buddy, and if you ever comes to the mainland, I sure hopes our paths cross again.

Charlie

John was relieved to see a lantern with six small drums of oil, candles, a big box of matches, tea bags, a mug, jars of meats and jams, pickled vegetables, and as many loaves of bread as could be stuffed into the remaining box space. His mouth watered, but he resisted opening any of it. John pulled up a hinged door hidden in the floorboards in the living room that accessed the root cellar. With no electricity or refrigeration, root cellars kept vegetables and other food items cool in the summer and prevented them from freezing in the winter. John hoped to find some of the potatoes, turnips and carrots he knew were stocked after the harvest to ration over the winter months.

Disappointment prevailed at the sight of the barren cellar, as John realized all the vegetables had been packed and taken to New Bonaventure. He brought down the burlap bag and the box of supplies from Charlie. He emptied both and then moved upstairs to Annabel's bedroom to grab one of the frayed mats to hide the cellar door from any more vandals. He brought the empty burlap bag with him upstairs and stopped when he reached the ladder to the attic. He climbed it, tentatively, and the first thing he saw was the godforsaken doll. He ran to get it and tossed it inside the burlap sack. He heard the muffled "Mama," and quickly tied a knot at the top and dropped it from the attic door to the hallway. It cried again. John needed to get rid of the cursed thing immediately. He couldn't bear to sleep with its presence in the house. He didn't want to take it out in the boat with him or burn it in the stove, so he decided to run through the woods and throw it over the cliff at Money Point.

He darted through the woods. The doll bounced and banged on his back with each heavy stomp. The relentless cry of "Mama" distorted itself into an evil, melancholic chant that could have been the voice of Satan himself. John pictured the blinking eyes of the doll, the fluttering eyelashes, the tangles of matted hair. The devil doll let out its last cry when John stopped abruptly on the brink of the cliff and hurled the bag into the ocean.

Sprinting back through the woods, John made it to Bill and Lillian's just before sunset. He knew that, masked behind the quaint harbour's flaring colours of orange and red, nightmares dwelt. He hurried inside, started a fire and lit some candles. He went down to his stash in the cellar and grabbed some bread and partridgeberry jam. In front of the stove, he opened the bread bag and set a slice on the metal hanger to toast. Unscrewing the lid of the jam, he used his index finger to smudge a heap of it over the toast. He salivated like a dog when he took his first bite. He wanted another slice, but he closed the bag and screwed the lid back on the jam jar. As he savoured the aftertaste, he noticed the dents and marks in the soft wood of the kitchen table, highlighted by the candlelight. John ran to Annabel's room, pulled the lone nail from the wall, then ran back to the kitchen and dragged its sharp point over the table until he scratched an outline of the harbour in front of him. He placed an *X* on each place he had searched. He studied the map and made a plan for the next day.

The days were getting shorter, the nights longer, and the dark frightened John. He tried to ration his candles and use them only when he needed to move around the house, so that left him in the pitch black of night in the living room. He kept the curtains partially open to keep watch for any movement at the window frame. He stayed awake, too scared to move around in the empty house, more scared to go to sleep. In the quiet living room, John heard the rush of the tide and then the loud cry. A shadow moved between the curtains. Fear gripped him as he approached the window and drew the curtain to one side. The doll's eyes stared at him, its dress and hair soaking wet.

"Mama!" it cried.

John's knees gave out and the curtain fell back into place. He stuck his fingers in his ears and hummed a long-forgotten melody to drown out the torturous cry. He held his breath so long he passed out. A forced way was sometimes the only way to fall asleep, when it meant trading the nightmare he was living for the night terrors that awaited him.

Chapter 10

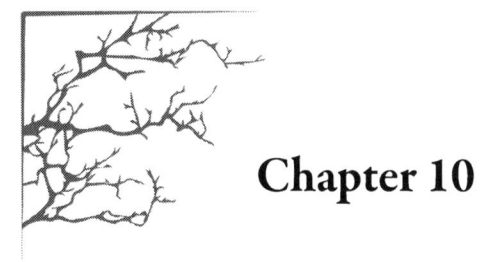

JOHN WOKE WITH HIS fingers still jammed in his ears. Fed up with his fearful state, in a rage he tore the curtains off the window. His heavy breathing produced a visible cloud of white mist. On the window, intricate patterns of frosted designs covered the glass. John saw what looked like hundreds of outstretched hands trying to claw their way from the depths of eternal damnation. He wiped the frosty glass and pressed his forehead against it. His eyes dropped to the bottom of the windowsill, then to the ground below.

John's heart sunk.

The doll lay dishevelled on the white-tipped grass. Its hair was a mound of icicles, its eyes frozen open. John ran through the kitchen and snatched his coat, hanging over a chair. He flew out the door and stopped abruptly when he saw the doll now propped up against the side of the house. It glared at him.

John looked around the perimeter of the woods, hoping it was a sick prank put on by the two young vandals he'd scared away. He saw no shoe prints surrounding the doll, but he did see small prints in the shape of cloven hooves. Footprints of the devil. John rubbed his eyes hard and shook his head, but the doll remained. He hoped he was living in a twisted nightmare that he would soon wake from. But it wasn't a dream. Resettlement had dismembered the community. Annabel was dead. He had killed her and their child. He was a murderer. He was sentenced to live within the solitary confines of the harbour, with no escape from the torrential torment that lurked in every corner of his subconscious.

He found another burlap potato sack inside the house and ran outside to collect heavy rocks, careful not to overfill and rip the bottom out of the bag. He kept the doll in his peripheral vision to make sure it didn't move. Once satisfied the weight was heavy enough to sink the devil doll to the bottom of the sea, he picked it up by the neck and threw it on top of the rocks in the sack. Its eyes were fixated on him, as the slow, drawn-out "Mama" startled him. John tied the bag together with tight knots, heaved it over his aching shoulder, and headed for the boat. He placed the bag gently inside so that it wouldn't damage the aging boards.

The sea was a mirror of the grey sky, reflecting huge cumulus clouds that charged in off the Atlantic like a pirate ship. The image rekindled his delusion of the notorious Peter Easton holding Annabel's soul hostage. The sight of the cloud formation coerced John to start his engine and zip across the water in the opposite direction of New Bonaventure, straight out to the freezing cold ocean.

John kept his eyes locked on the bag, except to glance occasionally over his shoulder until he could see that the island of Ireland's Eye was a speck on the horizon. The boat sped forward in full throttle until it chugged, sputtered and stalled when the gas ran out. When John lifted the bag, the rocks clunked together, and the doll continued its mournful lament. He dropped it over the side of the boat into the water, but the cry still echoed on in John's head. Tiny bursts of air from the bag rushed to the surface.

"What in the livin' name of...?"

The bubbles continued to rise in a steady stream. He pushed the anchor overboard, and it dangled like a giant fishing hook, suspended in the water, jigging with the rise and fall of the waves. The rope wasn't long enough to hook the sea floor, and it allowed the current to pull him and the boat farther into the Atlantic.

John took off his coat and jumped into the frigid water. He immediately lost his breath and started hyperventilating. Goosebumps shot up from every inch of his skin when he dunked his head to peer into the deep blue. Besides a lone mushroom-capped jellyfish with pink clover guts and tangled tentacles, he couldn't see anything. He resurfaced for air, and the stream of bubbles was visible once again, coming from the unending darkness below.

Immediately he dunked back under and heard fragments of Annabel's voice. The confluence of millions of bubbles orchestrated her screams; the same desperate screams from the night she drowned. John felt a new charge of adrenaline pump through his body at the sound of her voice. He kicked through the salt water that stung the inside of his nose and burned the back of his throat. As he came up for air, a strong force pulled on his leg. He kicked ferociously to free himself, but the grip only tightened. John struggled and sputtered as the menacing grasp dragged him under. Bubbles swirled above him. A circle of sunlight shone like the white of an eye; his boat, dead centre, the black pupil—like a Cyclops witnessing his descent into an icy hell.

As he sank farther, his peripheral vision went black. John could feel the pressure build on his lungs. His body was paralyzed, in shock from the bone-chilling cold that engulfed him. Bubbles slipped from his nose, but he held on strong to his remaining breath. Despite the pressure, he resisted the urge to suck in the salt water. The grip wrapped itself around his torso and made its way up to his chest and held on.

John looked up at the dying light of the sun and saw Annabel's face, her frozen lips blue against her ghostly pallor. For a moment, he wondered if it was the doll, a fairy doll, tricking him, breaking his heart once again. But there she was, and he felt her in his embrace. He leaned in close to kiss her. The interchange of energy, air and saliva in a kiss was absent; instead Annabel breathed a cool stream of salt water into his mouth and lungs. He tried to hold on to her, tried to let the force pull him down and kill him, drown him, but he was no longer in the confines of the grip. He kicked instinctively until his head breached, coughing up the water he had swallowed, choking for air.

He swam to the boat and grabbed hold of the side. He concentrated on Annabel's presence below. He wondered what she saw on the night she died, and whether she knew he didn't give up on her, until he didn't have any other choice. John knew she was a smart girl who wouldn't have panicked that night. She trusted John and would have waited for him as long as she could. But, he also knew she wouldn't have given up easily and wouldn't have died with grace. He tried to imagine the last memories that flashed before her eyes when she took her first breath of water. By that time, she would have known she was too far from John's reach, and with water in her lungs, she'd have no chance to fight her way up to the surface. She would have known she was going down with the momentum of a sinking ship.

John had always been told as a child that drowning was the most peaceful way to die. It was a lie, to soften the blow when someone from the community drowned at sea. Many clung to this belief to protect their broken hearts from the truth. But John knew that inhaling salt water burned and scraped as it entered the lungs. Tranquility only comes after the sting. He hoped she had passed out, to bypass the agony of suffocating in water. He could feel the terror in her heart, as a tingling sensation of thousands of goosebumps rose in waves up his thighs. His muscles were frozen, and as the blood in his extremities moved into his core, his strength waned. He visualized himself reunited with Annabel.

Alone, he floated like the buoyant, spineless jellyfish that bobbed nearby. Although he wished he had died with Annabel that night, he feared now that if he died, he would go to hell for what he'd done and be separated from Annabel forever. Even worse, he feared the possibility that nothing followed death. He floated until he could no longer bear the cold that chomped through his skin and gnawed at his muscles and bones. He struggled into the boat and wrapped his dripping body with the blanket he had stowed. Shivering, shaking, he fought the strong desire to lie down and go to sleep.

"Give me a sign, Annabel," John said, slow and slurred.

His mind was awash in confusion and he couldn't spot Ireland's Eye on the horizon. He had drifted far into the Atlantic. To add to his lack of direction, the clouds parted and opened up a blue sky, the sun at its zenith. As the heat of the sun permeated the cold breeze, a hot rush of fright fireballed through John's veins. A low fog began crawling toward him, rolling over itself, growing thicker and taller. He knew he had to get back to the harbour before the fog swallowed him into its white blindness, a fisherman's death trap. He put on his coat with clumsy hands and pulled up the useless anchor. His icy blood began to circulate, filling his arms with the excruciating sensation of pins and needles. The bubbles around the boat stopped, but the image of his wife burned in John's mind. The press of her hard lips and the taste of freezing salt water left him breathless.

As the sun began its departure, John rowed in its direction through the fog. He trusted his internal compass and rowed with heavy arms. The oars flopped out of sync with one another, and John sensed a dark energy following in his wake. He wasn't sure if it was Annabel's memory, her ghost, the demon doll, the pirates, or all of them teaming together to taunt and torture him. John harnessed his fears and rowed. Waves of nausea from hunger and thirst caused him bouts of dry heaving.

As he struggled to row, his eyes continued to search for Annabel. He prepared himself to see her hand dart from the water to clutch the lip of the boat. It terrified him to imagine her frigid body hauling itself aboard. The sound of her voice lingered in the cresting waves, as her scent lingered in his nose. She was a fire in his head, a fever that sucked the life out of him. She was all the beauty, strength and danger of the ocean, merged into one on the night she died.

In the distance, through the dense fog, John heard the murder of crows gathered around the rotting fish pile. Most of the fish flesh and guts now eaten, the crows scavenged amidst the bones. Their desperate caws led him to the opening of the harbour, back into the safe haven of Ireland's Eye.

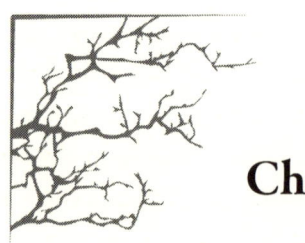

Chapter 11

LOW, HEAVY CLOUDS, engorged with the thick scent of rain, ruptured with a loud crack of thunder. John dropped the oars when the boat hit the rocky shoreline of the harbour. He touched his frozen knuckles to his windburned lips, and his hands felt waxy, as if they belonged to a corpse. He blew warm air on them, to little effect. His feet and legs were heavy and numb, a muscular paralysis from his plunge into the ocean. Though his pulse felt weak, his mind was sharp, and he knew he was soon going to freeze to death if he stayed in the boat. The cackling crows, ominous black messengers of death, spurred his desire to live. They sensed his weakness and told each other secrets filled with loathsome intentions as they flew near and landed on the ledge of the boat.

With fisted hands, John pushed one of his legs over the side of the boat. The sudden jolt didn't scare the birds that perched tight. With a little momentum, he rolled his body over the ledge and splashed into the crashing tide. The cold shackled his movements, and he panicked at the realization that his legs wouldn't obey his mind. He crawled with clubbed hands toward the house, his legs and waterlogged boots worse than useless behind him, like a ball and chain. The haze of fog lay over him like a heavy wool blanket.

Half expecting at any moment to succumb to hypothermia, John stopped to stabilize his breath. He was breathing so hard and fast he thought he might hyperventilate and faint, which would give the crows plenty of time to swoop in and devour him. He was able to calm his breath when he focused on the carnivorous pitcher plant on the pathway in front of him. It stood sturdy and tall against the cold wind and never succumbed to the snow that piled up on its stalk. Red veins stretched around the leaves, reflecting ultraviolet light to lure insects to the slippery lip so they would fall into its pouch. Little downward facing hairs prevented the insect's escape. The flower was sly and smart like the ocean, waiting patiently for sustenance.

The sound of multiple long caws, followed by a series of short caws, told John that the murder had left their perch on the boat, and were heading in his direction. A brave crow with fiery eyes emerged from the fog. John watched it peck at his leg, but couldn't feel the sharp stab of its beak on his frozen skin. The others must have been just at the edge of the fog, waiting for a signal from the brave one. John screeched, but the bird didn't flinch. It just tilted its head and watched him. All was still in the low-lying cloud that surrounded him, except for the movement of the eye of the crow. With a taste for blood, John knew it expected him to die, and that there were enough in the murder to torture him to death in his immobile state.

John drew back his top lip and barked and roared at the birds as they came too close. He swung his clubbed fists in the air until they flew away, but they were back the moment he stopped. They were hungry. He trudged his dead weight once again toward the pitcher plant. He needed to figure out which direction was homeward. In the fog, it felt like a blindfolded game of hide-and-seek. He grew colder with each passing minute and wondered if he deserved to die this way, eaten alive by the incessant pecking of the crows. He passed the plant and stayed within the rock path in front of him. Bill and Lillian's place finally came into view, and he managed to crawl through the doorway. As he was about to slam the screen door shut, a plague of flapping black wings gathered just outside. They cawed and rattled and clicked in a frenzy. John slammed the door. He knew they would perch around the house in defiance, scheming a way in.

John's boots made a sloppy sucking noise that echoed around the kitchen as he shimmied his feet out. Without the use of his frozen fingers and with a serious lack of hand-eye coordination, it took great effort to pull off his clothes and curl up in the sleeping bag on the chesterfield. Using his teeth, he pulled the drawstring tight around his neck to trap any heat his body might eventually produce. He longed to build a fire, but his body raged with tremors. As the hours passed, his skin burned as it thawed. Again, he welcomed the thought of death, an end to the pain that radiated through the awakened nerve endings in his leg muscles.

As John slept, the dead air trapped inside the sleeping bag heated up. His heart rate increased, and blood pushed its way through his frozen limbs and appendages. The frostbitten skin on the tip of his nose and cheeks turned black with warmth. When he woke up in the middle of the night, an unbearable thirst clutched his throat. He wondered why it was so hard to die. The room was dark except for the bleak grey light seeping in through the living room window. His tongue was swollen, his head reeled with dizziness. He had dealt with his share of frostbite as a fisherman, so when his fingers opened from his clenched fists, he knew they just needed time to heal. His dry, scratchy eyes blinked till they watered and washed out grains of sand.

A shrill cry came from outside the window. Too beaten and confused to be afraid, John pulled his naked body out of the sleeping bag. He brought himself to his feet, which still felt like frozen chunks of ice, and was relieved he could bear weight on them. Making his way to the window, he could see no source for the cry through the thick fog. It bawled again, and John pulled on some dry clothes, grabbed the flashlight he kept under his pillow, and headed outside.

John's flashlight flickered. It couldn't penetrate the foggy darkness. When it went out completely, he banged the butt of it against his palm, to no avail. He held his breath, listening for movement. He knew the fog wouldn't stifle the sound of the scream. It came as if on cue; a horrendous screech that shattered the silence. John braced himself as something rammed into his leg and sent him sprawling on all fours. Anticipating another blow from any direction, John closed his eyes and covered his face to protect himself from whatever penance the devil was about to deliver. He waited.

John knew his decision to pull in the fish was wrong. He had made the wrong choice. Until that point in his life, he had always believed the choices he'd made were the right ones. There were no wrong choices, only consequences that needed to be endured. But the death of Annabel and their baby was more than mere consequence. His decision became a life sentence. She was home to him, and that was the only place he wanted to be. The only thing standing in their way was his decision that night. But that night, on the boat, he didn't know Annabel was the choice. He didn't know then that the decision to pull in the fish would cost him more—would cost him everything. Three lives and a future together completely obliterated. John begged for forgiveness as he awaited, with agonizing guilt, due punishment for his sin.

He opened his eyes. The expected attack never came. John banged the temperamental flashlight on the ground till it shone. He flashed the beam all around, illuminating pockets of fog. The harbour was quiet, besides the gentle roll of the tide. Even the crows were hushed. He questioned his foolish mind and wondered if the incident was just part of his identity now, a delusional schizophrenic.

John scrambled to his feet, in the glow of his shaking flashlight a small figure emerged from the fog and darkness. Startled again, John dropped the flashlight, and the light made shadows on a scruffy face lined with a long, dirty beard, and topped with a broken horn. It lowered its head and rammed John's leg, tearing his pants and knocking him down again. It let out a shrill scream.

"Goddamn! You scared the living hell right outta me!" He kicked the goat away in frustration. His anger turned to pity when the animal lowered its ears and turned over on its side. John could see a xylophone of ribs under its raggedy coat. He suppressed the urge to kick the animal again and instead picked it up like a yaffle of wood and carried it into the house. The goat propped its chin on John's shoulder, its breath faint in his ear, its wild nature subdued.

John lit a fire in the stove and made a little bed for the goat with the crumpled white sheet from the chesterfield. He grabbed the water can from the stove and took a good swig before he filled his palm and let the goat lap at the water with its thirsty tongue. John watched the animal sleep and considered killing and eating it, though he knew there wouldn't be enough meat for a meal. He'd have to fatten it up first, but with winter approaching, that would be impossible with minimal rations.

The goat woke up and bleated as if plagued by the same nightmares that chased John. It came close and nestled its head on John's lap. John decided the goat would break the incubated silence of the long winter months ahead and help him ignore the sinister things that lurked in his mind and in the darkness of the harbour. Together, John and the goat slept through the night.

IN EARLY NOVEMBER, John had a few unwelcome visitors before the snow carpeted every inch of the harbour. Whenever a boat entered the harbour, John and the goat hid underneath the latched door of the cellar. More often than not, young vandals with nothing better to do harassed and scavenged the harbour. The demolition bothered John, but he saw the destruction as a distraction.

While he was busy one day hoarding his pockets full of matches and snacks, he heard an awful scrape and screech. He watched in horror as two young men worked vigorously to saw off the church steeple. It fell with a resonating crack. They jumped from the roof and rolled down the grassy bank to steal the copper weathervane.

As John made his way unnoticed back to the house, he heard the boom and clang of the church's pump organ crying out its last painful song. The violence escalated and he feared these hoodlums were the worst yet. A final violent blow silenced the organ forever. A short period of quiet ensued, until John heard the sound of his own windows shattering. He roared as he ran out of the house, bringing one of the hooligans to the ground. He pressed his weight on the kid and pushed his face into the ground.

"If I ever sees the likes of yous in this harbour again, you won't know what hit you."

He stood up, and the pair of them took off toward their boat.

The next day, John formed a plan to protect his solitude and defend his territory from further incursions. He placed piles of large rocks inside the church and on every corner of every house left standing. When unwelcome guests arrived, he would throw the rocks at the church bell. If that didn't scare them off, he'd present himself either crawling on all fours or hands high above his head. Sometimes he'd hide inside Bill's fishing stage and shake the walls, pretending to be a ghost, a tactic that frightened off many vandals before even reaching the shore. If they approached the house, John and the goat hid in the cellar. When they entered, he would pinch the goat's arse, and its blood-curdling bleat would send the vandals running faster than the speed of light. These were the only times John felt his face crack a smile. Scaring them had become the only thing that brought him pleasure.

One early morning, John heard yet another motorized boat turn into the harbour. He and the goat took to their usual hiding spot. When the door opened and the floorboards creaked, John immediately recognized Bill's voice.

"What a shame. What a bloody shame."

"John, my son," Lillian said. "Come on out if you're still here." Her voice shook. "Please, John. We just needs to know if you're still alive. Rumour has it you've got this place haunted."

Something thumped down on the kitchen table.

"Bill! Get in here!" Lillian said. "Look at this! He's carved a map of some sort on the kitchen table."

Bill's footsteps were heavy and sluggish on the floorboards.

"My good God, Bill. He hasn't given up! John? If you're here, my love, we've got to talk to you!"

John could hear Lillian's hurried footsteps through the house calling his name over and over. The little goat bleated at the ruckus above them. John lifted the floorboards, tossed the goat onto the floor, before he crawled out with his head bowed. He sat at the kitchen table without acknowledging them, even though Bill and Lillian's presence brought a warmth to the house.

"Oh, my son," Lillian said. She took a step back before she rushed in to give John a hug. "Look at you."

John knew he must have looked very different than he used to. His hair was greasy and unkempt, and mostly matted to his head. His beard was patchy, and the dirt on his face made him look dull, like a shadow.

Lillian grabbed him and cradled his head to her chest, unbothered by the stench of him.

Bill pulled out three chairs from the table, and he and Lillian sat down on either side of John. Bill pulled a flask of liquor and a box of cigarettes from inside his coat pocket and plunked them on the table. John sobbed intermittently.

"John." Lillian pushed his hair from his face and put her hands on his. "Come back with us, John. She's gone."

His eyes darted up to meet hers.

"We're heading to St. John's in a few days. Bill's health isn't good, so we're moving to town to get him the care he needs. It's his heart, John. I believes his heart's been broke right in two. Nothing's like it used to be. Everything's changed, and not for the better." She let go of John's hand and turned to Bill, whose lip quivered.

"Government was full of lies," Bill mumbled. "None of us should've given in, right from the get-go. None of this would have happened. It ruined everything. It just ruined everything." Bill walked to the door and opened it. He greeted someone.

"You remember Helen, Mr. Slade's daughter?" Lillian whispered.

John looked past Lillian, toward the doorway. He stood slowly.

"She offered to bring us here before we leaves." Lillian spoke quickly. "She's driving us to St. John's in the morning.

It's awful nice of her, if you asks me. I knows her father put her up to it though. Acts like he owes us something—but he knows the one thing I wants." Lillian's eyes grew wide as if she had said too much. "He's a lying son of a gun, and I don't trust him, is all."

It wasn't the merchant's daughter that made John rise from his chair. His eyes were fixated out the window. It was the sight of a torn burlap bag strung out along the shoreline.

Bill and Helen stood by the doorway.

"Come on in," Lillian said, waving Helen in.

Bill returned to his seat and lit a cigarette. He took a long drag before offering one to John. "Why don't you come with us?"

John finally took his eyes off the burlap bag and took the cigarette. Bill lit it for him, and both men took a long drag. Bill then offered his flask, which John nearly guzzled.

Helen stood opposite John, unmoving and quiet, though her cheeks burned red when John met her eyes.

"I can't leave," John said directly at Helen. "I watched her disappear out there. I can't leave." He took another long haul from the cigarette. "Her heart is like my own, and I can't let her go. She suffered out there. I knows it. Now it's my turn. I feels her presence here. She scares the hell outta me sometimes, but if it's her, then I'll stay. I was born here, and I'll die here. I'll take my chances, I guess."

"Come back with us, John. There's room." Helen's eyes never wavered from his glare.

He looked away but could feel her eyes on him. His hand trembled as he brought the cigarette to his mouth again. After a long exhale, he gathered his thoughts.

"I lies wide awake thinking of her, and I knows now that without her I'm empty. She's the girl of my dreams. When we were together, I never dreamt. I realize now it was 'cause I was living my dream. Just seeing Annabel completed my day. It was only after she left that my days felt incomplete, and I've started dreaming again. Nightmares mostly, but some nights she's in my dreams, and that makes me feel better."

"We knows exactly how you feels, my dear, but time moves on and changes everything," Lillian said. She wiped the tears from her face and shook her head. She grasped John's hand. "You can't stay in this house. It's too lonely; it's so empty. Annabel wouldn't want this for you."

"You're reaching for something that ain't there," Bill said. "You've lost her, and she's lost you. You done your best, but it's too late. We're all caught up in the whirlwind of life, and if you can find a bit of peace in your heart, hold on to it, b'y, then let her go. When we tries to control the things that ain't controllable, we suffers. We all gotta accept the hard realities life hands us and learn from them."

"It doesn't sound like you've convinced yourself," John said.

Bill looked at John, eye to eye. "You're stuck in a static moment b'y, smack dab after everything changed and before it will ever change again. You can't refuse to move on!" He smacked his hand flat on the table.

"Don't let yourself go to waste, my son. You have so much potential," Lillian said, trying to brush off Bill's anger. "You needs to come back with us. *Please.*"

John walked over to the kitchen window and looked out over the harbour.

"I'm all right knowing nothing will ever change again." John paused for a brief moment. "Beause no one in the whole world could make me feel like I did when I stood beside her. Whatever this energy is or was, I can't say. Alls I knows is, it exists. They say someone is looking over each of us. Now, I don't know who it is or where they are, but I think they gave me to her and her to me. And not just for the short period of time we had together; for something a lot longer and more meaningful. Whatever happens, my heart will be with her as long as I live. I love her with all my heart and soul. My heart rests with her."

"You gets one shot at this life, John. Don't stay here acting like a victim of untimely circumstances. It's not going to bring her back," Bill said, impatient.

"I have to stay." John didn't turn around. "I can't leave, 'cause I'd rather be here with her than any other place in the world without her. Even if it's just her memory, or her ghost."

Silence permeated the room. Lillian rummaged through her pockets.

Bill shook his head. "Waiting for something is the easiest excuse, but there will come a time when you can no longer deny the truth."

Lillian tutted away her husband's anger. "John, there's something I wants you to have." She handed him a picture. "It's my favourite picture of her, but I wants you to have it. I've got a dozen others, so I won't forget what she looks like."

The sight of Annabel nearly knocked John to the ground. His shoulders bowed and his chest heaved. It was a picture of the two of them dancing the night of the garden party.

"John, you needs to move on. Carry Annabel in your heart. Your shoulders aren't meant to carry such a heavy load, my love. The hurting will stop. She will always have our love and constant dedication, whether it's from this harbour or from anywhere on this earth. Or at least that's what I keeps telling myself. The love may be gone, but it'll never be forgotten. Just like this old house."

"You're wrong." John looked down. "Our love is not gone."

"Farewells should be sudden when they're forever," Bill said. He looked at his cigarettes and flask, then thought better of it, leaving them on the table. He pulled Lillian toward the door. "Come on now, Lill. Let's bring these trinkets to Annabel's gravesite. I knows she's not there, but. . . ."

"My darling Annabel," Lillian said.

They left with Helen and walked toward the graveyard. John sat back down at the table, transfixed on the image of Annabel he held in his hands. John's blurry mind's eye came into focus as he stared at the picture. He stroked the photo with his finger and felt such a loneliness knowing he'd never touch her skin or hear her voice again. The memory of that first dance looped in his mind, like a record player repeating the same groove over and over. She was completely out of his reach. He longed for her and didn't know what to do with the hurricane of feelings inside.

From the other room, a sloshing sound echoed through the house, like that from water trapped in rubber boots. The goat's ears perked, and John stood up from the kitchen table and listened. At the thought of the house being haunted, fear overwhelmed him, and he fled to the shore to investigate the

SALTWATER JOYS 129

burlap bag. The goat followed him like a lost soul. He looked up at the house on his way down and saw the curtain drawn to the side from Annabel's window. He wondered if it was the same thing Sarah had seen. John ran back into the house, raced up the stairs, and flung open the bedroom door.

"Annabel!"

The room was empty, the curtain back in place.

WHEN BILL, LILLIAN and Helen appeared from the woods a half hour later, John stared at them from Annabel's window. He tucked Annabel's picture in his front shirt pocket and left the house to follow them down to the boat.

"John, take care of yourself, you hear?" Bill choked up, and tears fell from his red, puffy eyes.

"I'll find her, Skipper. I got no plans to leave until I do." John shook Bill's hand and was struck by how slack and bloodless it was, a far cry from the muscled, calloused fisherman's hand he had worked with for years. It was yet another cruel reminder of all that had been lost.

Bill gave one firm nod.

"Get aboard, you two," Helen said.

The couple helped each other steady themselves as they stepped into the boat.

Helen stayed on the shore and looked at John. "I thinks you should come with us. There'd be something good waiting for you that you'll never discover if you stays here. I'd love to get to know you better. I always thought you and I could be great friends."

She looked sincere, but John shook his head. "I can't take you up on that offer."

"Are you sure you won't come with us?"

"There's no future without her. This is it."

Helen turned away, climbed into the boat and steered out of the harbour in a hasty departure. John's attention returned to the burlap bag. His heart lurched when he noticed the devil doll floating naked, face down in the tide. It bobbed against the rocks as the waves lapped around it, the cord of the bag tangled around its neck. He moved closer, the goat lingering close behind him. There were bald spots on the doll's head, and its hair was trimmed down to spikes. The goat hobbled over to sniff what was left of it and rolled the doll over. The eyes were gone. John turned away from the disturbing stare of the vacant black holes. In the bit of wet sand between the rocks, the goat left little hoof prints as it continued to sniff the doll then licked its head. It knelt down on all fours and pulled out some of the doll's remaining hair, chewing it like cud.

Chapter 12

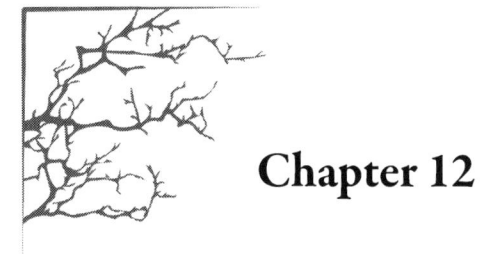

JOHN TOWERED OVER THE doll with a growing urge to pick it up. He stood still and stared for over an hour, not sure what to do with the wretched thing. A wild wind raged, shooting freezing sea spray from the breaking waves. Chilled, he knew he needed to make a decision. The doll's waxy appendages were twisted in an unnatural position, evidence of the struggle it had had with the ocean. He picked it up by the leg, and it was as rigid and cold as a dead body. He walked up to the house, the doll dangling upside down, its cry silenced by the ocean. The goat caught up to John, chomped down on a few strands of hair and tugged.

When John and the goat entered the house, John put the doll on a chair at the kitchen table, then retreated to the far end of the room. Its once demonic appearance was now stonewashed to a pitiful human figure with empty black sockets. His eyes darted from the doll to the kitchen stove. He contemplated cremating it, but it would take a long time for the water-logged body to burn, and he couldn't bear the thought of seeing a burning baby lying in the stove. Hours passed. The doll sat in the chair while John paced the kitchen, mumbling to himself, trying to formulate a plan to get rid of it for good. The doll didn't move, but the longer it sat, the more suspicious John became of it.

The click of the goat's hooves stirred John from his thoughts as it sauntered over to the doll and bit at its hair, until it tipped and crashed to the floor. The thud sent a hot rush through John's core and made him breathe heavy with fright. The goat dragged the doll across the floor to its bed in the living room and gnawed off more of its hair.

John followed the goat. "That was you, wasn't it? It was you all along? You're the goddamn devil with cloven hooves dragging the blasted doll around, scaring me half to death?!"

The goat continued to chew the remaining strands of hair on the doll's head.

In that moment, John's delirious mind riveted. He sensed now that the doll was not possessed by the devil, but housed the soul of his child. He touched the doll's arm. The goat bent its ears back and held on tight to the hair, a slight growl rising in its throat. John and the goat pulled back and forth in a weak game of tug of war until the last clump of hair ripped from the doll's head. The goat chewed the freed clump, with no further interest in the game. John pushed the goat off the white sheet and bundled the doll in it. He laid the baby on the chesterfield and forced himself to look away from its vacant eyes.

He grabbed a knife and a junk of wood from the woodpile and whittled two small spheres of wood. He pressed the wooden orbs into the gaping holes of the eye sockets until they slipped inside. The doll was still, and appeared to be sleeping, with forever unopened eyes. He carried the doll up the stairs to Annabel's room, imagining himself a father. He pulled the covers down on the bed and tucked in the doll. Taking the picture of Annabel from his front shirt pocket, he laid it on the pillow beside the doll. He gathered the strands of Annabel's hair he had left on the pillow and once again curled them around his fingers. John settled himself at the foot of the bed and felt his chest heave. He closed his eyes and tried to fall to sleep.

JOHN KNEW HE NEEDED supplies to sustain him through the long winter to come, so on a clear night, after most families would be fast asleep, he rowed into New Bonaventure to raid his abandoned home. As he walked along the gravel path to his old house, he insulated the noise of his footsteps by hopping onto grassy patches along the way. Arriving at the front door, he fished his house key from his pants pocket and, as soundlessly as he could, let himself in. He didn't want to draw attention from nosy neighbours who would mistake him for an intruder. He fumbled to turn on the flashlight, and its instant glow cast shadowy broken memories of his past around him. He seemed to float his way into the kitchen, like a ghost entering a museum of untouchable artifacts.

He ascended the stairs and stopped dead in his tracks in the hallway. In front of him were unopened cardboard boxes that Annabel had packed, belongings she didn't want to leave behind at her parents'. He carelessly lifted the flaps of one box, and the scent of talcum powder flooded his nose. Still-frame flashbacks flickered through his mind. He remembered the soft curve of her lips, the dimple in her cheek, the curve of her back, her jawline. Her eyes that looked up at him through long eyelashes. The frames sped through his mind in a line dominoes, each memory knocking down the one after it. The last domino stood, unaffected by the others. It lasted in his mind; Annabel's pale face with closed eyes, submerged in the Atlantic. He reached into the box and gathered a deep pile of clothes into his arms. He hugged them tight and breathed in all that was left of her.

John took Annabel's favourite wool sweater, the one she wore the night he proposed, and an armload of supplies that would help keep him warm: clothes, hats, mittens, socks, scarves, winter boots. He packed them all into one box; his fiddle and a deck of cards were last-minute additions. There was no food in the kitchen, and he considered breaking into a nearby house for some rations, but scurried unseen back to the boat instead.

As he made his way back to Ireland's Eye, John looked over his shoulder to what had been his favourite location to set nets, now tainted by Annabel's death. Blue and yellow flames danced above the water. The flames flickered and faded, only to rise again with fresh brilliancy, like a supernatural display. Reports of the mysterious lights struck fear in the hearts of fishermen; they were an early warning of an imminent storm. The ghostly lights lit the sea in a white sheen and silvered the few clouds above. John rowed toward the light. As he got closer, the lights flitted farther away. John pursued the lights in vain—they teased him until they eventually vanished into a dense mist. He wondered if this was the glow of Pirate Pete's ghost ship trying to lure him into deep water, where he waited to capture John's soul too. John turned around and rowed hard toward Ireland's Eye. He knew he'd have to hurry in case the lights did indeed foretell an impending storm.

Once John was inside the harbour, he couldn't help but notice how the moonlight lit the smashed windows of every abandoned house. They reminded John of the doll's empty eyes. Suddenly, another fleeting display of aurora borealis caught John's attention, except these were green and purple lights moving along the shoreline, not over the water. John pulled the oars inside the boat, careful not to be louder than the breaking waves or the rush of the tide.

John looked through the binoculars he kept in the boat and carefully turned the lenses to put the image in focus. He gasped. The dead walked, taking part in a mime-like performance. He watched women hanging invisible clothes on a clothesline. Searching in earnest for Annabel's face, John recognized one in particular among the weathered faces of the deceased: his father. He was playing out the routine of drying phantom fish, with empty hands. Like a small child, John's bottom lip trembled at the desire to grab his father's attention. The boat smashed into the side of the wharf, and John dropped the binoculars as he steadied himself. Just as a stone cast into a pool of water shatters the reflection of its surroundings, the halos of the dead were gone. The iridescent ghost town had faded into darkness.

John paddled the boat to the wharf, docked, then ran to the house with the box of supplies in his arms. The goat was waiting for him by the house. John balanced the box on his knee as he opened the door. The pair ran inside, and John dropped the box and locked the door behind him. He set a fire and listened to the cracking and popping of the wood. He lit a single candle from the burning belly of the stove, holding it as he would at a vigil as he went upstairs to make sure the doll was where he'd left it. When he found it was, he slipped Annabel's picture from the pillow into his shirt pocket.

At the kitchen table, in the glow of candlelight, John studied the map of the island etched into the table. He took the photograph from his pocket and laid it on the harbour. He placed his two pointer fingers on the photo like he would on a planchette, the heart-shaped indicator used in a séance, and waited in uncertain anticipation to communicate with Annabel's spirit. In this quiet state, John's senses were amplified, and each gust of wind that rattled the window made his eyes grow wide. He wondered if the chill that passed through the room was the wind or her ghost. Just when he doubted his efforts, John lifted his fingers, and the picture slid out from under his heavy touch. John stared in horror as the photo travelled from the harbour to the water, to the very location John and Charlie had been hauling in cod the night Annabel died. The sound of sloshing water in rubber boots once more filled the room. John jumped up from the table and peered around. He wanted to check every corner of the house but was stopped cold by the photograph's continued trajectory.

Deeper and deeper John's heart sank as the picture inched across the table until it reached the edge and fell to the floor. John grabbed the knife that was sitting on the table and carved a line marking the direction the picture had travelled.

JOHN REMAINED VIGILANT in his search for Annabel, but it was all in vain. He wondered how far she'd been taken out to sea, and he wondered if there'd be anything left of her. His soul pined for hers. His sleepless, watchful eyes were as desperate as those of a captain seeking a lighthouse on a dark and stormy sea. He spent every minute of daylight rowing and searching the hypnotic rhythm of the swells. Day after day, he replayed her death in his mind, and during the night, his subconscious reinvented it in nightmares. She infected his mind, but there was no antidote to cure him. Her love had been amputated from his heart, and now she existed as phantom pain, an invisible extension of his heartache. John wanted to lay her to rest, and to see her in the flesh one last time. But he knew the ocean wouldn't give up its dead, with or without a fight. Each time he paddled the boat back into the harbour, he longed to see her standing along the shore, or even washed up on the shore. He longed to see her just one more time.

AS JOHN PULLED THE boat up on the shore after a long day on the water, he heard the desperate cries of the crows. He caught sight of the goat as its stiff body rolled in the stagnant tide. The temperature had dropped exponentially, and John figured the poor thing must have frozen to death.

The savage crows swarmed and feasted on it like maggots. They didn't flinch as John approached. They were starving too. John fired handfuls of rocks at the murder until he hit one, and they dispersed. As usual, though, the moment he turned his back they returned to devour the lifeless goat. John watched from the kitchen window while the crows tore his companion apart. It was a foreboding reminder that John needed to get ready for winter. If he wasn't prepared, the crows would be waiting. The moment he died, they would find him and rip him apart too. He was the only reason they hung around.

Tired of the gruesome spectacle, John marched to the shoreline, a bag in hand, and collected the bloody bones and sinew of the goat. He took it to the graveyard. Sadness and grief overwhelmed him as he dug a shallow hole, cursing out loud for letting himself get too close to the animal. He decided to distance himself from any living thing to prevent further heartache. He scolded himself. He should have just killed the goat in the first place and gotten it over with.

After long days searching for Annabel, John would use the last couple of hours of daylight to pick buckets of partridge berries, sweetened by the autumn's frosts. After dark, he'd fill his stomach with steamed mussels and snails, a newly acquired taste, but he didn't have the tools to preserve them for winter. He dug through the gardens and collected broken pieces of carrots and potatoes missed earlier in the fall. He brought them down to the cellar, but he knew it wouldn't be enough to sustain him. He got to work and made some simple loop snares from some snare wire he'd found tucked away in Bill's stage. There was only enough wire to make a handful of rabbit traps he had to double wire them to ensure they wouldn't snap in the cold temperatures. His mouth watered at the thought of pulverizing a warm piece of meat between his teeth. He placed the snares over den openings and well-travelled trails, attaching the ends of the wire to heavy drag sticks. Rabbits would either strangle themselves to death or be held secure until John returned.

He checked the traps frequently, in an effort to beat the omnipresent crows to a catch. The crows were always faster. The sight of them violently stabbing the throat of the dead carcass of a rabbit amplified his anger. A profit unearned. He chased the birds away and stole what meat he could salvage. Perched high in the trees, they taunted him, mocked him, chittered and cackled at him. They were loud and rambunctious. An omen of death. Tricksters and thieves, they watched and waited. The crows knew what John knew, and John feared they knew much more.

During the evenings, John visited the graveyard, trying hard not to look at Annabel's wooden cross as he'd pay his respects to his parents.

"I'm still here, old man." The lack of response made John weep, acutely aware of the overwhelming silence death spawned. "I'm not sure what I should do anymore, but I told you I'd stay and do what I could to keep things going. All that work couldn't have been for nothing." John rubbed his temples at the thought of the dead beneath his feet, and the effort they'd made to preserve a culture and lifestyle, only for it all to die with them. "I wants to go where you guys are. To be with Annabel again. To breathe what she breathes, see what she sees . . . ." John's head lowered. "I'm nothing but a coward.

I'm still here." He stood up and touched both his mother's and his father's headstones, then walked away.

John needed a distraction, so he turned his attention to chopping wood to sustain him through the cold season. He made a fire pit of stone just inside the limits of the woods, closest to the house, and set a fire blazing. It kept him warm and provided light through the early darkness. As he swung his axe into the first tree, the clap of flapping wings erupted all around him, and a black mass swarmed above the treetops. He guessed there were at least twenty or thirty of them. Even after the crows left, the woods easily deceived him. Branches quivered in the chilly wind, and the rustle of the few dried leaves that held on made him look over his shoulder, often to catch a glimpse of a crow's malicious face flicking out from its hiding place. John tried hard not to be startled, but his fears would get the better of him. Like a clumsy bear, he pushed a loaded wheelbarrow with a deflated tire down the cowpath to the house. Too often, the wheelbarrow would overturn, and John would have to abandon the pile of wood as he took off to the house and awaited the morning light to fetch it.

The winter winds often blew too strong and kept John land bound. He'd use these days to bring stacks of wood into the house to keep a steady fire roaring. He filled empty hours by collecting kindling and dead twigs. He knew birch bark made a great fire starter with its highly flammable resin, so he piled up copious amounts. He would twist the bark back and forth until it was fibrous and malleable, then roll it until it became thin and light. John also busied himself insulating the house. He nailed pieces of wood over the smashed windows and stuffed any holes with curtains left behind in other houses. All the while, his thoughts never strayed far from Annabel.

Too soon, the harbour froze over, making it all but impossible for John to continue his search. He feared he had missed his opportunity to ever find Annabel, and that time was running out to rescue what was left of her. The ice had barricaded them, trapping Annabel on the inside, keeping John out.

John stood on the shore in the midst of a heavy snowstorm, watching millions of snowflakes swirl and fall to the ground. The white flakes stuck to his clothes, covered his beard, mustache, eyebrows and eyelashes. The snow muted the sounds of the harbour, insulating him with silence. His thoughts were as desolate as the season, his heart as cold as the sea. Like a lonely snowman pierced with cold, John stood and listened to the nothingness that lingered all around him.

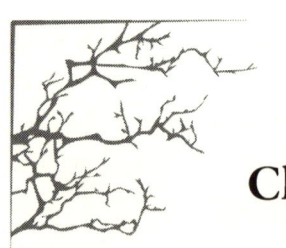

Chapter 13

JOHN DIDN'T KEEP TRACK of the days; still, the drastic dip in temperature and the amount of accumulated snow told him December had arrived. A harsh wind howled over the chilly harbour then calmed, settling into a freezing fog. An invisible master artisan sculpted ghostly white ice crystals onto every tree branch and twig. With sunlight reflecting off each crystal's surface, the trees glittered as if frosted with diamonds. John looked out the kitchen window and allowed the peaceful serenity of the quiet winter day to clear his mind. It hushed the strange echoes of Annabel, trapped between the veil of life and death. The winter months are full of deceit, though, as they merely cover up the dead leaves of fall. Winter became a superficial distraction from the truth.

Once the last of his rations was eaten, John was racked with hunger every hour of every day, especially as the days grew shorter and forced him to stay indoors. Busyness kept his ravenousness at bay, but there was only so much he could do outside in the below-freezing temperatures. He was thankful he had grabbed the deck of cards and his fiddle. He played solitaire for days on end, until his eyes were tired enough to sleep. Some days he played cribbage, without a board and with imaginary players. He loved to pretend Annabel sat next to him, and he talked to her as if she was there. He'd deal her in, put two cards from each of their hands in the kitty, and proceed to play his card then hers, in turn, pegging as he went. He'd try to make fifteen, or play a pair, or come as close as he could to make thirty-one. The kitty was never counted. He didn't play to win but to be with her. Other days he played the fiddle—sometimes gentle finesse, other times like a madman until his fingers bled. The screeching notes and upbeat tempo could never sound as happy as they once did. One by one the strings all broke, and he tossed the useless instrument into the fire.

Constant hunger cut like a sharp knife deep into his belly and his thoughts. Since the snow had buried the rabbit snares, and the crows killed or chased away any game birds worth eating, John turned to the sea. He set out lobster traps, through holes in the ice, to catch the "poor man's food." Each time he pulled in the traps, he'd hope Annabel would be caught. He'd take the feisty, muddy-coloured crustaceans home and put them in a pot of boiling water. He knew the friggers didn't have a brain and felt nothing as the heat scorched their shells a bright red. He wished himself a lobster, oblivious to such excruciating pain. He could only cook one at a time with the small pot he had scavenged from one of the abandoned houses, so he was never satisfied after he ate the few he caught each day. They weren't filling on their own, just enough to keep him alive.

The ceaseless cawing of the crows drove John mad as they circled above his house, spying on him, waiting for scraps, anticipating his death. John gave them nothing but empty lobster shells. The braver of the murder often perched on his windowsill, peering inside. John walked up to the window once and stared at the crow, eyeball to black, beady eyeball. The crow didn't shy away. Only its visible eye moved as it studied John's face. John banged his fist on the window, and the creature flew off.

Ravaged by hunger, John was forced to turn to a food source he despised. He would have to go ice fishing in the harbour, and to get there he'd have to trek through knee-deep snow. John knew he didn't have the energy to pull his legs from the suction of every sunken footstep—like trying to free a rubber boot stuck in a bog. He decided to make snowshoes from the tree nearest his house, its boughs weighed down by wet snow and shags of ice.

Before heading out, he covered his socks with empty bread bags, an old trick his mother had taught him to keep his socks dry. He pulled on his boots and took wide deep strides to the first tree. He was careful to select the smaller branches, where the needles were abundant and thick. He chopped six boughs, each about four feet long, fastened the bases together in two groups with twine, then tied a loose knot at the midpoint of each bundle. He secured his feet to the makeshift snowshoes around the toes of his boots. The crows looked on from atop the surrounding evergreens.

The day was cold but windless. John walked with difficulty at first, but had mastered his stride by the time he got to Bill's stage. John took off his mittens to unlatch and open the fishing stage door. He manoeuvred the snowshoes into the stage and found Bill's old auger. He slung it over his shoulder and grabbed a shovel, a loose-weighted fishhook and some tangled line, carefully tying the hook to the end of the line before putting his mittens back on. He closed the door and climbed down off the wharf to the ice. It was thick enough to hold his weight, despite the ominous cracks that boomed like thunder under each footstep. Near the middle of the frozen harbour, he removed his snowshoes to shovel and scrape away the snow, revealing slick black ice underneath.

The crows circled overhead, waiting. They knew what he was doing. They cackled and hopped and flew around him, until they were only a few feet away. Some landed as John drilled a hole through the ice with the auger. The helical bit sloshed water around his feet until there was a black hole of slush spilling onto the ice. John shovelled the slush and water until the circle of ice was cleared. The pool below was black, a portal to the ocean beneath his feet.

John set the hook and line through the hole in the ice, wrapped the line around his forearm, and jigged. He sat in silence, trying to recollect times he and Annabel had spent together, but nothing specific came to mind. Like the fish, his memories were getting harder and harder to catch and reel in. It was impossible to recall a memory when he tried too hard. Adding to the emptiness in his gut and his heart, there was nothing for his mind to devour.

Time passed without a bite. John's lack of movement permitted the cold to sink into his skin. He began to pull up the line, ready to give up, when he felt a tug. He wrestled to pull up a codfish. Its body flopped around on the ice until John struck it over the head with the shovel. The crows got louder, drew nearer, threatening John with their mighty calls. Frustrated with their boldness, John bellowed harsh profanities to scare them away. He stopped when a tiny stream of bubbles surfaced from the hole in the ice and caught his attention.

He leaned over the water until his nose broke the surface tension, and he caught a glimpse of Annabel's frantic, pale face underneath. He plunged his arm through the hole to grab her, until the pricking pain of the water took his breath away. He grabbed the auger and drilled another hole close by. He heard her gurgled screams. He drilled hole after hole, jumping all the while till his weight broke through, and he crashed into the hypothermic water. He thrashed around but could not feel Annabel in his outstretched hands.

He climbed out of the water and shivered on the ice. Not for the first time, he wondered if it was really her or if he was losing his mind. Caught between delusion and reality, a tiny wrecking ball banged so hard inside his heart that it went numb, as if shrouded in a cold chunk of ice. He looked over at the fish he caught, surrounded by the crows. They devoured it, blood from its guts staining the white snow. He tied on his snowshoes, grabbed the auger, and made his way back to the shore. John was freezing, exhausted, and longed to lie down right there in the middle of the frozen harbour, but his will was strong. He would not give himself up to the cackling black cloud of death that encircled him. The crows swooped and nipped at John, eager to see if he carried more fish. Their attacks added to his hotheadedness, kept his adrenaline pumping, and kept his legs moving.

He stripped off his wet things the second he got to the house, put on some warm clothes, and started the fire in the kitchen stove. He heated a pot of snow to a boil and dropped a used teabag into the water. He had used it so many times there wasn't any flavour left, but he used it anyway. Swirls of phantom scents of homemade bread teased John's nose. He closed his eyes and let himself pretend he was chewing the fish he'd lost, mixed with potatoes and scrunchions, little rinds of pig fat. He longed for a meal of fish and brewis. Before he left the empty table, he scratched Annabel's sighting onto his map, then went to the living room and fell asleep on the chesterfield.

Unsure if he was dreaming or awake, John watched an avalanche of snow spill through the window and all over the floor. The curtains danced with an intense sea wind. Annabel climbed through the window, dripping water, as John sat speechless. Her hair snaked across her pale, sea-worn face, and she shone with a ghastly glow through the dark, like the eerie light cast from the decomposing bodies of squids. She walked toward John, every step laden with the now-familiar sound of squishing water as she dragged her boots across the floor. He could feel her cold breath on his skin. John reached out to touch her, only to watch her vanish. She left him in complete darkness.

John ran to the cold rush of air from the opened window. A crow screeched on the windowsill, and John tried to shoo the bird back outside. It flew past him and into the dark room. Its outstretched wings hit the walls. John lurched for the crow, barely snatching its feathered body in his hands, and hurled it out the window. He brushed the window clean of snow and struggled to close it. He laid back down on the chesterfield and slept.

The deep chill of winter set in with swift fury. John hibernated inside the empty house, locked in the past with strained memories of the love he lost, the love that would never return. It was a time and space where he didn't have to deal with anyone or anything. John's hope to find Annabel faded as he grew weaker. The island was hit with repeated storms, with no lull in between. He lived like a ghost, among ghosts in the ghost town. Snowdrifts crept halfway up the second-storey window, insulating the house like an igloo. He slept away the days, and when he slept, he found Annabel. They found each other in his dreams and nightmares, and despite the cold and his hunger, she made the winter bearable. If John woke, he would incubate the dream, forcing himself back to sleep to see her again.

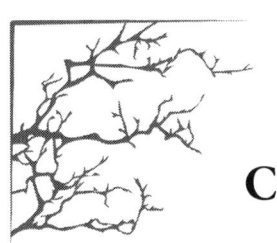

Chapter 14

THREE MONTHS OF HARSH winds and deep snow were soon met by March's spring sun. Tiny sprigs of delicate green pushed their way through the matted brown grass. Before its final surrender though, winter took one last desperate gasp. The ocean current delivered an ice shove that sounded like a freight train barrelling through the harbour. While massive ice pans filled the shoreline, John barely noticed the ice or the improved weather that month. His starved body had lost half its weight. He lived a waking nightmare.

In an almost drunken stupor, John went outside late one afternoon, his body hunched and shrunken. A long-haired woman rowed in a small boat into the harbour. John squinted to see, but his eyesight was blurred. The woman docked on the wharf and carried a basket to where John leaned alongside the house.

"Merciful God," he whispered. His heart stood still. In suspended disbelief, John thought he must have died and gone to heaven. He stood speechless, transfixed by the blurred silhouette before him. His heart, a faithful compass, believed it had found Annabel.

The woman didn't speak. She led John's frail body into the house and sat him down at the kitchen table. She opened the windows, and a fresh breeze swept out the foul stench of the house. John watched the woman light a fire, boil water from the creek and, finally, pour a shot of whisky and a little sugar in a cup. When the water came to a boil, she topped the cup with steaming water. The warmth of the hot toddy caused John to weep. The woman peeled some vegetables and added them to a pot of boiling water. She sat down beside him, and he reached out to touch her. His hands moved over her face and body like that of a blind person, taking in every detail with his fingertips. He felt her take his hands and felt the warmth of her lips as she kissed them. They held each other until the vegetables were cooked, and she put them on a plate with some warmed bottled moose meat. John ate sparingly, but he drank the alcohol she offered. He took a cigarette, lit it, and felt a rush of lightheadedness as he took a long drag.

As nightfall approached, the woman lit the lantern and warmed a basin of water. She gave John a sponge bath with soap she had brought. John breathed in the fresh scent and relaxed. The water in the basin turned brown from all the grit and grease, his hair shampooed for the first time in months. He welcomed the warm cloth she laid over his face that covered his achy eyes. The room was silent except for the drip of water from the cloth and the crackle of the fire. She dried him with a warm towel and helped him into some clean clothes.

John felt her hands on his arms, and he let her pull him up off the chair. She grabbed the lantern in one hand, tucked a flask under her arm, and let John put his weight over her shoulder as they climbed the stairs.

"You came back for me," John whispered. His voice cracked from not being used for so long. "You came back for me."

The woman didn't speak. She laid the lantern down on the far side of Annabel's room. John followed her. His vision was still poor. The air was filled with the energy of charged currents, until a magnetic force pulled the two of them together in the flickering glow of the lantern. John wrapped his arms around her and felt her shiver under his touch. His hands wandered up the back of her shirt.

"Oh, John," he heard. He pulled her close and kissed her.

He slipped off her clothes then his own, breathlessly awaiting the moment he could embrace her again. They slid into the bed sheets and covered themselves with the chilly blankets. He felt goosebumps rise on every inch of her skin as he caressed her body. She straddled him, and their reflection moved and danced, back and forth, in the smashed and bloodied mirror, until they collapsed on one another.

"I thought you'd forgotten about me," she whispered, handing him the flask of whisky.

"How could I forget you?" John said. "I haven't stopped searching for you. Just the thought of you pulled me through the long winter days." He drained the flask and dropped it to the floor. "Oh, Annabel." He closed his eyes and pulled her closer.

"Shhh," she said. "Get some sleep. We'll talk in the morning."

THAT NIGHT JOHN DREAMED the same silent dream that haunted him most nights. The same muted flashbacks fast forwarded through his mind: Charlie pulling in nets from his boat, Annabel showing up to warn of the storm then tumbling from his boat, her hand slipping from his.... This night, though, the dream shifted. John pulled Annabel's heavy, pregnant body into the boat and blew into her mouth. She lay lifeless in his arms, but he didn't give up. He held her close, his lips upon hers, breathing into her over and over. Charlie revved the engine and sped toward the harbour. Life miraculously returned to Annabel, and she choked out the water from her lungs. John looked upward to the heavens, thanking God. He sat her up on his lap to face him and straddled her legs around his waist, in an effort to keep their baby from freezing to death.

Charlie got them through the storm back to shore, and John carried Annabel's shaking body through the rain to her house. He undressed her and tucked her into bed. He undressed too, and they wrapped their bodies together. Lillian and Bill piled warm blankets on top of them and wrapped hot beach rocks in towels to lay at their feet. John fell asleep, thanking the Lord once more for sparing their lives.

John woke to the raucous cackling of the crows. He was bathed in a cold sweat, yet his fear was cast aside when he sensed Annabel lying naked beside him. He put his arm around her waist and something felt wrong. He rolled off the bed, onto the floor. Her pregnant belly was gone. He scrambled to his feet, peeked up over the side of the bed, and wiped his sleep-crusted eyes. The food and drink had pumped life back into his body and cleared his eyesight a little. The hair looked the same as Annabel's, but the curve of her shoulders and her slender hips weren't the same. When the woman stirred and turned over, John drew in a deep breath. He ripped the blankets off the bed and dragged the naked body onto the cold floor.

"Where's Annabel?" he demanded through gritted teeth.

"It's me, John. What's going on?" Helen grabbed for the blankets, but John pulled them away. She gathered her crumpled clothes and hastily shimmied into them, without taking her eyes off John.

"You tricked me," he seethed, without unclenching his teeth. "You made me believe you were Annabel." John stood tall, shadowing her trembling body. His volcanic heart erupted. Lava spewed through his veins as a sulphurous current shot through his lean muscles. The suppressed anger that had accumulated since Annabel's death was unleashed, if somewhat diminished by his weakened state. He slapped Helen across the face. She fell sideways, and he kicked her in the back. Her body curled up in the fetal position. In a sudden burst of rage, he grabbed her by the throat and pinned her up against the wall, her legs dangling.

"Please!" Helen choked and clawed at his hands.

"You're the spawn of the devil!" John's arm muscles gave out and he dropped her feet to the ground, his fingers digging deep into her flesh, leaving instant bruises. "How dare you!" His eyes blazed with fury. "How dare you!" He pushed her to the ground and heard a gruesome crack.

Helen whimpered and cradled her broken wrist. She scurried near him to grab her sweater.

"Get out."

"You ungrateful son of a bitch. I only meant to drop the supplies to you. The pitiful sight of you made me stay."

"Get out," John whispered. "Get out before I kills you too."

Helen wiped the blood from her gashed lip and swollen eye. "Bill was right, you know. You're holding out for something that's never coming back." She stood up and backed into the door.

"Go," he said, pointing at the door. His other hand was fisted behind his back.

John heard Helen's footsteps run through the house, until the screen door slammed. He watched from Annabel's window as she ran to the boat and sped out of the harbour. In the kitchen, he found a neat stockpile of supplies on the counter. Bottled moose meat, a pack of hard bread, a bag of vegetables, cigarettes, matches, soap and another flask. John lit a cigarette, took the flask, and pulled out a kitchen chair to sit down. He only took a few drags before he snuffed the glowing cherry out on the table. He wanted to make them last. He drank until the flask was empty. He needed the drunken relief to ease the heartbreak of losing Annabel once again.

The crows had gathered in the tree in front of the house. His madness, amplified by alcohol, helped him devise a plan to get rid of the taunting birds once and for all. He joined in their game of trickery, tossing a piece of moose meat on the front lawn. The loss would be worth the gain. The gluttonous beasts hoarded over the meat, making it easy for John to sneak up behind them and smash one over the head with a junk of wood. It chirped and folded its wings tight to its body before it died, its fierce black eyes staring up at him.

John picked up the crow and raised it high over his head. He stood silent, holding it like an offering until his arms could no longer bear the weight. The harbour was silent. Not a sound came from the murder that lingered. John hurled the bird toward the water and returned to the house.

He watched from the kitchen window as the crows gathered around their dead companion. One by one they visited the still bird, and one by one each crow left the harbour. The one thing they feared was death. John left the bird to rot. He cursed the cod and the goddamned crows.

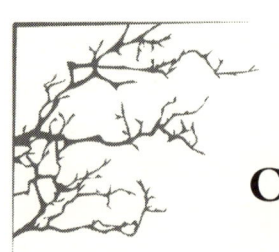

Chapter 15

AT LOW TIDE, JOHN TOOK a walk down to the beach to collect a feed of snails and mussels. He walked up to the dead crow, scoffed at its pitiful predicament, and kicked it off the path out of sight. The murder hadn't returned, and John took victory in their departure. He walked down to the beach and carefully stepped into the tide that washed over the slick seaweed-covered rocks. He plucked handfuls of snails from their suctioned grip, stuffing his pockets full. With one hand holding out his shirt, he used the other to rip blue mussels from the fibrous attachment that kept them anchored to the wave-washed rocks, gently placing them inside his shirt. He was careful not to crack the shell, or the mussel would die and be inedible. John collected just enough shellfish for a hearty meal and walked along the shore, making his way back to the house.

As he ambled, the purple gleam of broken mussel shells and the swirl of creamy seashells triggered a memory of Annabel. She would comb the beach for hours, searching for blue sea glass, driftwood coral, jet-black rocks, and intact shells strong enough to withstand the toughest of tides. She'd store her treasures in mason jars on the floor of her bedroom, jars now packed in boxes inside their vacant home in New Bonaventure. He peered down at the broken objects and loved them because they were pieces of her, glistening out from amidst the mundane. He couldn't shake the sinking feeling that, no matter the logistical acrobatics his mind conjured, he could never devise a way to bring Annabel back, to be as she once was. He couldn't retrieve what was supposed to be. He had never imagined his quest would be reduced to searching for any little sign or piece of his Annabel.

John wandered up the beach, holding tight to his shirt bulging with mussels. A high-pitched squeak from the direction of the woods assaulted his ears. It sounded like the chirp of a hollow rubber toy. The hairs on the back of his neck spiked as he passed by the lifeless crow. The cheeping grew louder. John let go of his shirt, his supper falling into a pile on the ground, and hurried into the forest.

John stood still to quiet the crunch of leaves and twigs beneath his feet. He heard the sharp squeal again, and it led him to the base of a tall pine tree. John climbed until he found a little crow nestling among five unhatched eggs. With no mother to incubate them, the others would never hatch. He listened for the call of a crow, but there was only silence. It was odd for the mother to abandon her young; odder still that concerned crow parents weren't making a ruckus with a human so close to their nest. A pang of guilt clutched John's heart. The dead crow must have been the mother of the nest.

Careful not to startle the lone nestling, John scooped up the nest and carried it down the tree. He didn't know what he would do with it. He hated the crows, but he couldn't kill another baby. The poor thing stretched its neck and opened its red triangular mouth. He knew it was too young to be left outside alone. John brought the nest in the house and made a place for it near the stove to keep the eggs warm in case they were still alive.

He emptied the snails from his pockets and put them on the table. He smashed open a snail shell with his fist. He picked off the broken bits of shell and offered the gooey slug to the nestling. The little bird gobbled it down. John offered more, noticing the blue in the bird's eyes, its fluffy down, and the tubes surrounding each long feather. The bird cuddled its head into the eggs when it was full, and closed its eyes.

While the bird slept, John went outside to retrieve the dropped mussels. Back in the house, he ripped the beards and barnacles off the crustaceans before steaming them in a bit of water. In a few minutes, the shells split open, revealing tan flesh peeking from the pearly white interior. He brought the pot to the kitchen table and pulled the shells apart, using half a shell as a spoon to scoop out the flesh. He relished the briny, sweetmeat.

Within a few days, John was pretty sure the eggs in the nest would never hatch. The little nestling was comfortable in the house, so John took the eggs outside and tossed them beside a tree. The baby crow made its imprint on John, begging him incessantly as it would its mother; maddeningly so at times. When the fledgling grew strong enough, he brought it outside and let it sit in the trees while he worked. John taught the little crow to be self-reliant, unlike the scavenging relatives that left it behind. If it ever begged for his food, he scolded it.

SALTWATER JOYS

JOHN ITCHED TO GET back out on the water to search for Annabel, even knowing it was no longer a rescue mission. He pulled off the weathered tarp that protected the vessel from the snow and found the boat in rough shape. John rebuilt and mended it as best he could while he waited for the ice pans to separate in the harbour. Signs of spring popped up all around him through the long days of his labour. Butterflies flew together in intertwined vortices. Flies filled the air, and robins nested in the trees. Green buds protruded from branches. John preferred the hush of winter, but he knew he'd need the spring and summer provisions to get him through another year.

When there was enough room in the harbour to manoeuvre around the ice floes, John pushed the boat off the shore and called to the crow. It perched obediently on the side of the boat as John's weak arms rowed to New Bonaventure. He yearned for some sort of closure so that he might rightfully reclaim at least his own lost life. There was no justice in Annabel's death, but finding her body was the only way he could know her soul was at peace, and perhaps heal his broken heart in the process.

An hour later, as he prepared to dock in New Bonaventure, John made sure there was no one around. He waved his hand at the crow.

"Get outta here!" He tied the boat to the wharf and jumped out. "Go find your friends."

The bird flew into the trees.

John found a piece of hose along a fencepost and decided to grab the empty jerry can from his boat. He syphoned some gas from a nearby car. The sweet aroma of petroleum rushed through his nose. The cracked blinds of a neighbouring house told him he'd been spotted, so he left the hose dangling from the car's gas tank and took off to his boat. He upended the jerry can and glugged the gas into his tank until every last drop was gone. The engine purred under him when he started it, and he sped back to Ireland's Eye, making sure the crow didn't follow him.

It was a calm day; the sun was shining—a nice break from the rain and cool weather. As John looked across the rolling waves, an iceberg came into view in the distance. He stalled the engine and began to row, careful not to get too close to the ice giant. If the berg tipped on its side, it would take him with it. He leaned over the side of the boat and used his jigger to break off a large chunk of ice to take home with him. When he peered into the deep, he came face to face with his irrational, pallid reflection—a stranger. He didn't recognize the long hair and beard, the sunken cheeks. His lip trembled as he pleaded with the figure below him.

"Who is it? Who's down there?"

His voice often calmed his racing heart when he became frightened of the shattered delusions that manifested in his mind. His leg muscles tightened in flight mode, but he had nowhere to go. His relentless need to find Annabel, coupled with the ongoing silence that engulfed him, drove him once again toward madness. His mind could not hold fast to the reality that one mistake could change the course of his entire life. He wished he could undo his mistake. But he couldn't rewind time—it plowed forth in only one direction. The truth hunted him down and he was easy prey. Once it had captured him, he could only be consumed by it.

The piece of iceberg he had broken off was floating now out of arm's reach, so he leaned over and used his fishing net to pull it closer. He picked it out and suckled the dense ice, as heavy as concrete. Keeping his eyes on his reflection, he savoured the prehistoric water. Suddenly the boat rocked, knocking the ice from his hands. Something had hit his boat, then disappeared in a puff of smoke. His stomach turned. He knew if the boat capsized, he'd sink.

"It's you, ain't it, Easton? You and that pirate crew you got down there. Wants me too, do you? Well, let me tell you, you lost your chance. I'm taking her back!" He stared past his unrecognizable reflection and saw something large move under the surface of the water.

He stood up and spun around, expecting the ghost ship to surface from any direction. He started the engine and slowly circled around the iceberg. He stopped moving and let the boat idle for a long time, until it sputtered and ran out of gas. The boat was rocked again, and John's nostrils flared as he girded himself for an attack. From behind came an immense splash and John turned just in time to see the tail of a humpback whale splash back into the ocean. When it surfaced again, its blowhole blasted out a cloud of sea spray, soaking John from head to toe. Salt water dripped down his face, eerily reminiscent of the endless tears he had shed.

John hastily rowed away, all the while thinking of Annabel. Suddenly the little crow, who like a shadow had been flying directly overhead the entire time, now landed on the ledge of the boat. It gave John a hard look, and its sharp beak let go of a shiny object.

"What the hell? What are *you* doing here?" John restrained his violent reflex to swat the bird away and instead leaned forward to see what the crow had dropped. He picked up a small gold band with a tiny diamond, and held it in disbelief. He knew the ring too well. It was the one he had given Annabel, the piece of tape still wrapped around the back of it. "Where'd you get this?"

John looked for signs of blood on the tape, wondering if Annabel might have washed up on shore, to be devoured by the crows. He found no trace of blood or other damage to the ring. It must have slipped off her finger in the water. He pulled a piece of hard bread from his pocket and cracked a chip off it and gave it to the bird. The little crow flew away.

John rowed as fast as he could to the harbour, where his feathered friend was already perched on a picnic table. As he approached, he saw a small pile of trinkets: a rusted screw, a bottle cap, a paper clip, a button. He picked it all up and put it in his pocket with the ring. He gave the crow another chip of hard bread, and the crow made a brisk dive for it.

"Don't get used to that, now. I don't have much left." John scowled as he went into the house. "Go on, now. Get outta here."

THE DESCENT OF EVENING made John conscious of his every breath. The silence drew him in and played with his head that night as he watched the shadow of the crow pace back and forth along the living room windowpane. John wondered if the rest of the murder had returned and was staying at the edge of his view, hovering like omens of his death, their very presence filled with innuendo of his sin. He sat paranoid until he saw Annabel sitting on the arm of the chesterfield. He tried to take in all the little details of her face. He remembered everything he never wanted to forget. He didn't move a muscle, afraid to disturb or frighten her spirit away with any sudden movements.

"I miss you," John whispered.

She didn't speak. Her silence was like the death that divorced John from his sanity.

"I miss you so much." His voice broke. He didn't take his eyes off her. "Stay with me, Annabel. Please, stay with me. That bit of time we had wasn't enough. Please stay." John proceeded with quiet footsteps toward her. "I'm sorry I made the awful decision to haul in the nets that night, Annabel. I'm so sorry I killed you."

John watched her conflicted eyes soften, and she shook her dim, expressionless face. He reached for a candle as he passed the wood stove and fumbled with a match until he lit the wick. The light chased the shadows from her face, but her figure did not cast a shadow on the wall behind her.

"How can we be together again? If I kills myself, will we be together?"

Annabel shook her head again, maintaining her hollow stare.

"How do I get to you? How can I find you? Tell me, please."

John knew his begging would have no effect. He knew she couldn't be real. Maybe his imagination ran wild from starvation, but he felt Annabel's presence. He knew he would for the rest of his life. John moved closer and knelt down on the floor in front of her. The flickering flame lit up the bronze highlights of her hair, and she looked as beautiful as ever. She was a perfect depiction of how he remembered her, only sadder.

"Annabel, I'm sorry." He reached for her hand but quickly pulled away. There was no flesh to touch. The empty space left him longing to touch her, something he had once taken for granted. He thought he would have a whole lifetime to hold her. "It's all my fault."

She shook her head and whispered, "It was mine."

It was a voice he knew so well. She was his heaven on earth, his fallen angel, his Newfoundland. Just the sound of her voice sent a shooting pain through his heart. Her soul was as tormented as his. She too bore the pain of guilt's sharp edge. It wriggled its way like a razor worm as it chomped through the dense terrain of both their hearts.

She opened her hand and dropped a gold coin. It clinked loudly and began to spin on its edge, sending an echo through the room.

John scrambled to pick it up. It was cold, heavy and wet in his hand. "Annabel, what are you telling me?"

A shadow flashed in the window beside her. The glass smashed, and a large, ominous figure cloaked in black grabbed Annabel by her hair and yanked her out the window. John heard the harsh caw of the crow, barking like a guard dog. The figure pulled her backward to the shore at an unnatural speed.

SALTWATER JOYS

John jumped through the broken glass and sprinted after her, but she was already in the icy-cold surf. The crow flew beside John and screeched its warning call. Annabel screamed the same scream as the night she died. He jumped the ice pans one at a time, following the tiny stream of bubbles that surfaced beside him. The ice pans came to an end, and John dove into the water. The shock of the cold kept him from going very far, and he knew he'd soon freeze to death. He scrambled back onto the ice and made his way up to the shore. It was the uncertainty of what came after his death that made his will to live so strong. There was no guarantee he'd find Annabel after he died. Life had proven there were no guarantees, so he figured that might be the same case in death.

As he made his way back to the house, John questioned his insanity. The weight of the coin in his hand was proof that he was living in reality, and that Annabel needed him. Once inside, he warmed himself by the fire and busied his mind to devise a plan to save her. The shadowy figure who had pulled Annabel to her death and held her captive in the ocean had to be Pirate Peter Easton. The pirate was smart; he knew John had been ripped off by the merchant. The coin's value was greater than the small diamond ring. John surmised that the only way to get her back was to play Pete's game. He needed to steal the treasure buried at Money Point and hold it as Annabel's ransom.

With an impulsive heart, John trudged through the dark woods illuminated by his lantern. The crow followed him like a watchdog. Together they went past the church, now fully collapsed from the furious snow squalls that had blown in during the winter. He passed the graveyard and headed straight to Money Point. He decided to dig and not stop until he found the rest of the treasure. He had a new purpose and a new drive to find Annabel. He really believed she was still in the harbour, held against her will.

John moved the heavy rocks, his weak muscles struggling under the shovelfuls of shale, dirt and pebbles. He dug a hole as wide and deep as he could, but his fervor diminished within a few hours. His energy dwindling, when the glow of the lantern blew out, fear defeated his desire. The branches creaked and cracked as the wind picked up. John looked around, terrified to be alone in the dark. He grabbed the extinguished lantern and bolted through the woods. The crow led the way while John tried to outrun the dark and his fear. He occupied his mind with memories of happy times with Annabel. He missed her so much. He ran, lost in his graveyard of memories, until he shot like a bullet out of the woods.

The cold penetrated his skin, but that didn't compare to the heartache that inflamed every inch of his body. He wanted Annabel desperately and cursed himself for giving up and hiding in the house like a scared child. He knew he would need food and drink for the next day of digging. In the soft glow of candlelight, he prepared jars of water and made a lunch from the provisions Helen had left. It would be just enough to get him through the day.

John ventured with the candle up the stairs and into Annabel's room to sleep. The blanket lay in a heap in the corner, and the bed was rumpled. The doll was face down on the floor. He picked up the blanket and the doll and tucked both into the bed. John was so lonesome for Annabel that he stuffed a pillow inside her sweater and placed it beside the doll. He stripped down to his underwear and wrapped his arms and legs around the sweater. He knew it was a pitiful sight, but his homesickness for her was overwhelming. John took whatever comfort he could find and, for a moment, pretended he held Annabel and their child.

AT DAWN, JOHN STRAPPED his provisions to his back and left the house. He tossed a few crumbs of dry bread on the picnic table for the bird and headed straight to Money Point. John blinked hard at the hole that was now filled back in, the rocks piled high. He knew he'd have to work hard to build up his strength; even more, he'd have to have patience to defeat Pirate Peter Easton. Though his hands bled, he worked through the pain, stopping for a drink of water only when he was parched. He ate small portions of moose meat and hard bread when he could no longer bear the hunger pangs. When he finished off the food, an even stronger voracity burned deep in his gut: a hunger for the treasure. He appeased his appetite for victory by feeding on phantoms; the taste of their defeat was the only thing that brought sustenance to his soul.

Like a gambler who plays just one more hand expecting a win, John dug each day, imagining he would hit the jackpot and find the treasure. Day after day, his muscles would ache after hours of digging. When darkness fell John would break, planning only to rest for a few moments, but he always fell asleep. And every time he awoke, the hole was filled in again. No progress, only endless defeat. He realized he wasn't enough; he needed more hands. But like a modern-day Sisyphus, who ceaselessly rolled a stone to the top of a mountain only to have it roll back to the bottom, John endured the self-inflicted punishment of futile, hopeless labour. John's passion to release Annabel became his torture, in a rebellious cycle of hope and despair. Every day, he dug at Money Point with fresh hope. He was no longer here to bide time. Annabel had become his reason to live and his reason to die. He was at checkmate with death. Some days he would dig a little deeper than the day before, but his body would fail him, his eyes would close, and he would fall asleep. He'd wake to face the full weight of his burden once more. The hole became a place between heaven and hell, a purgatory of his own making.

John dug when the ground thawed each spring, until it froze in the winter, for twenty years. He welcomed the torment that greeted him each morning. He continued to make no progress, and he continued to dig, finding cold comfort in the thoughts and memories and visions that tumbled around in his head. He planted his loyal heart in the empty outport and waited patiently for Annabel. In spring, memories of her proliferated like dandelions, plentiful and yellow and beautiful. But with time, the memories withered and blew away, like the billowing dandelion seeds. He sat in silence and fought to hold on to her. He counted the years and served his life sentence.

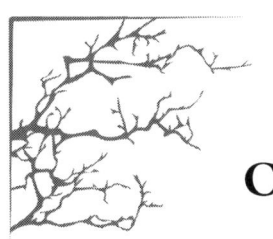

Chapter 16

TIME STOOD STILL FOR John. He endured the winters, survived the summers of constant digging, and looked forward to spring and fall. He never once gave up on his hope of rescuing Annabel. From any outsider's perspective, John had become a madman. He carried out his tasks quickly, intensely, sometimes violently. He mumbled to himself to drown the craziness out of his mind. His head hung low, as if weighed down by the mounds of hair that covered his face. His eyesight grew worse with each passing year. Without glasses, he relied heavily on his other senses.

Late in the afternoon, on a warm August day, a boat rowed into the harbour through a low-lying fog. From the open kitchen window, John heard the engine shut off, then the rhythmic slap of oars. He squinted, making binoculars with his fists to sharpen his vision, and was sure he could see the silhouette of a woman. He ran out the door, shirtless and shoeless.

John's frantic eyes tried to take in every detail of the woman who clutched the bow. It was Annabel, he was sure of it. She hadn't aged. She looked just the same. He stumbled and tripped and fell to his knees, but not once did he take his eyes off her. He waited, like an anxious child, on the shoreline. When the boat got close enough, he waded out into the crashing tide. He caught Annabel's eye and then turned his gaze toward the man who sat behind her.

Like a wild, rabid animal, John frothed at the mouth at the sight of what he could only presume was one of Easton's ghost pirates. When his squinted eyes unlocked from the man's bewildered face, he saw Annabel had the same nervous look. John realized he must have aged dramatically in his survival against the hostile elements of the outport. He wasted no time on personal grooming, and had grown accustomed to dirt, grime and the stench of himself. He cared only about surviving, for Annabel.

"It's all right, Annabel," he said, heaving. "Come with me. Leave this devil for good, and stay with me." He pulled the boat to shore, his arm and shoulder muscles bulging. He held on with a desperate grip, for fear of losing her again. She kept looking back at the man behind her. John held out his hand for her, and she hesitated. John studied her blurry face. Every curve and crevice was familiar. He twisted his jowls into a smile when she gave him her hand to step out of the boat. A citrusy perfume swirled into his nose. The man stood to follow them.

"Leave us alone! Just leave us alone!" John said.

The man raised his hands in surrender. "Mr. Lee, we—"

John put his hands on the boat in an attempt to shove it back out to sea.

"Wait!" the woman said. "His name is James."

As Annabel spoke, John noticed that the sound of her voice was the same but her dialect was different. Her tongue didn't carry the same quick inflection. Each word was pronounced to perfection. He couldn't process what she was saying.

"Can you hear me?" she asked. "I'm not Annabel. My mother was Annabel."

John let go of her hand and backed away like a wounded animal. "You tricked me again," John mumbled through clenched teeth. His hands squeezed into fists at his sides. His contracting muscles shook his entire body. John looked around the perimeter of the woods. The pirates and fairies had teamed together again to mock his suffering. He backed farther away and ran toward the house.

"Wait! You don't understand!" She started to follow him.

"Get back in the boat!" James yelled. "We've got to get outta here."

"John! John!" She ran after him.

"Leave me alone! I don't know what kind of sick joke this is, but—"

John tumbled forward as he stubbed his foot on a large rock. He shuddered at the throbbing, crushing pain that shot through his toes.

"Are you okay?" She crouched in front of him.

"I think I've broken some toes." He winced. The pain constricted his lungs and made it hard to breathe.

"There's a first-aid kit in the boat." She looked back toward the shore. "James! Grab the first-aid kit, please!"

She held John's foot, and he was surprised she wasn't appalled by the state of his repeatedly frostbitten feet and overgrown toenails, not to mention the unbearable stench. James approached with the first-aid kit, as well as a bag of tea buns.

She accepted the kit, fished out some supplies and bandaged his foot. John caught her eye, and he couldn't look away. She had the face and eyes of Annabel.

"Who are you?"

She looked him square in the eye. "Your daughter."

"Evelyn?" John scurried to stand up.

"Yes." She took a step back, a twinge of grief permeating her heart at the sound of her name.

"You can't be my daughter. My child drowned in my wife's womb twenty years ago." John raised his voice without breaking eye contact.

"I was adopted from Ireland's Eye twenty years ago."

"Well, you got the wrong person," John said, his voice void of emotion. "Some sick joke, I tell ya." He turned his face from hers. She looked like Annabel—the spitting image of her. His mind, made powerful by the assault of the elements and circumstance and time, was quick to construct a make-believe reality when he let it run wild. Isolation had made him psychotic, but he had learned to quiet the voices in his head. The only voice he didn't quiet was Annabel's. John rubbed his closed eyes with the palms of his hands, expecting to be alone in the harbour when he opened them. But Evelyn and James remained.

"What do you mean I have the wrong person?" Evelyn asked in a gentle tone. "You knew my name." She gave John a pensive look.

John watched her furtively. His toes throbbed. "Annabel and our baby died. They have been out there ever since the night I killed them." His chin trembled as he stared past Evelyn to the ocean. "Annabel came out to warn me, told me to come in." He paused. "But I kept hauling in the fish. I never wanted the fish over her, I swear." He placed his hand over his heart. "I hauled in the fish to square the debts with that scoundrel, Slade, so we could live with a clean slate. But I went against her, and so I knows it was me that killed them both." Tears brimmed the bottom of his unblinking eyes.

"Thomas Slade was my father."

John's face tightened and his brows drew closer. "That son of a bitch?" He sneered at the thought of the man. "You said he *was* your father."

"We held his funeral here. That's why I'm back. I'm so sorry, John. I had no idea until last week that you were alive. I was told you were both dead," Evelyn said.

John felt her grab his hand and hold it when his body started shaking. Her hands were cold and tiny. John looked at her. "You're a figment of my imagination. That's all this is—a dream. How am I supposed to know what's real anymore?" He looked around, crazed. His stare turned cold, his eyes hard and flinty.

"You know it's real because of the consequences." Evelyn stepped lightly on his toes and eased up when John winced. "That rock there is pretty real, and your throbbing toes are pretty real."

A grave expression blanched his face. His breathing slowed. A memory long forgotten surfaced and hijacked his mind: Sarah telling him that Annabel had had the baby. He put a hand over his mouth when a sudden urge to throw up overcame him, remembering the crying baby in the merchant's ship the morning after Annabel died. He looked at Evelyn in disbelief, completely lost for words.

"I only found out before my father died that you were still alive. He warned me not to look for you." Evelyn wiped her watery eyes. "My sister, Helen, and I came back from Calgary for his funeral. I had to come find you." She reached for John.

"I don't deserve to have you here." John shook away her hand. "I'm in exile, my punishment for what I done."

"I'm here, John, and I know for a fact that you didn't kill my mother." She stroked his forearm.

John's chest tightened and his shoulders began to quake. He hesitated before speaking, as though weighing his words. "I thought I lost you too," John said. "I thought I lost both of you." John choked and sputtered in a coughing fit. All these years he had thought his baby was dead. He should have believed Sarah and Charlie. He felt a surge of release from the clutches of guilt as he pulled Evelyn close and hugged her tighter than anyone could ever have held her. She smelled like her mother.

"I know," Evelyn whispered. "I feel the same way. I thought I lost both of you. My father told me you both died in a storm at sea when we moved to Calgary fifteen years ago."

John held her delicate face in his dirty, calloused hands. "I'm still searching, you know. Her spirit's still here. They've got her, but I'm not going to stop until I saves her. I've tried to kill myself to be with her, and I've been cursed with health, but—"

"Who's got her?" James asked.

"Those good-for-nothing pirates! They took her from me. We found a piece of their gold, and I bartered it for a ring, and that's when they took her." John noticed the frightened look that James gave Evelyn. He knew his delusions often fused with reality, but he knew he was right this time. "I've outsmarted the buggers though, and now I knows how to get her back."

"Evelyn, I thinks it's about time we heads back," James said, pulling her away from John. "It's gonna be dark soon, and we don't want to end up staying here tonight."

"There's no rush." John pulled Evelyn back alongside him. He felt surprised when she didn't resist, though she still looked terrified. "You have to believe me. I knows how crazy this sounds, but I'm not telling you a word of a lie." John watched as she studied his face. He sensed a gleam of Annabel's wild eyes in Evelyn's.

Without taking her eyes off John, Evelyn spoke in a matter-of-fact tone. "James, I have to know more."

"Are you sure that's a good idea?" James asked.

Evelyn looked over to James, then back to John. "What if you came with us back to St. John's, so we can catch up? There's so much I could learn about my mother. And you."

John's eyes darted up to the house.

"We'll bring you right back," Evelyn said. "We could get you fed and cleaned up. You'll feel brand new."

John shook his head. "I can't leave her."

"Do you remember Charlie and Sarah?" Evelyn asked, raising one eyebrow.

John's curiosity piqued.

"Sarah sent these out for you." Evelyn snatched the plastic bag that James was still holding.

John gave Evelyn a sideways glance before opening the bag. He breathed in the warm baked scent of tea buns. He picked one with lots of raisins and bit into it. The light but crispy texture melted in his mouth. He savoured each morsel, rolling it around on his tongue until he couldn't help but swallow.

"These are my favourite, you know."

"Well, the buns are from his parents." Evelyn motioned for James to say something when John turned and looked at James with scrutiny.

James shrugged his shoulders.

"Well, I'll be damned. Little James Hodder." John slapped him on the back.

"Why don't you come with us, then? Come and see Charlie and Sarah?" Evelyn grasped his hand and tried to lead him to the boat, but he stood fixed.

"I can't leave Annabel. She's still here. I can feel her beside me when I lays down at night, until the pirates comes to get her. They're holding her hostage, and I knows where the ransom is. I've dug for the treasure every spring and summer, day in and day out, but I needs extra hands to get to it."

"It will all be here when you get back," Evelyn said.

"I can't go. I can't let you go." A crazed look returned to his eyes.

"Come on, Evelyn!" James said with renewed urgency. "We have to get outta here now!"

"If you go, I'll never be able to keep the promise I made to her. I can't get it outta the ground by myself. If you go, I'm sure I'll lose her again." John stood up straight and pushed his shoulders, feigning composure. "Why don't you come up to the house? I've got something to show you."

"I don't know if that's a good idea," James said with great hesitation. "We gotta get back before it gets too late."

John didn't wait for Evelyn's response. He turned his back and started walking, favouring his broken toes.

Chapter 17

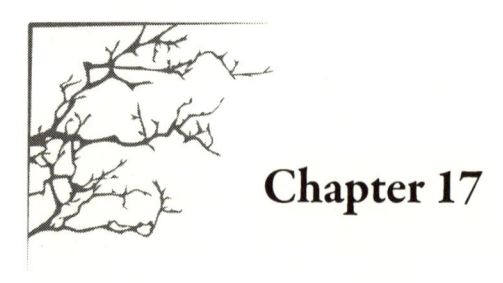

EVELYN FOLLOWED JOHN up to the house. Wisps of fog hung in the air close to the ground, weaving themselves around the trees that surrounded the harbour. The smell of seaweed and soggy grass mixed with the saltwater air made Evelyn feel like she had never really breathed a breath of fresh air until now. In a bittersweet moment, Evelyn felt like she had journeyed back centuries in time while simultaneously arriving at the future, to see the shadow of what Ireland's Eye once was, before Confederation. She felt the forlornness of a place that used to bustle with people, now abandoned and hushed. She had an unsettling awareness of her own heartbeat as she ascended from the shore, where the wind and the tide partook in an intricate dance.

Under her footsteps, bright yellow buttercups sprinkled the overgrown cowpaths that twisted around the outport. The abandoned homes had disintegrated and folded in on themselves, collapsed like houses of cards. Others were disembowelled, their sides split open so that she could see the inside and outside at the same time. The few sagging wood-framed houses left standing stared out to the harbour through broken windows. Wind-tolerant lichen climbed up their sides. Empty foundations, like gravestones, marked the phantom houses moved during Confederation— a sad testament to the lives and legacies sacrificed in the "government's game." Ireland's Eye was the epitome of a ghost town.

To Evelyn, it looked as if the heart had been ripped out of the harbour. The outport, once the soul of Newfoundland, was in ruins. Red paint chips on the bleached skeletal remains of an abandoned boat looked like bloodstains from the slaughter of a culture. High on the plateau of the harbour stood the remnants of what must have been a church. She could see the upside-down steeple on the grass.

Evelyn watched John's mechanical movements and assumed it was because he had lived without a companion for so long. The weathered house that John headed toward was a mirror image of his tormented soul. Its exterior was like something from a horror movie: boarded-up windows, shredded and bleached curtains poking through the boards, and a leafless, blackened tree in the front yard with a lone black crow perched among the branches. The wretched bird stretched its wings and broke the silence with a piercing caw, just as John entered the house. Evelyn saw the curtain move from the only upstairs window still intact. She elbowed James and pointed up.

"Did you see that?" Evelyn asked him. The curtain immediately fell back into place.

"I did, and I don't know if I wants to go in," James said. "But I will, if you still wants to."

"We'll go in for a few minutes." Evelyn grabbed his hand to inch him forward and was surprised at how sweaty it was.

"You don't think that was a prisoner, do you?" James asked. "John seems a little foolish, if you asks me." He stopped and pulled Evelyn back.

"You can't be serious, James. He's an old man." Evelyn laughed and pulled him to follow her.

"Pretty strong for an old man." James didn't budge.

"Don't worry. We'll make a run for it if he does anything out of the ordinary." Evelyn let go of his hand and walked backward in front of him. "He's my father, and I need to establish some sort of relationship with him. I have to know more about my birth mother, and this might be my only chance. She's always been kept a secret, and I've always wondered if I'm anything like her. I need to fill this void with memories and stories of her, and I think I've found my opportunity."

"I can understand that." James rubbed his hands together with hesitant anticipation and followed her to the house.

The harbour stirred a forlorn feeling in Evelyn, like an accumulation of lost dreams and untold stories from past generations. Evelyn's hand moved over the torn screen door that once protected the house from bugs and mosquitoes but was now full of holes. The buzz of houseflies welcomed them as they stepped onto the porch. She and James stood at the entrance to the kitchen and hesitated. It was not what Evelyn expected. The interior of the house was kept neat, although a stench of strong body odour filled the stagnant air. Evelyn held her breath and peered inside, noticing the small carved wooden figures and boats that lined the kitchen countertop. Small collections of knick-knacks, shells and sea glass were organized in piles on the kitchen table. She was thankful when John's voice broke the awkward silence.

"Day after day, she's right outside my doorstep, and I can't get to her," John said. He stood in front of the kitchen stove and lit a fire before sitting down at the kitchen table.

Evelyn let go of her breath, inhaling the scent of the burning wood that helped mask the stink of the house. She pulled James's arm to follow her inside, and they both sat down with John at the table. John stared at Evelyn with eyes that exuded a kind of translucence. When she took a seat next to him, he squinted until crow's feet wrinkled the outside corners of his eyes. She felt a little uncomfortable, but she didn't falter from his stare. She studied John's hairy face, thinking that the skin uncovered by his hair and beard, his nose and cheeks, looked like a tanned hide. His calloused, veiny hands were folded on the table in front of him, his fingers deeply cracked and obviously worked to the bone. He pulled something from his pocket and held it in a fisted grip on the table. On his left hand was a tarnished ring.

"What did you want to show me?"

"I told you I killed your mudder." He said, in a tone that suggested he had changed his mind.

"John, I know you didn't kill her," Evelyn whispered. "I heard the story after my father's funeral."

Evelyn couldn't believe she was sitting in front of John. Yesterday she had buried her father and, that afternoon, had her first experience at a pub on St. John's legendary George Street, a lively strip with more bars and pubs per square foot than any street in North America. Her father's friends and family were dancing and drinking. They were friendly enough; still, Evelyn felt completely out of place. Helen and her son, Ethan, had flown back to Calgary immediately after the funeral to make Ethan's university football tryouts. So, Evelyn sat by herself, listening to the fast-paced music and lilting accents surrounding her. She had heard Newfoundland stories from her parents, but had only visited the island once, for her mother's funeral. She wished her mother was still alive to help her navigate the city, the people and her grief. Millie had loved the island; she'd dreamed of retiring in Newfoundland. But when Evelyn turned twelve, the dream faded. Cancer had spread like wildfire through Millie's body, and the trauma of her mother's loss left Evelyn never wanting to come back. She saw Millie's gravestone that morning when she laid her father to rest, and apologized to her mother for not returning sooner.

"What can I get you, pretty lady?"

Evelyn was shaken from her thoughts and looked up at the bartender. "A little cranberry juice, please." She dug through her purse for some change.

He frowned. "No alcohol tonight, love?"

"Not tonight." She didn't crack a smile.

"Funny place to be if you're not drinking."

"I buried my father today, and this is the last place I want to be." She nodded over her shoulder at the rowdy bunch dancing behind her. "They're celebrating his life." She rolled her eyes to hide the tears she tried to suppress. "I catch a flight back home to Calgary in a few days."

"I see," he said and put out his hand. "I'm James. Nice to meet you."

"Evelyn." She didn't offer her hand.

"Nice to meet you, Evelyn." James picked up a glass and filled it with ice. "Who was your father? I might have heard of him."

"Thomas Slade."

"Ah, the merchant?"

"Seems everyone knows everyone here." Although her words rested on an air of sarcasm, she was immediately interested in the conversation. James was quite handsome, and she blushed at her rude demeanour. "I was adopted when I was a baby. Just before my father died, he told me my biological father was still alive. I'm hoping to meet him, but I can't seem to find anyone who knows anything about him."

"What's his name?"

"John Lee."

"Oh."

"Do you know him too?" Evelyn sat a little taller in her chair, disguising her vulnerable curiosity with confidence. "He lives, or used to live, in Ireland's Eye." She studied James's face for any sign of deception.

"Matter of fact, I do know someone by that name. Not personally, by no means." He filled a glass with red liquid, swirled it with a straw, and pushed it toward her. "I mean, there might be a hundred different John Lees around. If you wants to find out more to see if it's him, there's some folks you should meet. They used to live in Ireland's Eye, and by the sounds of it, they can probably tell you what you'd like to know about him."

"Who are they?" Despite her skepticism, Evelyn played along.

"My parents." He scratched down an address and telephone number on the back of a receipt. "Geez, what's the odds of that?" He smiled. "I'm off in a half hour. You can meet me at this address, or you can follow me, if you like."

"How do I know you're not some psychopath?" Evelyn took the receipt and fished through her purse again, calling him out on the uncanny coincidence.

"Drink's on the house."

She put a five-dollar bill on the bar. "You could be setting me up and just saying they're your parents."

"Setting you up for what?" James snorted.

"To rob me or something?"

"Now, why would I want to do that? All the same, I likes the way you thinks." James winked at her. "You can catch a ride with me, if you'd like," he said nonchalantly, wiping the countertop.

Evelyn eyed him with suspicion as he peeked up at the clock on the wall. He seemed a little too friendly and hospitable. She questioned his motives, but he looked harmless.

"What are you looking at me like that for?" James asked. "There's no need catching a cab if I'm going there anyways." He seemed to sense her wariness. "I'll meet you out front in a half hour, once I'm finished up back here. You can let me know then what you decides."

Evelyn made her way around the bar and said goodbye to the tipsy crowd, telling them she was heading back to her hotel room for the evening. She stood outside the front door and waited for James with her arms wrapped around herself to stave off the brisk wind. When James exited the bar, he jauntily tucked one arm through hers and walked her to his red pick-up truck.

"After you," James said, opening the passenger door.

Evelyn was impressed by his chivalry, but alarmed by her irresponsibility. It was not like her to trust a stranger, nor to take such a risk as going with James, in a place she was unfamiliar with. He waited until she got in then closed the door for her. He seemed to have a bounce in his step, a liveliness in his eyes and a constant smile. It felt like he wasn't putting in any extra effort to impress her; it just seemed like that's who he was.

James jumped in the truck, started it, and they sat in silence for a moment.

"I'm sorry to hear about Thomas." James leaned over the bench seat and patted Evelyn's hand. "You seems like you're holding up all right." His tone was less certain than his words.

Evelyn knew he sensed her turmoil. He had pinpointed the reason for her wishy-washy behaviour, her impulsiveness and poor reasoning: she was still in shock over her father. She realized she hadn't had time for reality to sink in, to let herself feel the pain of his loss. She couldn't reply to James's instinctive observation. In an attempt to sidestep her grief, she pretended that her father was still alive. She wasn't ready to say goodbye.

"But I knows the difference though." James gave her a nod and his hand retreated back to the steering wheel.

Evelyn wondered how James seemed to have the ability to see right through her.

He popped a cassette tape into the stereo.

"I knows what will cheer you up. I'll give you the full Newfoundland experience." He cranked up a traditional accordion-laced folk song and sang along until they pulled up to his parents' house. Evelyn welcomed the distraction of the colourful line of Victorian-style townhomes. She had heard about "Jellybean Row," but the picture she'd painted in her mind didn't do justice to the beauty of downtown St. John's. She marvelled at the candy-coloured houses infused with the vibrant spirit of Newfoundland. The heart of downtown St. John's was radiant in spite of the grey, foggy weather and bleak, rocky backdrop. James parked in front of a tall blue house, sandwiched between a yellow and another blue one, all of them trimmed with what looked like thick gingerbread icing. The bold houses reminded her of the spirit of her mother Millie.

They walked together to the front step, and James opened the unlocked door. Evelyn could hear someone scurrying about inside, then the porch light flicked on. The two of them stepped inside, where an attractive woman with strawberry-blonde hair smiled at them.

"Evelyn, this is my mudder, Sarah."

Sarah's smile disappeared and her knees buckled. "Oh, merciful God, I can't believe it!" She flopped backward onto an armchair.

"What the devil has gotten into you?" James's face grew red as he peeked over his shoulder at Evelyn. "Come in and sit down, Evelyn. Don't mind her. She's not in her right mind tonight."

Evelyn didn't move from the doorway. She watched Sarah struggle like a turtle overturned on its shell as she tried to roll out of the chair.

James leaned in close to his mother and whispered in her ear. "Mudder, what's gotten into you?" He pulled her up from her awkward position.

Sarah grabbed Evelyn by the hand and pulled her through the house, not even giving her time to take her shoes off. "Charlie! Charlie! Where are you, for God's sake?"

The two women stumbled into the kitchen. A man was sitting at the kitchen table, smoking a pipe.

"My nerves, woman, what's all the fuss?"

Sarah put her arm around Evelyn's shoulders. Evelyn tried to shrink from her grasp, but Sarah held on to her.

"Well I'll be!" Charlie dropped his pipe onto his pants and leapt from his chair, smacking his pant leg to extinguish the burning tobacco.

"I'm so sorry," Evelyn said, oblivious as to why she was apologizing.

James came in behind them. "Mudder, stop being rude!" He snatched Evelyn away from Sarah's grip and turned back to the front porch.

Sarah was giddy as she rummaged through some drawers in the kitchen. Charlie picked up his pipe and returned it to his mouth.

"Tell her to wait, James! Don't let her go anywhere!" Sarah threw papers and odds and ends from the drawers to the floor. "I knows it's in here! I have to get around to cleaning out this junk drawer one day."

"Clean it out? But where would you put everything?" Charlie laughed, his arms folded across his chest.

"Will you wait a minute?" James asked Evelyn. "I promise you, if they pulls anything foolish, I'll personally escort you outta here."

"I found it! I found it!" Sarah lifted the glasses that draped from a cord around her neck and put them on the tip of her nose. She held the picture up in front of her face. "Well, I knows you're not her, but you're the spitting image of my best friend, Annabel."

Charlie leaned over and looked from the picture to Evelyn. "My good God. She came back from the dead!"

Evelyn turned around and stepped toward the couple, their eyes glued to her. James took the photo from his mother, glanced at the old black-and-white image, then handed it over to Evelyn. She had never seen a picture of her biological mother before. She studied the photo. The woman was petite but capable looking, she thought. Her long, wavy brown hair cascaded below her shoulders. The same smile, the same petite nose. It was as though Evelyn was looking at a picture of herself.

She blinked back tears. "This is my mother? This is Annabel?"

"Yes, my darling." Sarah rushed to Evelyn and hugged her with all her might. "How in the world did you end up on my doorstep? All these years, all these years . . . ."

Sarah let go of Evelyn and rummaged through the drawer again. She handed Evelyn another photo.

"Here she is with John, your father. My God, he loved her some lot, let me tell you." Evelyn stared unabashedly at the photo. The couple looked like her and James. When she handed it to James, his eyebrows shot up his forehead. When their eyes met, she knew he thought the same thing.

"Let me show you this one," Sarah said, passing Evelyn another photograph. "These folks were Annabel's parents, Bill and Lillian Toope—your grandparents. Fine folks, they were. I loved them like they was my own parents."

"Where are they now?" Evelyn asked.

Sarah collected her thoughts. "Bill passed ten years ago, I daresay, and Lillian followed him by just a couple of months," Sarah said. "Poor Lillian didn't know how to live after Annabel drowned and you were taken by Mr. Slade. Without Bill, her heart couldn't take it. Broke clear in two."

"Do you know why they put me up for adoption?" Evelyn steadied her shaking hands in her lap. It was something she often wondered about. Before her adoptive mother died, she'd posed the question but was only told it was because there was no one to take care of her.

"To this day I scold myself for not taking you with us. I was young then and wasn't bold enough to stand up to the likes of Thomas Slade. You don't know how much Bill and Lillian wanted you back. Lillian wasn't in her right mind when she let you go, and it happened so fast. She only wanted what was best for you. You were going hungry at the time, and we were all in shock at the thought of losing Annabel."

"I never knew any of this." Evelyn took a seat beside Charlie to let the information assimilate into the stories she'd been told. "What about my father?" she asked. "Where is he?"

The room silenced. Sarah leaned against the kitchen counter. Charlie puffed on his pipe.

"If John's still alive," Sarah said, "he'd be living in a ghost town."

"A ghost town?" Evelyn asked.

"I believes the old man's still alive," Charlie said with the pipe between his teeth. He took it out and continued. "But he's likely gone mad living all alone for so long. I don't blame him. He's probably like a wild animal out there now. He told me once that it was his life sentence for what he done. It'll be twenty years in October since Annabel died. People swears his ghost haunts Ireland's Eye, but I knows it's him hiding out. The bugger doesn't want to be found. I heard tell the house he lived in is the only one left standing, being somewhat maintained, so that there tells you something."

"Does John know about me?" She wanted to hear the answer, but she knew she would be heartbroken if he did but had never reached out to her.

"He was so heartbroken over Annabel. Charlie and I told him you were alive before we left the harbour for good, but he didn't believe us. He didn't have a level head. We figured in time his heart would mend enough to let Annabel go, but he never came round."

The news pricked Evelyn with an intense sting. She excused herself to use the washroom, following James's instructions: upstairs and first door to the right. She splashed some cool water on her face and reached for a tissue. She stayed a little too long in the washroom, trying to compose her chaotic heart. When Sarah knocked lightly on the door, asking if she was all right, Evelyn opened it and accepted the comfort of Sarah's arms. She walked with heavy feet back to the kitchen, but with renewed strength to continue deeper into the conversation.

"How did my mother die?" Evelyn asked.

Charlie, Sarah and James looked to one another, and Sarah clasped her hands in front of her, preparing herself to retell the tragic story rarely spoken of, but never forgotten.

"She died at sea just hours after you were born. She went out to warn John and Charlie of a bad storm when they were out pulling up nets. She loved your father fiercely, and . . . ." Sarah started to cry.

Evelyn felt as though a fog had lifted all around her. The truth quieted her racing thoughts, and a stillness came over her.

Charlie rubbed Sarah's back, trying to comfort his wife. He puffed on his pipe. "John made a deal with your father, and to this day John would tell you that's what killed Annabel. It would have killed him to know that Mr. Slade had you."

"What kind of deal?" For a moment, Evelyn lost her breath. She wasn't prepared to hear of her father portrayed as a villain. She knew the general perception of typical merchants, and while her father was firm and a man of few words, she believed he would never purposefully hurt or take advantage of anyone. She braced herself defensively as Charlie spoke.

"John wanted to clear his debt with your father before he resettled, but there wasn't enough dried fish to pay for what he owed. He wasn't close to breaking even, so they came on an agreement for a load of fresh codfish that Mr. Slade would pick up on his return trip to St. John's. That's the night I was out hauling fish with him, when Annabel came out and was swept to sea." Charlie choked on his words at the memory of that night.

Sarah patted Charlie's arm. "I don't know how many times Lillian said she did the wrong thing. Poor thing was in shock that morning Mr. Slade came into the house. I heard him pestering her, but I didn't know what to do. I was pretty young myself."

"We were all young then," Charlie said. "Thought we were all making the right move. Twenty years ago, we all left to find something that we're still searching for. Resettling didn't give us a better life. Government was full of empty promises, making us believe we were missing out on something better. Matter of fact, it's no better at all. I misses the harbour and how we used to live back then. I'd do anything to get it back, you know, to the way it was. Life's supposed to be a vicious circle, but I knows I'll never get back there." Charlie shook his head, stood up and walked out of the room.

"Didn't know how good we had it back then." Sarah lamented.

James sensed Evelyn's mounting discomfort. "That's enough, now. With all due respect, Mr. Slade was just buried this morning. There's no need bringing up the past. You can't blame anyone for what happened. Bad things happen sometimes, and we just does what we can to get through."

"Oh, my darling." Sarah rushed to Evelyn's side. "I'm so sorry to hear. James, you're right. Let's not fret over the past. Let's celebrate that you're here with us now. I'm thankful he took such good care of you. Look at the darling woman you are."

Evelyn stiffened in Sarah's embrace, then felt her grief explode. Until now, she had protected her heart as best she could. The thought of life without her father created a heaviness in her soul. She felt now like her heart was being dragged behind her, anchoring her to her memories. She had taken his presence for granted, so caught up in her own life that she didn't realize he was dying. Evelyn felt the strong urge to defend her father. "He would never do these awful things intentionally to hurt people. He was a good man. He and my mother treated me just like their own daughter, my sister Helen. I loved him so much, and I'm just going to miss him so much."

Evelyn saw the knowing look Sarah shot over to Charlie.

"I want to go to Ireland's Eye and meet my biological father," Evelyn said with reverence. She wiped her tears with her sleeve. For twenty years she and John had grieved and mourned one another, unaware the other was still alive.

A look of shock swept over Charlie, Sarah and James.

"Now that would be the surprise of a lifetime." Charlie relit his pipe.

"I'll take you there tomorrow," James said, "seeing as you only got a few days here."

"I'm going to make up some tea buns for you to take to him." Sarah looked in a tizzy, and her voice trailed behind her as she raced around the kitchen.

JAMES KEPT HIS WORD, and brought Evelyn to Ireland's Eye the next day.

Now, watching from across the kitchen table as John dug through his trouser pocket, Evelyn's curiosity was piqued when he pulled something out and held it in a tight fist in front of her.

"Son of a bitch threw this to me after your mudder died. Told me it was cursed. He must have had you in his boat that morning." John banged his fist on the table. His eyes blazed with contempt as he opened his hand.

A gold coin rolled across the table. Evelyn and James looked at it in recognition.

The crazed look returned to John's eyes. "The treasure is at Money Point, and I knows how to get it. I needs it for her ransom, but I can't do it alone. I needs your help."

Evelyn was afraid of the insane look in his eyes. "Why don't you come back with us? Come to St. John's and get a hot shower and a good meal. We can talk as long as you want. How old are you? Fifty? Early sixties?"

John thought for a moment and looked down at his fingers. "Well, I was born on June fifteenth, 1939, so that means I'm forty-five or forty-six, I suppose."

Evelyn couldn't believe it. He looked so haggard and old. She shook her head and reached for him.

"You're too young to throw away the rest of your life," James said. "You got to get outta here. It's making you crazy. Come with us."

"I can't."

"But it wasn't your fault! It's time to move on." Evelyn wondered if she could push him hard enough to convince him to leave. "You can't be captive to unfortunate circumstances."

John gazed at his daughter. "You're as headstrong as your mudder. Does my heart good to see that."

Evelyn felt tears prick at her eyes.

"But I'm searching for the one thing that ever meant anything to me. Annabel's still here. The only thing I'm a prisoner of is time and the seasons, but I keeps a watchful eye while I waits. I thinks of it like this: I wouldn't be happier anywhere else while I wait. I takes small pleasure in the things I used to take for granted."

"What are you waiting for?" Evelyn asked.

"I'm waiting to rescue Annabel. Then waiting for my death, I suppose, so I can see her again. But aren't we all?"

"That's a pretty depressing way to put it," James said, chuckling nervously.

"How long can you stay?" John asked Evelyn.

"I'm heading back to Calgary on Saturday."

"You don't live here?" John frowned.

"No, I don't." Evelyn could see the hurt in his eyes at the thought of losing her again.

"Well, then, what day is it today?" John jumped to his feet.

"Thursday," James said.

John counted on his fingers, like a child rehearsing the days of the week. "Well, we better get to work then. We needs to dig in shifts so that someone's looking over the hole constantly. Those pirates might be ghosts, but they don't do any of their funny business when they're being watched."

"How do you even know you're going to find her?" James asked.

"I don't know for sure," John replied. "What I do know is that the coin came back to me and that's proof that she's still here and needs me to find her. I knows her soul ain't at peace while it's out there with the pirates." He looked out to the ocean.

"It's been twenty years, John. There wouldn't be anything left of her," James said.

Evelyn cleared her throat. "Geez, James, that's—"

James shrugged. "I'm just saying, after this long her body would be gone."

"It's not her physical body I'm after." John stared, his eyes as deep and blue as the Atlantic. "It's her soul I needs to rescue."

"What if you just dreamt it?" James asked.

John slammed his fist on the table again. "If it were a dream, how do you explain me getting back the gold coin?"

Evelyn sensed John's growing irritation. "John, I want to believe you, as hard as it is," she whispered. She watched James's expression from the corner of her eye. "I'll stay."

There was a sense of mistrust in James's skeptical smile. "If you wants me to stay I needs to know what I saw from the upstairs window. I mean, if you plans on keeping us here locked up like prisoners, I don't want no part of it."

"You saw her?" A light came to John's eyes.

"Who?" Evelyn asked.

"Your mudder. Breaks my heart every time she escapes them damn pirates, even though I gets to see her for a bit." John walked over to the staircase and looked upstairs. "They hauls her back out every time, and it's torture watching her. You'll likely get to see her later, if you're around when they comes back."

"What do you mean?" Evelyn followed him and peeked around the corner of the staircase.

"When they comes to get her," John said. "They don't leave her for very long. It's a pretty awful sight to watch the love of my life carried away by the demons of the ocean."

Evelyn turned to look at James. He had visibly paled.

John gritted the few teeth he had left. "You'll understand once you sees them come for her. Let's head down to Money Point right now." John stroked his beard and started pacing the kitchen floor. "We'll take a shovel to dig it up and an axe to chop wood for a fire. They got me so fired up, I just might dig it all up myself tonight." He cracked the knuckles on both hands. "Follow me." James and Evelyn didn't move as John nearly pulled the screen door off its hinges.

"You sure about this, Evelyn?" James asked. "Sounds like he might get us killed, too."

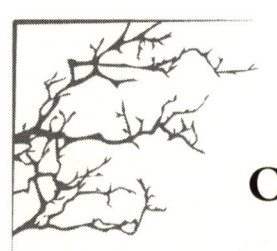

Chapter 18

EVELYN WAS NOT PREPARED for the hike to Money Point that night. She wore only a light windbreaker that was no match for the blasting wind. Her worn-out sneakers slipped on the damp ground, making each step a struggle, but she did her best to keep up with John. She loved the roar of the ocean as the waves slammed against the shore, not far in the distance. It was clear to Evelyn that this was a well-travelled path for John. His familiarity and endurance were obvious as he weaved through the dark woods without hesitation, even with broken toes. The lone crow flew above him, cawing and clicking, also used to the route. When Evelyn and James fell behind, they followed the dim glow of John's lantern through the trees. Evelyn held a flashlight James had taken from his boat, and James had insisted he bring his axe. He told Evelyn stories of people who were nice and kind one minute and losing their heads the next. He wanted to be prepared, as it seemed to him John fit that bill.

They passed the unkempt graveyard, where a wooden gate creaked and slammed with each gust of wind. Evelyn shone her flashlight toward the cement crosses and oval stones standing in rows, barren vines twisting over each one. Some were fractured and slanted, on the verge of crumbling to the ground. She wondered about the inscribed names and dates of the dead, abandoned and forgotten. Her eyes searched for her mother's name. Evelyn felt a rush, like a shot of alcohol, charge through her veins when she saw it—Annabel E. Lee—etched on a wooden cross. Fear and desire filled her chest when James grabbed her hand to guide her through the tangle of trees, swinging the axe to chop larger branches out of their way. The thrill of chasing John and holding James's hand made her feel alive and carefree. She tried hard to silence her rational mind, telling her the likelihood of finding a pirate's buried treasure was zero, ridiculous even. The thought of a quest for a supernatural pirate treasure and her mother rekindled a sense of adventure she had only ever felt as a child.

"Jump on my back," James said. He knelt down on one knee with his back facing her.

"Why would I do that?" Evelyn didn't try to contain the bubbling giddiness of a schoolgirl.

"We needs to catch up to John. He's moving too fast now." James was serious, lowering his other knee and signalling her to climb on his back. "Hurry up, before we loses sight of him and gets lost in the woods."

Evelyn climbed on his back and wrapped her arms around his neck. She pointed the flashlight straight ahead of them. James's forearms clutched her thighs as he hoisted his body up, keeping the axe in his hand.

"Hold on tight!" James hollered as he dashed like a deer through the twisted trees.

Evelyn closed her eyes and tucked her head into his neck to protect her face from sprung branches. The smell of James's cologne mixed with his sweat sent her head spinning;

she felt like she was falling in love with a man she barely knew. She wondered if he was seeing someone or married with a beautiful family, though she hadn't noticed a wedding ring.

"I really appreciate this, James," she said close to his ear. "I bet you didn't know what you were getting into when we met."

"I don't mind one bit," he said, panting.

After a while, John's bobbing light came to rest ahead of them. James stopped and Evelyn climbed off his back. He threw the axe down and bent over with great exaggeration as he tried to catch his breath. Through the last few trees between them and John, Evelyn could hear the sound of John's shovel scraping rocks.

She peeked around a tree to see John digging so desperately it made her want to cry. She could feel the pain that tore up his heart.

"Come on," James said, picking up the axe and leading Evelyn from the edge of the woods to where John was digging. James tossed the axe aside and scrambled to the top of the rock pile. He started throwing the largest rocks to the ground. Evelyn propped her flashlight on a twig to brighten the pile of rocks.

"How on earth did you survive out here this long by yourself?" Evelyn asked John, perplexed. Her teeth chattered behind closed lips. She warmed up as she climbed the pile of rocks to where he stood and began slinging rocks from the top of the pile to the ground below. She waited impatiently for John's delayed response.

"I never really thought about it," John said, without slowing his pace. "Just did whatever I needed to. Sounds foolish, I know, but I didn't want to survive at first. I thought the ocean and the weather were monsters for the longest time. Still do at times. I guess I learned the seasons weren't always out to get me. I just prepares for the months as they comes and hopes it's enough to keep me from starving to death."

"Aren't you afraid out here all alone?" James asked.

"I used to be." John forced a laugh. "Boy, did I ever get scared sometimes. But it don't bother me so much anymore. Mostly 'cause I can't see so well. I wouldn't know if something was after me till it was up in my face, for God's sakes. I hums to myself when it gets dark like this to drown out the nerve-racking noises around me." He peered into the woods. "I knows they are there, that they're watching me. That bird is awful good at warning me if she sees something suspicious."

"I thought it odd to see a single crow in the harbour," Evelyn said, uneasily following John's stare to scan the dark tree line for any sign of movement.

"I killed its mudder." The twinkle in John's eyes extinguished. "Had no choice but to take care of it." He kicked a few rocks to diffuse the surge of remorse, wincing at the impact on his broken toes.

James took a break from his rock clearing, wiping his sweaty forehead with his sleeve. "How far down do you think it is?"

"Once we gets into the ground, the rocks aren't as big, and it goes a little faster. I've gotten as far as six feet down before I crawled out. Felt like I was digging my own grave. Scared me to death thinking they'd bury my alive if I dozed off in there." John spoke with a devilish scowl. "Not this time though."

After a couple hours of heavy lifting, Evelyn tried to stifle a yawn, but her exhaustion prevailed, triggering the involuntary reflex as she opened her mouth wide and inhaled.

"Well, it's time for you fine folks to head back to the house," John said. "Grab some sleep for a couple hours. I'll dig till you gets back. Those friggers don't scare me anymore." He shook a quivering fist over his head.

"It's a long way back," Evelyn said. "What if we get lost, James?"

"What? You don't trust my sense of direction?" James asked.

"I do, I just never had to walk through the woods in the dark," Evelyn said, not knowing how to respond to James's playfulness.

John pointed through the woods. "Remember, that way. Keep your ears open for the sound of the ocean to your right, then just keep on going straight. You'll come out of the woods and hit the harbour."

When John wasn't looking, James picked up the axe then took the flashlight from Evelyn. "Follow me, my lass. I'll protect you." Then he whispered, "I don't trust the old man with a weapon of sorts so the axe is coming back with us." He held the flashlight like a sword, slashing its beam through the air in a mock battle.

"Get going before that moon decides to hide out in the clouds; it'll get darker than pitch black out here." John paused. "Those ghost pirates gets pretty pissed off when I'm out here digging, but don't let them scare you too much.

Whatever you hears, they're harmless. Haven't touched me once." John whistled to the crow. "She knows her way home. Follow her back if you can keep up."

The bird took flight into the woods, as James and Evelyn ran through the darkness with the flashlight illuminating the immediate path ahead of them. Occasionally they'd stop and listen to be sure they could hear the ocean at their right. Neither spoke. They kept their eyes peeled in front of them, careful not to trip.

Evelyn became acutely aware of every crack of a branch and crunch of the ground. Whispers and moans grew loud around them, until Evelyn, mistaking the thudding of her heartbeat for the pirate ghosts' footsteps, envisioned pirate skeletons chasing close behind with outstretched bony fingers ready to snatch them up in an instant. She imagined them pulling her into the ocean. Avoiding the urge to keep watch over her shoulder, she forced her legs and slippery shoes to outrun her imagination.

Evelyn and James finally emerged from the woods and made their way to the haunted-looking house. The crow called out before it headed back into the woods.

"Do you believe all this?" Evelyn asked, out of breath, when they were safely inside.

James hurried to make a fire in the wood stove. "As a matter of fact, I do." James cleared his throat. "I grew up with these kinds of stories, so I can't help but believe them. Scary as hell, if you ask me."

"Do you think John's a ghost too?" A shiver ran down Evelyn's spine, imagining John as a disembodied spirit.

"Come on, now. Don't go letting your mind get away with you." James laughed. "But I sure hope not."

From behind James's flashlight they explored the frigid house like ghost hunters. They made their way up the stairs and James peeked into Annabel's room.

"Do you want to sleep in here?" James asked.

"I'm too scared." She pressed herself into his back, peeking over his shoulder. When she was sure the room was ghostless, she pushed James inside to escape the dark hallway.

"I can bring a chair up and sleep beside you, if that makes you more comfortable."

"I'd like that." She turned down the blankets on the bed and was startled by the decrepit doll with stubbly hair and blank wooden eyes. The glow of the flashlight cast its shadow across the bed.

"What in the world would he keep an old doll for?" James stammered.

Evelyn picked it up and shuddered at its unnatural pose. She motioned for James to follow her into the hallway. "Let's put it outside the door. It's going to give me nightmares if it stays in the room."

When they returned to the room and stood over the bed, Evelyn noticed John's head imprint in the pillow, surrounded by dirt, grease and a dried blood stain. She scrunched her face and looked at James. "Probably hasn't been washed in a long time."

"I highly doubt he's got any soap."

Evelyn's scrunched face grimaced.

"Didn't your mudder ever tell you that your face will stay like that if the wind changes?" James snickered, but tried to stop when Evelyn shot him a look of trepidation. "I got some sleeping bags and a tent in the boat. You know, just in case a storm rolled in. Standard precautions in case we got stuck somewhere."

"Maybe just the sleeping bags." She accepted the flashlight James offered.

She sat alone in the room while James ran to the boat. She was intimidated by the darkness but watched out the window while James ran with just enough moonlight to guide him. Evelyn stopped breathing when she heard the sound of sloshing footsteps echoing down the hallway. She peeked around the corner of the doorway, flashing the light into the hall. Finding it empty, she darted from the room, down the hallway and out the front door to meet James.

"James! There's something in there! There's something in the hall!" Evelyn gasped for air as she looked back to the house. The curtain was now drawn to the side from Annabel's window.

James had the sleeping bags in his hands. "Do you really want to go back in there?"

"What else would we do?" she asked, looking around the harbour. "I think it would be even worse out here."

"True enough."

They walked back to the house keeping their eyes on the window with the curtain drawn to the side.

They went back up to the bedroom, each carrying a sleeping bag. The room was empty, but the curtain was still pulled to the side. They hesitated outside the doorframe. James threw the sleeping bags onto the bed. The curtain fluttered but didn't drop.

"What's holding it back?" Evelyn whispered.

"What, or who?" James corrected.

Both were hesitant to enter the room.

"Where's the washroom?" Evelyn asked.

James busted out a hearty laugh. "You think John's got a bathroom with no power or running water?" He snorted as he tried to control his breath. "There might be an outhouse. If not, you just might have to use the bushes."

Evelyn was horrified. She needed to pee. She wasn't going alone in the woods, and she didn't want James to go with her and watch. She followed James through the hallway.

"In here," he said.

Evelyn grabbed the flashlight from him and shone the light inside the room. It was empty, except for a tall white bucket in the middle of the floor. It reeked of pungent urine.

"It's a salt-beef bucket," James explained, "a kind of toilet."

"I guess he wasn't expecting company." Evelyn plugged her nose.

"Not too bad for twenty years of use." James laughed again. "I can see if there's an old Sears catalogue here somewhere."

"What for?"

"Toilet paper."

Evelyn sneered, but when James pulled out a half roll of toilet paper from his coat pocket, she smirked, snatching it from his hands.

"You never know when nature's going to call." He winked and closed the door.

Evelyn let go of her nose and laid the flashlight on the floor. She squatted awkwardly over the bucket. As hard as she tried, she couldn't make herself pee. She had a case of stage fright, knowing James was on the other side of the door. She closed her eyes and tried to relax. When it finally came, the tinkling sound seemed to go on forever, echoing loudly. A tiny fart reverberated off the walls of the empty room.

"Almost done in there?" James called out, amidst a burst of laughter.

"Stop it. I'm going as fast as I can!"

"Good, 'cause it's getting kinda creepy out here in the dark hallway with this doll."

She finished up, disgusted there was no sink to wash up, then opened the door with a jolt, shining the flashlight under her chin so that the light cast distorted shadows over her face.

James's eyes bulged and his body jerked at the sight of her.

"You're not afraid, are you?" Evelyn laughed.

"Not one bit." He grabbed her hand and hurried her into the bedroom. "Wait here."

Evelyn pointed the flashlight at the opened curtain and didn't move.

James ran downstairs and returned a moment later with two kitchen chairs. He placed them just inside the door to Annabel's room. "Comfort is key."

Evelyn unrolled and crawled inside one of the sleeping bags, and James did the same, except he laid himself out on the kitchen chairs, placed seat to seat. When James switched off the flashlight, the curtain dropped, filling the room with blackness, sending a shiver through both of them. Evelyn sidled to the edge of the bed, until she and James were shoulder to shoulder.

The wind picked up, howling like a banshee through the old house. It reminded Evelyn of a braking freight train, metal grinding on metal. She covered her head with the sleeping bag when she heard a "rat-a-tat-tat" on the windowpane growing louder. The sound of sloshing footsteps echoed from downstairs.

"James?" Evelyn whispered through complete darkness, her stomach now in knots.

"Probably just a tree branch. Nothing to worry about."

"I don't remember the tree outside being high enough to reach the window." She held her breath. She could tell James held his too as they both tried to make sense of the sounds.

James scrambled for the flashlight beside the chair, flicked it on and laid it on the bed pointing toward the door. Still in the sleeping bag, he hopped over to the door, holding the sleeping bag up with one hand, gripping the chair in the other.

"John?" he called loudly out the door.

No response. He closed the door and put the chair under the knob to keep it secure.

"Like that's going to keep out pirate ghosts." Evelyn snorted a nervous laugh.

"Now there's the spirit."

Evelyn sat on the edge of the bed until James motioned for her to hop over beside him at the window. He pulled the curtain aside. The eerie glow of the moon lit the room. They exchanged a look of dread as they saw there were no tree branches outside the window. On the horizon, a fog bank grew. From downstairs, they heard the latch of the screen door open and bang shut. Moments later, the scream of a woman echoed up the stairwell.

"Oh my God!" Evelyn buried her head in James's chest. His heart pounded in her ear. They both jumped when the screen door slammed shut again.

James and Evelyn watched from the window as a dark phantom dragged a woman by the hair at an alarming speed into the ocean. Her cries rang through the harbour as she was pulled into the crashing tide.

"Holy shit," James whispered. "Holy shit. Holy shit!"

"Was that Annabel?!" Evelyn asked, terrorized, drawing in deep, shaky breaths.

"I'm pretty sure." He reached for her hands and squeezed.

"Do you think it'll come back for us?" she asked in a long, dragged-out whisper.

"John says they're harmless. They would've taken him long ago." James wrapped his arms around Evelyn as she cried, hyperventilating.

"I really didn't believe him," Evelyn said, breathless. Her eyes were still glued to the waves. "It's horrific. I can't believe it's true. I mean, I assumed he was making it all up."

"I wouldn't have believed it if I didn't just see it with my own eyes." He held her tight. "I can't believe what we just saw."

"Should we go out there and try to help her? I can't help but feel like we should do something."

"I'd say she's long gone now, by the looks of it."

"Should we go tell John, then?" Evelyn turned, and her lips accidentally brushed James's cheek. The sensation tickled until she licked her lips. She quickly turned to look back out the window, speechless, when she noticed he was staring at her mouth.

"We could, but I think he knew it would probably happen. We needs to get a little rest so's we can dig and keep watch," James said. "Geez, I just can't believe it."

"You think John's okay out there?"

"He's survived this long. I'm sure he's fine."

Evelyn turned around and sized up the bed. "I know it's only a single, but I think it's big enough for the both of us." She crawled into her sleeping bag, careful to place a layer of the sleeping bag between her head and the pillow. "The extra body heat will keep us from freezing."

"Sure thing." James smiled a brazen smile.

"Just keep your hands to yourself." She tried to hold back a smile.

James switched off the flashlight, and Evelyn felt the bed heave as he crawled into his sleeping bag next to her. They both lay still for what felt like a long time.

"Are you asleep yet?" Evelyn asked after only a few minutes.

"No," he answered. "I feels wide awake now."

"Me too." Evelyn tried to move but almost slipped off the bed. "Maybe we're both dreaming?"

"Now that would be the strangest thing." He put his arm under her neck. "You all right with this?"

"Yes," she said a little too quickly. When she turned to face him, her nose brushed his. She could feel his warm breath on her lips. She felt the desire to kiss him but instead turned her head to the ceiling. "Thanks for making me brave enough to sleep in this haunted house."

James made spooky sounds, and within a few minutes, they were both in fits of laughter.

"How on earth did he stay here for twenty years by himself?" James asked.

"I have no idea. He must really have loved her." Evelyn yawned.

"Good night, Evelyn," James said, squeezing her tight.

She thankfully fell asleep before he did.

Chapter 19

EVELYN AND JAMES WOKE up in each other's arms. Even wrapped in separate sleeping bags, they'd managed to get their legs tangled together, anchoring themselves to one another to stay on the bed. The blush of dawn shone through the closed curtain, and a cold breeze blew through the room. Evelyn shivered when she crawled out of her sleeping bag.

"James! We overslept!"

"Shit!" He jumped to his feet.

"Listen," she said.

"What is it?" James turned his head. "Do you hear those ghosts again?"

Evelyn laughed. "No, listen."

James looked out the window.

"The waves. They're so peaceful." She loved the sound with all her heart. She wished she could bottle it up and take it home with her. The white noise of its ebb and flow held something special. It was so simple, yet it filled her soul and cleared her mind. It was hard to believe it could ever be murderous. She pushed the curtains to look out the window. "Hurry, we have to get back to him."

"Oh, geez. I was expecting you heard something other than that." James tossed a pillow at her and quickly rolled up the sleeping bags.

"Doesn't look so scary in the morning," Evelyn said and threw the pillow back. She raked her hair with vigorous strokes of her fingers and looked across the bed into the broken, bulging mirror, trying to find a place to see her reflection between the cracks. Her mascara was smudged under her eyes, giving her the appearance of a meerkat.

"You're right about that," James yawned and stretched. "What are you up to?"

Evelyn looked back at him. "I'm not much of a morning person," she laughed. "Trying to make myself look presentable."

"Don't worry about what you looks like," James said. He pulled her down with him to the bed. He kissed her forehead.

Evelyn's heart quickened, and her stomach fluttered. James looked just as good in the morning as he did the night before. She could only imagine what he saw when he looked at her. She longed for a brush and her make-up bag, not to mention a toothbrush, or even a facecloth and water to wash her face. She looked down at her wrinkled, frumpy clothes.

"I'm quite the vision today." She stood up and walked to the bedroom door, waiting for James to follow her.

"You don't got to impress me." James gave a half smile. "You already have."

Evelyn rolled her eyes at him. "Let's go."

"Aren't you hungry?"

"Not really." Evelyn's stomach grumbled, but she was anxious to get down to Money Point to relieve John. "But let's bring food with us. I'm sure John's hungry."

James walked over to her and gave her a hug. "That sounds perfect."

Their eyes met, and he slowly leaned in. Evelyn closed her eyes and let him kiss her. She froze, unable to breathe for a moment, as his soft lips caressed hers. A million silver-bellied thoughts swam through her mind like a capelin roll—a phenomenon her father had told her about as a child. Tens of thousands of small smelt fish would wash up on the beach each summer to spawn, and she recalled her father's stories of people flocking to the beach with dip nets and buckets to catch them. It was something she wanted to experience, one day. She ran her hands up James's strong back.

"That was a pretty risky thing to do," she said, looking at his lips.

"A risk I was willing to take." He pulled her in close again. "I wanted to do that last night, but I didn't want you to get the wrong impression."

Evelyn kissed him back, despite being self-conscious about her morning breath. "It's lucky you didn't. You would have been sleeping by yourself on the couch in this haunted house."

James took her hand and led her through the hallway to descend the staircase. "Do you think we dreamt it all up?"

"Maybe," she said. She followed him down the stairs and to the kitchen. The floor was icy cold, and Evelyn shook, both from the chill and from the thrill of James's kiss. She hugged into herself to try to calm the shivers, but she could still feel the pressure of his kiss on her lips.

James took off his jacket and put it over Evelyn's shoulders. "Here, I'll be warm enough."

Within a few minutes, they gathered the two knapsacks loaded with supplies that they'd brought from St. John's: matches, instant coffee, tea bags, tin milk, mugs, spoons, a small tub of margarine, bread, canned sausages. James ran down to the boat and grabbed the tent he kept in the storage box, while Evelyn went to the creek to collect water in mason jars. She splashed her face with cold water, hoping it was enough to wash off the mascara.

Like the ocean, the woods looked so much more innocent in the daytime. But when they reached Money Point, they were aghast to find the huge pile of rocks put back in place. John was nowhere in sight.

"My good God, they must have buried him," James said.

They searched the trees for any sign of John and circled around the freshly stacked pile of rocks.

"Or maybe he was never here." Evelyn shuddered at the thought. "What if that was him last night hauling her out of the house?"

"I wouldn't doubt any possibility right now."

"Do we stay or head back to the harbour?" Grief hit Evelyn when she considered losing John. It wasn't the same mourning she felt for her father but more of a feeling of regret. Regret that she hadn't tried to learn more about him or her mother. She hadn't tried hard enough to revisit her connections to Newfoundland. If she had, she could have met her grandparents and learned so many things about her mother, leading her to John sooner. She wanted to know more about her past, a past that would remain hidden if John were only a ghost. A surge of disappointment flared through Evelyn's heart as she scanned the perimeter of the woods.

"Look!" James stood by a nearby tree. "He's over here!"

She ran to James's side to find John toppled over next to the shovel.

"Do you think he's dead?" A loathsome feeling quickened in her heart. To be given something and have it taken away felt worse than not having it at all.

"I hope not." James picked up a stick and poked him.

"Oh, James, what do we do? I don't think he's breathing." She reached down and touched John's cheek. "He's cold as ice! I think he's dead!"

James poked John again, but harder. John sat upright, moaned, and Evelyn let out a high-pitched scream that sent her flying backward, landing hard on her tailbone.

"Morning, John." James laughed. He offered him a hand to get up.

Overcome with gratitude, Evelyn sprung from the ground and hugged John with intensity.

"Damn, I must have dozed off after I chopped up some wood." John returned Evelyn's hug, though he soon removed himself and walked over to the pile of rocks. "Told you they were sons of bitches." He picked up the shovel and threw it. "Goddamn it! I can't tell you how many times they've done this!"

Evelyn could tell from the muscle tone in his arms that what he said was true.

"We brought a tent. That way, you don't have to walk all the way back to the house."

James pulled the tent from its case, unfurled the heap of wrinkled green nylon, and set to work assembling the poles

SALTWATER JOYS

to hold it up. "Someone will always be able to keep watch through the night if we're all here together."

"Now you're thinking." John smirked. "We'll outsmart them, one way or another."

"I'll start a fire and put on some tea," Evelyn said. She walked around and gathered dry branches and bark. The wind gusted in sharp blasts, and the cold nipped at her through James's jacket. She built the branches into a little teepee on top of the ashes from the fire the night before, then tried to light one with a match. A tiny trail of smoke swirled from the branch, but the match blew out. She tried again and again, but the wind defeated her best efforts. Meanwhile, she noticed James had already built the tent and was pegging the corners to the ground so it wouldn't blow away.

"How's that, Skipper?" James asked. He unrolled the sleeping bags inside the tent.

"Oh, best kind," John said as he crawled into the tent without hesitation and immediately started snoring.

"I'll let you in on a secret, m'lovey." James bent forward and cupped his hand around the teepee of small sticks. "Like this," he said.

Evelyn held her hands the way he showed her and then lit the match and pressed it to one of the sticks. She exhaled softly and steadily until it caught fire. When a stream of smoke rose from her cupped hand, she lit another match and added some bark to the kindling. She was careful not to let the wind blow out the small sticks now glowing red.

"The secret is to give the fire a little oxygen, but not too much all at once." James looked impressed as Evelyn's fire grew high. "Usually it's pretty hard to light anything in this wind."

Small bursts of flankers whizzed by their heads as the fire burned hot, warming them up. Evelyn boiled some water, and James toasted a couple pieces of bread from a long stick. Evelyn grabbed the mugs, while James carefully removed the boiled water from the fire. James offered her a slice of the burnt toast he had smothered with margarine. Evelyn scrunched her nose.

"Best way to eat it, sure!" James took a big bite and rolled his eyes up in his head. "Seriously, though. It's the best toast you'll ever eat. You don't know what you're missing."

Evelyn took a bite and was surprised how the toast stayed crunchy and soft at the same time. The burnt parts added a comforting smoky flavour to the bread. Delicious. Although they weren't doing anything spectacular, Evelyn's senses were stimulated like never before. The crash of the tide, the wind rustling the towering pines, the birds chirping, James's melodic humming—little things that turned the quiet day into something extraordinary. Evelyn especially loved each sip of tea, splashed with tin milk. In the middle of nowhere, in what felt like a million miles from civilization, she felt invigorated. She'd never forget this simple pleasure, and hoped someday to experience it again.

"You fits right in here, Ev," James said. "Is it all right if I calls you that?" James's smile revealed black flecks of charred toast between his teeth.

Evelyn laughed. "Yes." She smiled and pointed to her teeth. "You got a little something there."

James smirked and gave his teeth a quick wipe with his tongue.

Evelyn covered her mouth with her hand and laughed a deep belly laugh.

"You ever think you could live here?" James asked.

"In Ireland's Eye?" Evelyn tried to think of something serious to tame the laughing fit so she didn't wake John.

"Well, no. That boat sailed some twenty-odd years ago. I mean here, in Newfoundland?" His voice faltered.

"I was born here, but I don't remember ever living here. I love the hustle and bustle of the city, the convenience. Though it lacks all this." Evelyn spread her arms wide. "I've never experienced anything as charming as this island. The grandeur of the mountains is comparable, but I've never seen anything as vast as the ocean. I mean, I think I could live here, but don't have anything or anyone here, besides John, and he doesn't sound like he'd ever leave this harbour."

"What's kept you from coming home?"

The word *home* struck a chord with Evelyn. She wondered whether home was the place where you lived permanently, or the place your heart longed to be. Her home was in Calgary with her father, but with her father gone, she felt homeless.

"My father loved the city. Loved Newfoundland more, but there wasn't much for a merchant to do when the fishery was taken over by the trawlers and longliners. He used his business experience to make himself a decent living out west. I lived with him, cared for him after my mother died, and now he's gone." She began to cry. She thought of having to go back to their house, without him, and she didn't want to face it.

"You miss him," James said. "And you will for the rest of your life."

"I do. I should be able to just go back to Calgary and continue where I left off, but it's going to be hard without him. Without him, I don't know where I belong. I can't explain it, but since I found out about John, my mind keeps making up a new history that seems so much more exciting than what's waiting for me in Calgary. I don't want to spend my life wondering about possible family members. I want to know where I came from, where I would have belonged. I need to find my roots."

"I likes the sound of that," James said. He put a couple more slices of toast on the stick and set it over the fire.

"It feels like a part of my past has been exposed and it's unravelling a whole new world for me. I'm constantly wondering if I might have more relatives here that could help me piece together my family history. I can't help but wonder what my life would have been like if I hadn't been adopted."

"Well, I'm sure glad you're here now."

John groaned from inside the tent, rustled around a little, then resumed his intense intervals of snoring.

"Do you think he's going to be all right?" Evelyn asked.

"What can't be cured must be endured, or at least that's what Fadder tells me. By the sounds of it, John's heart will never be cured of Annabel. Though I'm sure having you here might be a start to that."

"Have you ever had a love like theirs?" Evelyn's cheeks flushed at her boldness in asking such an intimate question.

James thought for a moment and shook his head. "I thought I did when I was younger, but nah. I forgot her pretty quick."

"Why?" Evelyn couldn't help but pry.

"I just never had that feeling for her. You know, the one where you gets all obsessed and wants to spend every waking moment together. I've actually never had that feeling until a couple of nights ago." James gave her a wink. "How about you? Is there a special boy you loves?"

"No, I'm . . . ," she started. "I haven't had much time for that." She swallowed hard when she thought of her father and his overprotective love for her. She was kept so busy, so focused, raised to know that she was capable of doing anything a man could do. So much so that she'd never had a serious relationship.

"Well, I suppose we should get at 'er then?" He gestured to the towering rocks, heavy and deep.

They cleaned up, let the fire die down, and set to work. James followed Evelyn to the top of the pile.

"You push those medium-sized ones and roll them off to the side," James said. "I'll roll these bigger ones. Let's see how far we can get down before he wakes."

"I wonder how far down he dug last night."

"Hard to say, but by the looks of the gravel over there, he dug into the ground."

"Do you think the pirates really put it back?"

"In my right mind, I knows it's impossible, but I can't see the old bugger putting it back by himself." James mused. "That means it had to have been the ghost pirates." He made spooky ghost calls until Evelyn jabbed him in the side.

Evelyn enjoyed the chance to talk with James. At first it helped make light of the heavy workload, but as the hours passed, they got to know each other. She found out that bartending was a gig over the summer months when he wasn't teaching. She shared her dreams to teach when she graduated university. She asked him questions about his life and childhood to keep the momentum of their budding relationship going. Evelyn couldn't help but feel that when James listened to her, it was with his whole heart. They were in tune with each other, and fed off each other's energy as if they were somehow connected.

Evelyn was conscious of her bare face and greasy hair, but James made her feel like she was the most beautiful person when he looked at her. Even though her muscles ached and her hands were dry and cut from the sharp rocks, she felt like nothing mattered but the moment they were sharing. She pushed past the stinging pain and unleashed her inner child, full of excitement to find the pirate treasure buried deep beneath the rocks.

Chapter 20

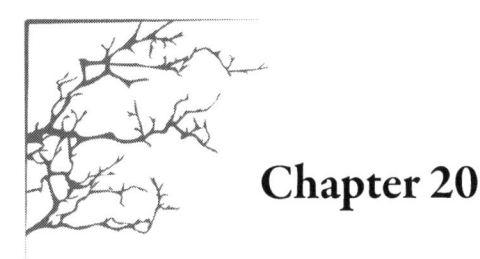

"BY GOD, HOW LONG HAVE I been asleep?" John stuck his head out of the tent. "I thought I must have been dead when I woke. I didn't know where the heck I was."

Evelyn looked down at her watch. "It's two o'clock. Let me make you a little burned toast." Evelyn chuckled under her breath, as she climbed off the rocks. "You're going to need something to eat."

"You've made some progress here," John said, looking impressed and picking up the shovel. "I thank you for that."

Evelyn glowed inside as she gathered broken twigs for a fire. James was at her side, with the excuse to help light the fire. Proud of her repeated accomplishment, she put on some water to boil for instant coffee. The crackle and hiss gave way to the smell of woody smoke. From the corner of her eye, Evelyn noticed John watching her and James.

"Now, I'm no prophet, but I dare say if the community would've voted against Confederation, you two would've grown up together. Just the same as when me and your mudder grew up and fell in love. I knew her from the moment she was born. My gut tells me you two would've followed in our footsteps. You know, your mudders and fadders were best friends." He raised one eyebrow and glanced sideways at both of them. "And I knows for a fact you two would've been married by now if they had any say." He smiled.

"Oh, John. You don't know what you're talking about." Evelyn blushed.

"I sure as hell do."

He spoke with a big smile, and Evelyn noticed for the first time that he had large gaps of missing teeth. "Annabel and Sarah would have found some way to make you fall in love."

Evelyn was surprised to see James with a serious look on his face.

"Funny you said that," James said. "Mudder said the same thing." He looked contemplative, but snapped out of it when he looked nonchalantly at Evelyn. "But I don't know if a pretty girl like you would have anything to do with the likes of me."

Evelyn focused her attention on the kettle over the fire, pretending not to hear James. She grabbed a long branch to take it off the heat. James was at Evelyn's side to help pour the steaming water into cups, already prepped with a sprinkle of instant coffee.

"Don't want you to burn yourself, young lady." He gave her a quick kiss when John wasn't looking.

"Thank you." Evelyn was relieved James didn't seem bothered by John's bold statement that they would have been married. She carried two steaming cups toward John and didn't think twice before she blurted out what she was desperate to ask.

"John, could you tell me a little more about Annabel?" She prepared herself for the same ache that filled her heart when she thought of her adoptive parents. She longed to see them again, knowing she never would.

John stopped digging for a moment and stuck the shovel straight into the ground. He held the long handle with both hands and rested his chin on top. He stood speechless, staring into the distance for the longest time before he let the shovel fall and crossed his arms across his chest.

"There's so much I misses about that girl. Let me tell you, I fell right in love with her heart. Pure gold, it was. I put her high above everyone else. There's not enough I could ever say to describe what a wonderful person she was. She was fearless and carefree. Prettiest thing I ever did see." He turned and looked at Evelyn. "That is until I saw you. And I knows she wouldn't mind me saying so."

"Tell me more." Evelyn blushed as she walked over to stand in front of John and offered him one of the cups. She sipped the weak coffee, peeking over the rim of the mug.

"She wanted you more than you could ever imagine. We'd talk about our future together, and it always revolved around you. She was my world, Evelyn. Everything I loved, I found in her." He took a sip of coffee and shrugged his shoulders. "And she loved me—the most stubborn person in the world. I don't know why she loved me the way she did, but she did. I'm not much for the emotional stuff, but she really got to me. I was, and still am, crazy over her. Makes it hard to ever think of letting her go, even if it means I'll never physically touch her again. I'll hold onto her memory 'cause I knows her spirit lives here, and that's the reason why I'll never leave this harbour. I finds her in the strangest places, even after twenty years gone. She's my harbour now, and she's the ocean that washes up on the shore. But until I knows her soul's at peace, I won't rest. The thought of her beautiful soul in the hands of that pirate kills me."

"We saw her last night, John. Just like you told us," Evelyn said. "It was the most disturbing thing I've ever seen."

John uncrossed his arms. "Once we gets her ransom, I'll find her on the other side of this dream, this nightmare. Or maybe I'll die and find her in heaven, if I makes it there. I'll probably be sent to hell for eternity for killing her. And for what I done to Helen." He paced in front of Evelyn.

Evelyn straightened up at John's mention of her sister.

"I don't ever ask for forgiveness. What I did was unforgivable. But until I figures out how to make things right, hopefully enough to be forgiven, this is where I'll take my chances." John started digging again.

"Helen? You knew her?" She paused. "And she knew you?"

"Yes." John hesitated. "I guess you would have been just a baby when Helen came to me, the spring after Annabel died. She came with provisions. In my head, I thought it was Annabel back from the dead." John hung his head. "I beat her, Evelyn. I don't know what got into me, but I thought she was tricking me to make me believe she was Annabel, I got so damn angry, I beat her." He closed his eyes. "I thinks about her every now and then and wonders if she knows how sorry I am."

A desolate feeling came over Evelyn. "She never told me anything about you." Evelyn thought of her sister as her greatest confidant and now she felt a jolt of betrayal.

"I don't blame her. She probably thought me a dangerous man. Maybe she told your fadder, and that's why he told you I was dead." He shook his head. "Our actions cause waves of consequences that can't be stopped."

AS THE NIGHT APPROACHED, Evelyn tended the fire and prepared snacks and drinks to keep the men going. She hung the sleeping bags on the evergreen's wide branches to air them out. Her hands felt so dry and cracked from handling the rough rocks that she longed for the bottle of hand lotion in her hotel room. She sat down near the edge of the hole and used the flashlight to keep the shadows from getting too close. Whenever she heard branches crack or murmurs of echoes and whispers rise behind her, she'd whip the flashlight toward the unfathomable forest, retracting the figments of her imagination.

James climbed out of the hole and sat next to her.

"You looks tired, Ev."

"My eyes are getting pretty heavy. I'm not used to all the fresh air. It feels like there's been a power outage, and the darkness terrifies me. It feels confining, like I've been blinded by it. I guess I'm just used to the glow of city lights." She laughed. "I'll crawl into the tent and sleep for a while, if you guys are okay?"

John's voice rose up from inside the hole. "Yes, indeed. Get some rest."

"Are you scared?" James asked.

"Not since you mentioned it." Evelyn stood and walked toward the aired-out sleeping bags. She grabbed one, trying to hear James and John's conversation as she entered the tent and zipped it up. She crawled into a sleeping bag, shivering as she laid on the cold, hard ground. She felt a hard rush pulsate through her body when she heard footsteps draw near and the zipper of the tent reopen.

"Whatever you does, wake me up before you falls to sleep this time, Skipper," James yelled out before he crawled in. "Enough room in here for me?"

"Yeah. It's pretty cold though." Evelyn's teeth chattered uncontrollably. "What about John?"

"He's gonna take the first shift and keep digging until he wears himself out." James knelt down. "Why don't we zip both sleeping bags together? I'll keep you nice and warm that way."

Evelyn's silence told him she didn't like the idea.

"Don't worry. I'll keep my hands off you. I'm thinking more for survival so we don't freeze to death."

"All right then."

They each unzipped their sleeping bag and zipped them together. Evelyn crawled in first, then James crawled in and pulled her near.

"Brrr! Holy frig, it's sure cold in here. You're like an icicle." He turned off his flashlight. He kissed her and then pulled away. "You know, I heard that people stayed alive after they stripped down and held onto each other. Creates more body heat."

Evelyn remained silent. She loved how she could hear him smile as he spoke in the darkness.

"Not saying we have to, but if you feels like you're about to die of hypothermia, I'm game to keep you warm any way I can."

"Thank you, James, but I'll warm up in a few minutes."

"Can't blame a boy for trying," he said. He held her close and twitched with sleep as soon as he laid his head on the ground.

She closed her eyes for what seemed like only a few minutes, and when she opened them, she could see the outline of the sun through the tent. James was gone, so she went unseen to the woods to pee.

"Good morning, gorgeous." James flashed a goofy smile when she came back.

Evelyn slipped back into the tent to fix her hair. She groomed herself as though she were a cat, licking her hands to flatten her hair and wipe her face. She longed for a mirror. When she came out, James had a fire started, and set the pot of water over it to boil.

"Where's John?" She took a seat on a rock next to James.

"He's still down there." James cupped his hand to his ear. "I still hears him moving the dirt."

"All night?"

"He knows you got to leave today, so he's determined, let me tell you. I never saw the likes."

When the water boiled, James dipped the spoon into the instant coffee jar and put a heaping amount into a mug. He stirred it after adding a splash of milk. He offered Evelyn the steaming cup of coffee. "I made it good and strong."

"Did you get much sleep last night?" She accepted the coffee, testing the temperature with her top lip before taking a sip.

"I slept for an hour or so but kept waking up. I was scared the old man would fall asleep again. I don't want any part of having to lift all those rocks for a third time. He stayed up all night though. This instant coffee must be pumping through his veins still."

"Why don't you have a rest—"

James hopped up and looked over the ledge of the hole. "What's going on down there?" He looked back at Evelyn. "He's stopped digging. I can't hear anything."

Just as James set his coffee down and was about to jump into the hole, John climbed like a zombie from the earth, his eyes glazed. He stumbled to his knees and crawled into the tent without even seeing James and Evelyn.

"Frigger was down there sleeping. That's all we needs now is for him to get buried and then have to dig him outta there," James said with the fiery temper of an overtired child.

"You need sleep too." Evelyn laughed. "Why don't you go to the tent, and I'll keep watch and dig for a while."

"I'll lay down when he wakes up." James finished the last drop of his coffee, grabbed the shovel, and headed toward the hole. "Those pirates might make off with a pretty thing like you." He winked.

Evelyn followed him and dangled her legs over the edge of the hole before she jumped in.

James put his foot on the base of the shovel and put all his weight on it. He tried to drive it down, but it didn't move. On the third try, he hit something.

"B'ys! B'ys!"

John jumped out of the tent and sprung down into the hole before Evelyn even realized what was happening. She watched James dig around the object, while John madly scraped with his hands. When more of it was exposed, they heaved and hauled until they finally freed it.

"I can't believe it! I can't believe it!" James yelled.

They brushed it off and James heaved it from the ground. John grabbed it and didn't flinch under its weight. He let out a victorious guffaw and gave the chest a good shake, then threw it down when it didn't rattle like he expected it to. The rock actually resembled a treasure chest.

"Damn it!" John climbed out of the hole and headed back toward the tent. "They tricks me all the time. Gets pleasure outta it."

Evelyn stopped him. "John, do you have the coin with you?"

"Carries it everywhere I goes," he said, pulling it from his front shirt pocket.

"This might sound a little absurd to you, but instead of stealing the treasure for Annabel's ransom, why don't you just give the gold coin back?"

He turned toward her with his face agape. "That's something I never thought of." He looked at the coin. "If you're right, and that's all they wanted, that means I've kept her captive twenty years." He didn't look away from the coin that weighed heavy in the palm of his hand. "She brought this to me all those years ago. Why the hell didn't I think of that? You just might be right. She told me to find her, but I never did. When she gave me the coin, I never thought to give it back. I just wanted it all. Show them what it feels like to have everything you ever wanted taken from you. What if that's why they've kept her away from me all these years, 'cause I didn't give it back?"

"It wouldn't hurt to try," James said, stretching out his sore back.

A crazed look came over John's face. "She's the only thing I ever wanted, and when I lost her, I lost the only fortune in the world worth something to me. If it's true, I've been deceived by my own self." He fired the coin down onto the ground. "Take it! Take it! Lord tunderin'—take it!" The coin landed beside James's foot.

"Now what do we do?" James looked at John.

"Bury it." John said.

The three of them climbed out of the hole, and filled it up, which was much easier than digging it out. Evelyn looked to John once they finished.

"Now we wait," he said.

"Wait for what?" James looked around and wondered if they were being watched.

"Wait for some sign from her. Her soul is tied to it. I've been doing the wrong thing. I might have had her release in my own goddamn hands the whole time." His nostrils flared, and he ground his few teeth together.

"How will we know if it worked?" Evelyn asked.

"Every single time she escapes, they always takes her back that night. If she's up in the window when we returns, and they don't come for her tonight, I'll know it worked." John picked up his shovel and headed along the path, anxious to see if Annabel would be there. "Meet me back at the house."

It didn't take long for Evelyn and James to pack up the tent and supplies, and make their way back to the harbour. When the house was in view, they noticed the curtain wasn't pulled to the side. Inside, they found John sound asleep on the chesterfield.

"I don't want to say goodbye to him," Evelyn said.

"Take your time," James said as he plunked himself down in an armchair. "You could cancel your flight, you know."

Evelyn knelt in front of John and repeated his name, careful not to startle him, until his eyes opened.

"Annabel?"

"No, John. It's me."

He squinted. "Oh, yes. Now I sees you." He sat upright, and his eyes darted around the room.

"Why don't you come with us to St. John's? My flight leaves tonight, but I'd love to spend more time together."

"You're leaving already?" A sullen look filled John's eyes as he counted on his fingers. He walked to the kitchen table, sat down and lit a cigarette.

"I really wish you would come with us." She followed him into the kitchen and motioned for James to join them. "You deserve so much more than this. Running water, electricity, plumbing, heat, proper meals . . . ." She pressed even harder when John shook his head. "If I'm anything like my mother, or if she was anything like me, I know she wouldn't want you to punish yourself any longer for something you had no control over."

"I can't go. I needs to know if Annabel will return to me tonight, without those goddamned pirates to drag her off into the sea again. I got to know if it worked."

"I want to know if it worked too, and I don't want to leave you," Evelyn said. "I thought you might have lost your mind when you told me about the pirates, but when we saw her the night before last, I knew it had to be the truth." Evelyn looked at James aghast at the horrifying recollection.

James rubbed the back of his neck. "That was the spookiest thing I ever saw. Wouldn't have believed either it had I not seen it with me own eyes."

"You're welcome to stay here as long as you want. And I sure want you to." John dug into his pocket and pulled out the little diamond on a band of gold. "Your mudder's ring is the only thing I has left of her." He pushed it across the table. "Take it. It won't do me any good. I wants you to have it. There's no one else I ever wants to marry. She's the one love that is going to take me whole life to get over."

John winked at James as Evelyn slipped the ring on her finger. It was too big, so she undid the necklace she wore and looped the chain through the asymmetrical circle.

"So, what do you say, are you going to stay a little longer?" John pressed.

Evelyn sighed. "My flight is leaving tonight, and Helen would worry if I wasn't at the airport."

"You get going, then. It'll take you a while to get back to St. John's. I'll stay and make sure they leaves her alone."

James walked over to John and shook his hand. "Nice meeting you, Skipper. Hope to see you again sometime."

John reached for Evelyn, holding her for a long time. "I'm sorry, Evelyn, but this is the only place that's fit for a person like me." His cheeks were streaked with saltwater tears.

"I feels a little left out, you guys," James said.

John stepped away from Evelyn. "Before you goes, I want you to have one more thing." He took off up the stairs and returned with the nightmare doll. "It was your mudder's. I thought it was possessed for a spell, but now I know different. It's been out in the ocean, washed up on shore, and chewed by a goat, but I'd like you to have it. I think it was your mudder's way of telling me you were still alive."

Evelyn cringed—she could hardly look at the wretched thing—but the hopeful look on John's face made her reach for the doll and tuck it under her arm. "I'll have it refurbished when I get home so it looks like it would have when Annabel had it."

James gathered the sleeping bags, flashlight and tent and joined John and Evelyn as they walked to the boat in silence. The ocean was quiet, just a flap of surf on the shore. James and Evelyn boarded the boat and were soon on their way. Evelyn waved, taking with her the history and feelings of those who used to live there. Her eyes were the eyes of the generation before her. She felt like she was leaving home. That word pulled at her heartstrings; she felt such a connection to this place where she had never lived. Ireland's Eye was like a *hiraeth*, a feeling of homesickness for a place that never was home. She took one last long look at John before he was out of sight, sensing the turmoil he felt. She looked up to the house and saw the curtain in the bedroom window drawn to the side.

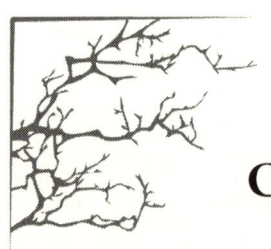

Chapter 21

EVELYN LOVED FEELING the rise and fall of the ocean beneath her, the sound of the waves slapping the side of the boat, the way the wind sprayed salt water in her face. The lonely beauty of Ireland's Eye captivated her. From the bow, she admired the rocky coastline pounded by unrelenting waves, the moss-covered spruce trees growing sideways from muddy banks at the edge of the woods, held strong by deep-set roots that resisted the harsh winds.

As they made their way toward New Bonaventure, Evelyn grabbed the sides of the bow. When James killed the motor and the boat slowed, she panicked at the thought of potentially being stuck in the Atlantic. She feared reliving the same fate as her mother. She looked back at James, afraid of being swept to sea by a sudden rogue wave.

"What's going on?" Evelyn didn't let go of the edge of the bow. "Why did the motor stall?"

"Calm down, Ev." James pointed up.

High in the sky, a bald eagle soared. Its white head and tail contrasted with its chocolate body, which looked tiny compared to its massive wingspan.

"It's beautiful!" Evelyn let go of the boat. Her hands were trembling as she watched the distinguished bird swoop close to the shore and perch on the branches of a tall evergreen. It sang a single, soft, high-pitched note as it watched the boat with piercing eyes.

James started the engine, and they continued their trek along the Smith Sound. The sunless wind was cold, and Evelyn breathed easier when James slowed the engine and docked at the wharf in New Bonaventure. He helped her out of the boat, and passed her the keys to his truck so she could start it and crank up the heat to thaw her hands. He carried their supplies from the boat to the truck, then jumped in the truck, backed up and jumped right out again to hook up the boat to tow it back to St. John's. She turned up the radio and smiled when James jumped in the driver's seat.

"So?" he asked.

"So what?"

"So, what do we do with the doll?" he asked, cringing as he held it up by its neck.

"Just put it on the floor." She looked out the window as the truck pulled away from the wharf.

He slapped the seat beside him. "Scooch over. You seems so far away over there."

Evelyn slid across the cold leather bench seat. She played with the ring on her necklace.

"I knows a guy who'd fix that up real nice."

"Well, if you think you can get it back to me before my flight." She undid the necklace, slipped the ring off, and put it in James's hand.

"I daresay I could do that."

They listened to the radio. Evelyn curled into James's shoulder and closed her eyes. Although the drive was a few hours, Evelyn wasn't ready to get out when they pulled up to the hotel. He leaned in for a kiss, and Evelyn gave him a quick peck on the cheek.

"I really need to brush my teeth." She slid over to the passenger side and hopped out. "The lady working at reception is going to think I was kidnapped, walking in there looking so ragged."

"What odds?" James winked. "Give 'em all something to talk about. You want me to walk you in?"

"I'm fine." Evelyn hesitated to get out.

"What time's your flight?"

"Ten o'clock." Evelyn looked at her watch, disappointed to see it was already six-thirty.

"Well, you call me when you're ready." He examined the ring in the palm of his hand.

"Ready for what?" She resisted the urge to jump back in the vehicle.

"I got somewhere to take you before I drops you off at the airport. It's a surprise." He put the ring in his shirt pocket and patted it to mark its security as he smiled at her.

Evelyn was on the verge of inviting him into the hotel, but one glimpse of herself in the truck's side-view mirror made her close the door. "See you soon."

"And I means as soon as you're ready. I needs every single second to make you fall in love. I wants you to love it so much that you'll never want to leave." His smile grew when she looked back. "Don't forget this." He handed her the doll. He waited until she was in the door before pulling away.

AS SOON AS SHE ENTERED the room she put the doll in a plastic bag and tucked it in her suitcase. It gave her the creeps and she was glad she wouldn't need to sleep in the room with it. It took only twenty minutes to freshen up and pack her things. Evelyn showered, brushed her teeth, and dressed quickly. She stood in front of her makeup bag and opted for a little powder, mascara and lip gloss. The few days in the sun had made her skin flush with a natural glow, and she examined the sprinkle of freckles across her nose.

As soon as she zipped up her suitcase, she called James on the rotary telephone. Sarah answered and pleasantly informed her that he was already out the door and on his way back to pick her up. Evelyn smiled, thanked Sarah, and hung up. She had one more person she had to call. She picked up the receiver again and dialled.

"Hello," her sister voice demanded through the line.

"Helen, it's me."

"I've been trying to get ahold of you for two days, Evelyn." Helen growled through the wires. "I was getting really worried."

"I'm sorry." Evelyn felt a twinge of guilt, but she also felt a deep rage surfacing. To calm herself, she pulled the curtain to the side to look out for James's truck. "I'm soon on my way out again, but I wanted you to know that I found my birth father." She waited for Helen's response but none came. "I was in Ireland's Eye yesterday. His name is John Lee, and he was shocked to see me, to say the least. He thought I was a woman named Annabel, my mother."

"I'm happy for you, Evelyn." Helen's angry voice softened. Silence amplified the intermittent crackling noise on the landline.

Her sister's lack of emotion told Evelyn everything she needed to know—she'd been lied to by everyone in her family. "It's hard to believe you didn't know he was still alive."

Helen cleared her throat. "I'm coming back to Newfoundland, and I think it might do us good to have a heart-to-heart, face-to-face."

"You're coming back?" Evelyn's surprise surpassed her anger, momentarily.

"I shouldn't have left so soon. I spoke with Dad's lawyer in St. John's about the will, and I have to meet with him. I'm going to try to talk Ethan into coming with me. I'm happy you called. I was hoping to catch you before your flight tonight to see if you want to wait there for me. We'll be there Saturday morning. Today's Thursday, right?"

"You can't see a different lawyer in Calgary?" Evelyn asked, skeptical despite her desire to stay in Newfoundland a little longer.

"I guess Dad owns multiple properties in St. John's. It's his request that we choose one property. The inheritance is held up until we do. So that means we'll need to meet with a real estate agent while we're there too. I wish I would have known that while I was there."

As Evelyn listened to Helen digging through papers, she reluctantly dropped her petty grudge.

"I still can't believe he's gone," Evelyn said. She looked up to the ceiling and tried to prevent the tears that welled in her eyes, but they poured like rain down her cheeks. Their mutual tears cleared the brief intensity that had arisen between them.

"I know. I can't believe it either. It's not the same here without him." Helen cried softly into the phone. "I think you should stay and wait for me. We need to be together to do this. I'll change your flight when I book mine. Could you book another room there from Saturday to Tuesday?"

"Until Tuesday?" Evelyn's heart buzzed with anticipation to tell James. "I can do that." Evelyn saw the lights of his truck pull into the hotel parking lot.

Her sister spoke, but she wasn't listening.

"I wish you would have told me about John," Evelyn said. Before Helen could answer, Evelyn said goodbye and hung up the phone. She made a quick call to the front desk to prolong her stay, standing at the window watching James nearly run from his truck into the building.

He waited for her in the lobby, flashing that same big smile as she walked toward him with her suitcase in tow, as she needed to do something with the doll since she was staying longer. She hugged him and kissed his clean-shaven cheek. His skin felt so smooth and soft as it brushed against her lips. The smell of his aftershave lingered.

"Where are we going?" Evelyn asked, bouncing on her toes.

"There's so much I wants to show you, in so little time." He leaned in and kissed her. "And I thought about something on the way to my parents and all the way back here. I wants you to stay. I can't explain it, but I don't want you to go. There's a special place that I knows you'll love, and it'll make you want to stay."

Evelyn wanted to tell him she was staying longer, but his kiss left her breathless.

They walked into the cool night, hand in hand. James opened the passenger-side door and gave her another kiss before he let her get in. He hoisted the suitcase into the back of the truck, jumped in on his side and handed Evelyn a handkerchief from his front pocket.

"You gotta cover up those pretty eyes though. I wants it to be a surprise."

Evelyn tied the cloth around her head. It was saturated with the scent of his cologne. She felt the truck pull forward, and within minutes they were climbing a hill, taking long swerves as the truck ascended.

"Where are we going?" She moved over until she sat right next to James.

"Trust me, you'll like this surprise." The truck didn't hesitate when he floored the gas.

She felt James rest his hand on top of her folded hands. When the truck stopped, he turned the key but kept the music playing.

"I'll be back in a minute. No peeking," he said before slamming the door.

Evelyn was tempted to peek but kept her eyes closed underneath the handkerchief. When James opened her door, she could hear the flapping of flags and the rumble of a faraway surf. James took her hands and led her in front of the truck. She felt his hands on her waist as he hoisted her on top of the hood. She felt him hop up and sit beside her.

"All right, you can look now." He gently untied the handkerchief.

Evelyn kept her eyes closed for a few seconds longer. She opened them to a bird's-eye view of the historic landlocked harbour of St. John's. Her soul filled with awe at the kaleidoscope of colour before her, the large ships docked along the edges, the beautiful houses, the ornate architecture. And overlooking it all was the Cabot Tower.

"Spectacular," Evelyn whispered. She revelled in the majesty for a while, then looked around, behind them, across the parking lot. "What's over there?" The wind whipped Evelyn's hair around her face.

"I'm glad you asked. Let's go find out."

They walked across the parking lot toward a blanket stretched over the grass, held down by four large rocks to keep it from flying away in the wind. All the edges ruffled and reminded Evelyn of a magic carpet. A picnic basket sat in the middle. Although they were precariously close to a ledge overlooking the wild Atlantic that plummeted into a steep cliff of long grass and rock, James didn't seem fazed. He patted the blanket, telling her to take a seat next to him. He pulled a couple of cans of pop from the picnic basket.

"Mudder might have helped me out a bit when I told her what I was up to." James opened the can. It hissed, and he sucked the fizz that sprayed out. "She told me she'd like you to stay just as much as I do. She told me everything about you reminds her of Annabel, except your accent, of course."

"What accent? I don't have an accent." Evelyn shoved his shoulder.

"You do to us. You sounds just like a Mainlander," James said, in a clear voice with no intonation.

"I guess I can't argue with that, b'y." Together they laughed at her feeble attempt to sound like a local.

"Well?" James looked at her.

"Well, what?" Evelyn sensed he knew she was holding something back.

"Well, what do you think of this place?" He stretched his arms out wide.

Evelyn looked far across the stretch of ocean in front of them. "I love the ocean. I could sit and watch and listen to it all day."

"Funny, that's the same way I feel about you."

The mounting chemistry intensified between them. Their mutual attraction was hard to ignore, but Evelyn pretended she didn't hear him.

"What's this place called?" Her question broke the tension.

"Signal Hill. The first transatlantic communication was right here."

"I didn't know that." She was simultaneously relieved and saddened that the conversation took another direction.

"Read that on a plaque in the museum. Impressive, ain't I?" Without giving Evelyn time to react, James grabbed a couple of sandwiches and a small cardboard box from the picnic basket. "Here you go, as promised."

Evelyn opened the box and sucked in a quick breath. She touched her fingers to her parted lips. Inside, she found her mother's ring. It was a perfect circle.

"Try it on," James urged.

She slipped it on her finger and was shocked that it fit. She lifted her eyebrows and looked at James. "How did you do that?"

"Fadder took it out to the garage, sawed it, soldered it back together, and polished her up in no time. I guessed the size of your finger."

She admired the small lone diamond on the thin gold band. It no longer resembled a tarnished keepsake. Now it was a thing of beauty that she was excited to wear. She was happy and sad in the same moment to have something so meaningful given to her, but a dark thought came to her. "What if the ring's cursed?" Evelyn asked, quickly slipping it off her finger. She wondered if it was best to give it back to John. She thought of how the ring was once worn on her mother's finger in life and death.

"You're just being superstitious." James pinched it from the palm of her hand and carefully examined it. "It didn't cause your mudder's death, if that's what you're thinking. Her death was bad timing, poor judgment, and bad luck more than anything."

Evelyn nodded. "I hope you're right, but I can't shake that thought."

"You know, I think I got John's permission to marry you," James said casually examining the ring.

"What are you talking about?" Evelyn felt her heart flutter.

"After he slid the ring over to you, he gave me a wink when you weren't looking." He glanced over at her and then back to the ring, not ready to give up, with a persistence to pursue Evelyn.

"Did he?" Evelyn teased. "I think you misread his cue. It seems everyone winks around here." She gave him a wink and laughed.

"What are you going to do with it?"

"I'm going to wear it," she said. "Cursed or not, it's special to me." She felt a jolt of electric impulse when James lifted her left hand.

"On your wedding finger?"

"Is this my wedding finger?" She wiggled her ring finger. She could feel his hands tremble as he slid the ring on her finger.

"What if I asked you to marry me, Ev?" He paused. "These last couple of days have been like nothing I've ever experienced with anyone before."

"James, you can't be serious. We barely know each other." Evelyn looked him square in the eye.

"I'm serious, if you wants me to be." He swallowed hard, his Adam's apple bouncing down then returning. "Then what if I asked you to stay? You've been kissing me, so that makes me believe you likes me too. I'd love it if you moved back here." He looked at his watch.

Evelyn blushed and rolled her eyes when a wave of emotion hit her, similar to when they first met. She gave a dismissive wave of her hand, despite the unrelenting flutter she now felt in her stomach. His words hit a nerve. *Move back here*. She didn't remember living here in the first place. "I can't stay, James. I don't have anything here. I don't fit in."

"What if I told you that you did have something here, and that you would fit in?"

"But I don't, really. I mean, John is here, but there's no way he's going to leave Ireland's Eye."

"You'd have me. I'd take good care of you, Ev. I can't afford much right now, but I makes a wicked batch of moose stew. Tell me if you feels the same, or tell me I'm crazy. Just don't hide the truth, either way. I knows you're leaving tonight—in fact, we got to get going this very minute to gets you to the airport on time—but I can't let you leave without telling you how I feel. I'm afraid you'll forget about me." James looked to his hands. "I'd give you a good life here, just in a different way. It's not all about the riches, Ev. I'd take you to a different beach along the ocean every day and sing to you. I'd make it so you'd never want to leave me."

"James, stop it," Evelyn said, without conviction.

James offered her a bite of sandwich made with thick homemade bread. Her taste buds perked at the flavour of peanut butter mixed with a slightly sweet and tangy jam. She washed it down with the ice-cold pop.

"What kind of jam is this?" She'd never tasted anything like it before. Her taste buds were alert, and she loved the robust flavour. She opened the sandwich to discover a dark magenta-coloured spread speckled with little red berries on top of the peanut butter.

"Partridgeberry, my dear. Don't tell me you never had it before?"

Evelyn took another bite, and shook her head as she chewed.

"You like it?"

Evelyn slowed her chewing to savour the little gem-sized berries bursting with flavour. "I do."

"They grows all over the place here, and I knows some great places to go berry picking. Best to go and pick them in November, when they're sweetest. Mudder makes it herself, and I'm positive she'd love to show you how to make it. And you haven't tasted anything as good as Mudder's toutons with a spoonful of her jam.

"Touton?" Evelyn asked.

James looked appalled. "Don't tell me you don't know what they are either?"

"Yes, I do." She laughed. "My Mom used to fry up bread dough for us, when I was a little girl."

"I can't help it, Ev. I'm crazy over you. I've never felt like this before, let alone talked to anyone like this before." James thought for a moment. "It's times like these that I believes in some higher power. Call it God or fate or whatever, but it brings people into our lives who are supposed to be there. I believes what John said. We would have been married by now if we had grown up together. I kid you not. If I'd known you all along, I would have asked you to marry me a long time ago. There's just something about you, Ev."

She looked at her watch to distract James from saying more and to distract her mind from its tendency to overthink things, which often left her more confused. "Where did the evening go?" she asked. The sunset cast intense hues of flaming reds and flicks of orange through the sky—a horizon on fire.

"I know. Time flies with you. I suppose I should bring you to the airport so you don't miss your flight."

"There's no rush," she said, trying to hide the smile that lit across her face. "I talked to my sister when I was at the hotel, and I guess I'm here for a little while longer. We need to meet with lawyers about my father's will on Saturday." Evelyn's smile faded when her father's death crept into her mind and another surge of grief crashed over her. "I don't know what I'm going to do without him."

James looked stunned. He wrinkled his eyebrows and searched her face for confirmation. "How much longer?"

"Until Tuesday."

James wrapped his arms around her and kissed her hard.

"I can imagine how sad you feel, but Mudder always told me that when there's rain, look for rainbows, and when it's dark, look for stars. Come on now, it's getting dark, so follow me." He helped her up, gathered the picnic basket, rolled up the blanket, and walked with her to the truck.

Just as she was about to jump in, James pulled down the tailgate.

"Wait now," he said and motioned for her to come over. "I still have the sleeping bags in here." He spread them out in the bed of the truck, still zipped together. He gave her a hand up. "It's going to get dark, so let's look at the stars. Crawl in beside me, and we'll keep each other warm."

They lay together, talking for hours, with their heads propped up on the suitcase, until the stars blazed brilliant, and it seemed there was not a black empty space left in the sky. James wrapped his arm underneath her, and she closed her eyes and nuzzled her cold nose into his cheek.

"I want to fill your heart with Newfoundland. The temperature might be a little cold, but it's the warmest place to rest a weary soul, let me tell you." James held her tight and kissed her over and over again.

Evelyn closed her eyes. His arms felt like home.

Chapter 22

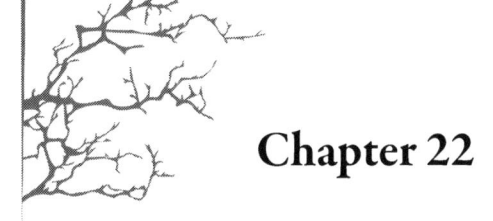

AS DAY AND NIGHT MERGED, Evelyn woke exactly how she fell asleep: tucked into James's arms. The rush of the tide and the sweetness of the cool morning air encouraged her to sit up. She yawned loudly and stretched her arms and legs, stiff from the hard bed of the truck, purposefully exaggerating her movements to wake James. She peeked over the edge of the box of the truck to survey the expansive stretch of ocean, and saw the sun swell just above the horizon, its straight golden reflection blazing a path through the water ahead. Pink ribbons of clouds caught fire as the sun's rays beamed stronger, lighting the entire sky with vibrant hues of red, orange and yellow.

"I've never seen anything so magnificent," Evelyn said when James woke.

"You're right about that," James said, without taking his eyes off her. He sat up and pulled the sleeping bag over their shoulders to protect them from the breeze.

Evelyn still didn't know how to respond to James's feelings for her. His impulsive nature was the inverse to her logic. She struggled to think of something to say, until an awkward silence made their presence together uncomfortable. Pulling her hair from the clutches of the wind, she tied the swirling strands into a ponytail and looked off into the distance.

"Come on, let's get going." James finally said, disheartened. "We're going to blow away if we stays any longer." He offered his hand to help her climb down off the tailgate.

It felt like her tongue was paralyzed. She got into the truck while James rolled up the sleeping bags and slammed the tailgate shut. As they drove back to the hotel, Evelyn kept her chin propped in her hand as she looked out the passenger window. While just a short drive, it seemed like James was intentionally driving slowly and hitting every red light. He stopped at the lobby door of the hotel and put the truck in park. He leaned over and gave her a quick kiss on the cheek. She opened the door.

"I'm really sorry if I said too much last night," James said.

She shook her head, jumped out of the truck, and closed the door behind her. She felt strange that she had developed a sudden case of mutism. Regret welled in her chest when he jumped out of the truck and gave her the suitcase. He offered to take the doll out and leave it in the truck. She nodded, eager to leave the doll. She zipped the suitcase back up when she handed him the doll in the plastic bag. She turned away, walking toward the hotel and heard his truck pull away. Her pride kept her from looking back. He hadn't asked to make plans for the day, so she feared he might have changed his mind.

She wrestled with a whirlwind of confusion as she walked through the empty lobby to her room. She closed her eyes, remembering the way James looked at her, like she was the only person in the entire world when they were together. She knew if she moved back to Calgary that she would eventually forget what her heart felt for him. As her head, heart and gut battled for dominion, Evelyn concluded that falling in love with James wouldn't be the end of the world if their impulsive feelings for one another turned out to be a mistake. It might be a greater risk to let him go, leaving her with a benign haunting her entire life, wondering what might have been. Just like John.

She took a long, hot shower and hoped she would have the courage to call James. She made a mental list of everything she would say and then planned to jot it on the complimentary hotel notepad so that she had something to reference if she became tongue-tied.

After she switched off the hairdryer and was putting on a little makeup, she heard a loud knock. She raced to the hotel door, in only a towel, and peered through the peephole. James stood on the other side, sporting the same outfit and messy hair from their windy excursion.

Without hesitation, Evelyn fumbled to unhook the chain and open the door. James smiled a tired smile. A crumpled newspaper was tucked under his arm, and he held a tray covered by a white cloth napkin.

"I thought you might be hungry for something." He waved his hand over the tray like a magician performing a trick, and when he pulled off the napkin he revealed a platter full of coffee, milk, muffins, bananas, cereal, yogurt and juice.

"You came back!" Evelyn awkwardly manoeuvred herself around the tray to hug him. She held on longer than either of them expected.

"What's gotten into you?" James asked. "I never really left. I just parked the truck. You can invite me in so's I can put down this heavy load."

"You've been out here the whole time?" She opened the springy door wider and let him squeeze by her.

"Just long enough to read this entire newspaper." He gave her a kiss on the forehead as he walked in. "I could hear the shower, then the hum of the hairdryer, so I knew you weren't ignoring me. I was going to ask for a key, but I figured that might be a bit too brazen. They didn't have much to choose from down at the free continental breakfast buffet." He shrugged his shoulders. "I grabbed one of everything."

"It's perfect." Evelyn ushered him to the small table in the corner of the room. She excused herself to get dressed in the bathroom, and when she came out, they sat together in the same awkward silence. They ate breakfast and sipped warm coffee. She felt an overwhelming feeling to hug him, to curl up next to him, to just hold him in her arms.

"Well, what's the plan?" James looked hopeful as he dusted the crumbs on the table onto the floor.

Evelyn felt the same chokehold of muteness clutch her throat. She tried in vain to recall the mental list she had made in the shower. She looked at the blank notepad on the nightstand, realizing she didn't have a backup plan. Her thoughts seemed to be sucked into a vortex of disorder, and she couldn't hold onto one long enough before it shifted, making it impossible to speak. She closed her eyes.

"There's something I want to tell you." She looked away.

James put his coffee cup down and seemed to prepare himself for what she was going to say.

"I've had a little time to think, but I find it really hard to find the right words, as you may have noticed." Evelyn looked past him to the window and noticed a large murder of crows perched on the power lines.

"Go on," James said, a little shakily.

Evelyn hesitated. She kept the beady-eyed birds in sight.

"Just say it," James said.

"I'm trying, but it won't come out!"

The crows flew off in one large, black mass, as if they had heard her snap at James.

"Just relax then. I've got all the patience in the world." James picked up his coffee cup, trying to seem unfazed by the intense energy buzzing between them.

Evelyn sighed, took a deep breath and wrinkled her nose. "James," she said, exhaling slowly. She shook her head. She walked over to the window to catch a view of the receding crows.

"I feel the same way about you as you do about me." With her back to him, Evelyn cringed at her childish words. She heard James release his breath. He turned her around to face him.

"That's what you had to tell me?" He laughed. "Well, I've known that all along, but it sure feels good hearing you say it. I thought I might have scared you away last night, and you were going to tell me to get lost." He hugged her and nuzzled his face into her shoulder. "Is there anything else you wants to tell me?"

"I don't know." She shot James a sly look. "There is something I'd like to ask you, though." She gave him a sweet smile so he couldn't say no. "I'd like to surprise John and tell him I'm here for a few more days. But tell me if it's too much to ask you to bring me back to Ireland's Eye."

"I can leave right this minute, if you wants."

"Do you think I'm just as crazy as he is, for wanting to see if the pirates left Annabel alone?"

"Not at all. I've actually been dying to know if your idea worked too."

She also wanted to see John again. He was her anchor to Newfoundland. He offered her a place to belong, with the hope she could call the island home someday.

"What about your work?" she asked.

"I can switch my shifts at the bar with someone while you're here. I does it more to help pay off my student loan. Mind if I makes a call?"

"Go ahead." Evelyn motioned toward the phone. She took the opportunity to sneak into the bathroom to braid her hair. She gathered what she needed for the day and put the remaining breakfast in her purse to snack on during the drive. She reached for James's hand when he put down the receiver.

"Good to go," he said. He didn't let go of her hand until they reached his truck.

After they picked up James's boat, they drove nestled together, listening to the radio. Evelyn couldn't help but be distracted by the sound of the doll banging around in the bed of the truck, and by her thoughts as she contemplated her choices and repeated the pros and cons of going back to Calgary or staying in Newfoundland. She thought of her father and the reasons he had left the island. He was forced to migrate west for work when the fisheries dwindled, but he always told her it was his dream to return home someday. In the end, he did return home, just too late.

When she thought of going back to the city, she envisioned lines of city houses like headstones with garage doors that swallowed the cars whole. She considered the relationships she had built up to this point, which were, at best, kind of robotic. Love and kindness were tied like a superficial lasso around her heart. Her friends listened only to talk, gave only to receive, and used any means to climb the ladder of success—all reasons why she had yet to enter any kind of serious relationship. She was able to see through the men she did date: heartless skill drowned in ineptitudes of passion. She thought of the buildings, the concrete, the traffic, the coldness of strangers. She thought of all the nights she had fallen asleep to the sound of heavy traffic. It wasn't comparable to falling asleep to the lull of the ocean.

When she looked up at James as he drove, she knew he had nothing to offer her but himself, yet she felt like she'd follow him anywhere. He made trivial things marvellous. He challenged her goals, just as Newfoundland shifted her perspective. She saw everything from a different angle, in a new light, and it felt like her eyes were open for the first time in a long time. Things looked clearer, and she realized she'd been living on autopilot. The same urban routine, day in, day out, hadn't bothered her until Newfoundland's picturesque landscape took hold of her senses and attuned her to the finer details of life. This eastern province, imbued with unexpected turbulence, forced her to switch off autopilot and take charge of navigating her life. It set a fire in her heart that sparked a longing for a lifestyle of adventure, and a burning to explore a history so rich and unique.

Grey clouds gathered as they drove, and raindrops plinked on the windshield, like the staccato beat of a snare drum. The windshield wipers kept time with the haphazard thrumming of the rain, until the rhythmic screech of the synchronized blades lulled Evelyn to sleep. She woke when the truck suddenly shifted direction, as James stomped on the brake then put the truck in reverse.

"We're here," he said, smiling. He expertly backed the truck onto the launching ramp and, pulling on a baseball cap, jumped out to unhook the boat and push it in the water. He returned to the truck, soaked through, and leaned over the backseat to dig around for a toque, some trigger-finger mittens, and a raincoat. "You'll need these." He rubbed his hands together, trying to build enough friction to heat them up. Evelyn put on each item of clothing. "The wind's got a good bite," he said, pulling the toque down over her ears. "It's going to be a heck of a cold ride to the harbour. Should've brought a couple of wetsuits." He laughed. "Maybe a snorkel too."

Evelyn couldn't help but laugh.

The rain pelted their faces as they sped toward Ireland's Eye. The lashing wind threatened to take Evelyn's breath away, so she turned her head to tuck her mouth and nose inside her jacket, but she dared not close her eyes. White caps swelled all around the boat as the ocean heaved the bow, giving Evelyn a sensation of free falling when the boat hit hard on its descent back into the water. She tried to tell James to turn around, but her voice was lost in the roar of the wind, the rain and the motor.

When they finally pulled into the harbour and docked the boat, Evelyn looked up to the bedroom window and saw the closed curtain. Evelyn called John's name through the drizzling rain and then through his house, but he didn't answer back.

"Where do you suppose he went?" James asked.

"I'm not sure. Perhaps the plan didn't work, and he's back digging at Money Point."

They headed toward the woods, both soaked and shivering, the trees offering scant refuge from the rain. When they came upon the graveyard, it was nothing like it had been just the day before. The twisted vines had been cut and gathered, the bushes pruned. Evelyn stood beside the wooden cross inscribed with Annabel's name. One vine remained with the purpose of holding intertwined daisies and dandelions. She knelt in front of her mother's empty grave and gently touched the name. She could feel her knees sink into the cold, spongy wet ground.

"Looks like John's been busy," James said.

The crack of branches and a bear-like grumbling startled them. Out of the woods came the familiar sight of John, hunched over, moving fast, talking to himself, holding a small bouquet of wildflowers in his hand.

"Hiked all the way over to Black Duck Cove for nothing. I needs building supplies, but that harbour's been all scavenged too. Nothing left worth using. Hard to rebuild anything with rotted boards and bent rusty nails," John mumbled. He walked right past James and Evelyn.

"John?" Evelyn fumbled to stand.

He stopped short and looked at them with surprise. "What are you doing back here?" He bowed his head as he approached the graves.

"I'm here for a few more days until Helen arrives. We have to meet with lawyers about my father's will." John didn't react, and Evelyn felt a twinge of disappointment. "I'd like to take you into St. John's until I have to leave for Calgary. It's only for a few days, but it would be good for us to have some time together. We can get you fed and get you the supplies you need to rebuild."

John looked Evelyn in the eye. "I can't." He didn't move a muscle when the rain turned to a downpour.

"James and I will bring you back." She covered her brow with her hand to block the rain, raising her voice to be heard. "Come on, let's go to your house to wait until the rain stops." John stood planted in the ground. Evelyn grabbed his hand and tried to pull him toward the house. "You can't let this place remain your prison, John." As she wiped the rain off her face, she wished she could unshackle the chains wrapped around his heart to free him of his guilt.

"You don't understand." His clear eyes were full of torment.

"Did they come back for her?" Evelyn's heart raced.

"It worked," John whispered.

"It did?" Evelyn hugged John. She expected him to be happier in the midst of such a triumph. She stepped back when he didn't return her embrace.

"How do you know it worked?" James looked nervously over his shoulder into the woods behind them, then up to the house.

"They never came back for her," John said.

"I knows she's your wife and all, and she's the last person I should be afraid of, but where do you think she is now?" James inched closer to John and Evelyn.

"I sees her in the window, but when I goes up, she's gone." John let go of the limp wildflowers he held. They fell to the ground. His sullenness magnified his madness. "I'm afraid I'm going to lose her. Selfish of me to want her back so desperately that I sometimes thinks of digging that gold coin back up."

"Come with us," Evelyn asked gently. She sensed John's escalating heartache.

"Skipper," James said. "If Annabel is here, she'll still be here when you gets back."

"But what if she's not?" John scratched his thick-bearded chin. "This place is both heaven and hell, and this is all there is for me. I don't deserve to leave and go anywhere without her. I'll keep on taking my chances and wait here with her ghost, or whatever it is I'm left with, even if it is just her memory. She'd be all alone and lost without me if I went." He picked up the wilted and soggy flowers, walked over to her cross and tucked them into the vine. "I don't want to leave them either." He pointed to two nearby graves.

Evelyn read the inscriptions: Ned Lee, Beloved Husband and Father, 1909–1958. Marylou Lee, Beloved Wife and Mother, 1919–1939. She had only been twenty years old, Evelyn realized, and she died the same year John said he was born.

"My parents. Your grandparents." John cleared his throat. "I never knew my mudder."

"What happened to her?" Evelyn asked.

"She died in childbirth." John's lip quivered.

"I'm sorry," Evelyn said.

"You got nothing to be sorry about, m'love. Nothing you did."

"Sounds to me like you guys got something in common," James said.

"Losing her was hard on my father." John spoke without taking his eyes off Evelyn.

"Sounds like history repeating itself." James commented.

John looked peculiarly at James and then Evelyn before he turned his back and started walking to the church.

In that moment, Evelyn knew something had shifted in John's frozen heart. She waved for James to follow her, and they caught up to John, who was mumbling to himself.

"I wants to try to make right for all my wrongdoings, if that's even possible. Find a way to say I'm sorry for what I did to Annabel and for smashing these windows that used to shine so beautiful from inside the church. But I've still got a streak of anger that lives in me, and I can't make it go away."

Evelyn grabbed his shoulders and shook him out of his stubbornness.

John looked at her, then looked up, as if noticing the rain for the first time.

"Your nose and cheeks are red, Evelyn. Let's get inside and outta this storm."

The three of them hurried toward the house.

Evelyn and James were relieved to finally take shelter inside. They removed their soaking outer clothes and sat at the kitchen table while John quickly started a fire in the stove.

Evelyn moved closer to the fire, and closer to John. She mustered all her courage to open up her heart.

"John, I have something to say right now that is too important to leave unsaid." She wiped away loose strands of wet hair. "I believe some things in life are beyond our control. You didn't mean for Annabel to die—I know that, everyone knows that. You need to somehow learn to forgive yourself. Your anger is just a response to your hurt, John, and you need to give yourself a break so you can start to heal." Evelyn was surprised at her words. "To tell the truth, I've felt that same streak of anger ever since I was a little girl, believing that if it weren't for me, both my parents would be alive. I've held that guilt my entire life. It's only when I found out you were still alive that I could have a hope of forgiving myself. I think I'm a lot like you."

"It wasn't you that caused it." John stood and pounded the table. "It was the goddamn Confederation and the government forcing us to resettle. Taking away the essentials one by one, necessities that we couldn't survive without so we'd have to leave. We would all still be right here with all the people we loves. I am hurting, 'cause death can never be undone. The decision I made that evening had consequences that I can't wind back and change. There's no turning back. I'm mad at myself for what I took away from you. I can't give your mudder back to you. She would have made such a good one. It breaks my heart all over again when I looks at you. Whether I forgives myself or not, she'll never come back." He sat down heavily and released a pent-up cry.

Evelyn pulled her chair close to his and hugged him.

"I believe there is something waiting for us after we die, John, and I believe I will meet my mother when I go to heaven. Until then, I believe in angels that guide us. From the time I was told you were both dead, I imagined you as my guardian angels, looking out for me, and I'd talk to you every day. Whether it's coincidence or not, I think Annabel has been my guardian angel, and I'm pretty sure she's the one who brought me here to you. There's no other explanation. The things that had to transpire to get me here to you have convinced me that some sort of divine power is orchestrating this. It's nothing short of a miracle the way I met James, Sarah and Charlie, who led me to you. I know in my heart she would want us to be together, even if she can't be with us." Evelyn felt like a child as she tucked her head into John's neck and felt him stroke her hair. "You are my father, John, and I can't abandon you, and I won't let you abandon me. I'm hurting too. You hold all the secrets about my history that I want to know.

John sniffed back his tears. "Okay, but I'll need to make a quick stop if it's not too much trouble." He spoke with a sense of urgency. "I don't have a penny to my name, but I have a house in New Bonaventure. The house me and your mudder was going to raise you in. Let's go explore it. It's been locked up, so hopefully untouched."

"You mean you could have stayed there all this time?" Evelyn asked. "You had another choice?"

"To me, it was never a choice."

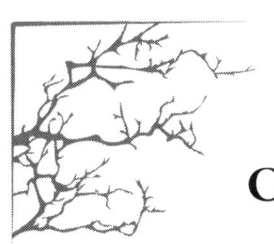

Chapter 23

WITH JAMES AND EVELYN'S help, John gathered all the trinkets that lined the kitchen countertops and all the belongings he didn't want to see stolen. Vandals hadn't come in a while, he told them, but he could never be too careful with the possessions that had taken him twenty years to collect. When everything was in the cellar, under the living room floor, John slid the rug over top the door. Evelyn thought it a pitiful sight to see how little John owned, with no material value in what he did possess.

The rain had subsided and the sun now peeked through some low clouds. Its rays, refracted by the raindrops, created a stunning rainbow over the two hills on either side of the harbour's entrance. When Evelyn looked a little closer, she could see another dim arc over top of the rainbow.

"Never seen anything like it," John said. He slipped his hands into his pockets and stood in awestruck wonder.

"Maybe there's a pot of gold at either side." James chuckled. "Maybe we was after the wrong ones for treasure. I heard those leprechauns are pretty rich." He let out a spirited laugh.

"But you can't ever get to the end of a rainbow," John said. "I've tried a few times. It's one of those things you can never reach, even though it's right in front of you." His eyes set out over the water.

Once on board the boat, making their way through the harbour, they neared the double rainbow, shining with radiance. Evelyn watched how it moved with them. She noticed the dimmer rainbow had a reverse colour scheme, like a mirror image of the primary rainbow that shone so much brighter. The sun's warmth radiated on her skin, until the clouds overhead shifted, blocking the sun's light, and a coolness swept over her. The rainbow disintegrated.

"The rainbow's like Mom," Evelyn said, blushing when she realized it was the first time she had referred to Annabel in that manner. "She's here with us, even though we can't see her, like an optical illusion—so close but so far."

"It's a little scary, if you thinks about it," James said. "To try to imagine what's on the other side of life."

"That don't scare me anymore." John kept his eyes on the rolling waves. "It's not the unknown that I fears anymore. It's what's real that scares me. I'm afraid of what I do know. I wants to believe she's here, but the truth is she's not. That's what terrifies me. She never will be." He looked a little farther out over the bay. "She comes to me in dreams, you know. But that's just what it is: a dream. Life is all about figments of the imagination. Things will happen if you believes it enough and thinks about it enough. You can bend your mind to see anything. Tricks is all it is, but sometimes I wonders 'cause she seems so real, even though I can't touch her. Too complicated to make any sense of it. I sounds crazy to myself talking like this."

"What I saw was no trick or stretch of my imagination," James stammered. "We all witnessed the same thing, so if you've gone mad, so have we."

"Exactly," Evelyn nodded.

In the distance, the call of crows grabbed John's attention.

"I saw a bunch of crows this morning, perched outside my hotel window," Evelyn said. "They scared me to death." She thought it seemed like they were waiting for her. It reminded her of the Alfred Hitchcock movie she had watched as a child, the one where all the birds attacked people. "I don't trust them." Evelyn looked for the source of their cries, scared the crows might fly out from the trees and attack them in the boat, knowing they had nowhere to go.

"They knows I'm a murderer. I murdered one of their own, and they never forgets a face. Somehow passes it down to the next generation and now they're plotting their revenge. Payback time."

"John, you're scaring me." Evelyn shrunk down as the caws grew louder around them. "Do you think they're following us?"

"Hard to say. They're smart and knows what I did. Even the young is supposed to recognize the faces of danger. They don't forget. Look, there they are."

"Come on, John." James scowled. "No need to scare us."

"Wait, now." John stood up, his strong legs keeping him upright even though the boat was moving fast. "You little rascal!" John shouted to the trees.

Evelyn watched the birds with suspicion. "James! Get us out of here!"

"Look at that." John grinned. "There's my old friend." He pointed up to a crow perched high on top of a pine. "I knows it's her 'cause she's as ragged and ugly as me." John extended his arm and whistled a sharp note. The bird returned his call and at once the entire murder left its perch.

Evelyn screamed as the crow descended from the circling swarm of black birds. It landed on John's arm. The other birds called out louder above them. Evelyn covered her head with her arms and tucked herself into a ball.

"What's wrong, Ev? Those birds aren't going to hurt you," James said in a tone that poked fun at her.

"I thought you must've died," John cooed to the bird. "She must have followed you two out yesterday and found her friends." John shooed the bird off his arm.

The crows didn't follow when they docked in New Bonaventure. John led Evelyn by the hand to the old house that stood just as crooked and weather-beaten as John's house in Ireland's Eye. She looked back to James, who followed close behind. Even in the middle of the day, the house looked haunted. Evelyn noticed the curtains of nearby houses drawn to the side, held back by the silhouettes of nosy neighbours. A few people on their front porches stopped what they were doing and watched with prying eyes. After twenty years with no sighting of him, John was rumoured to be dead. The animal-like man would surely stoke up great stories for those who witnessed his emergence from Ireland's Eye.

"This is where you'd have grown up," John said to Evelyn. He fumbled with the key and unlocked the door. The rusty knob was hard to turn, so John gave it a good squeeze and hip-checked the door to open it.

Inside, Evelyn saw wallpaper that had warped and loosened from the glue that once held it, pictures hanging askew, and a ceiling that was ready to collapse with a good gust of wind.

"If you wants to know more about Annabel, you'll find it upstairs in boxes." John's voice held a hint of pride and sadness. "I've only come back once to get winter supplies, but it was too painful sifting through all her stuff. I couldn't bring myself to do it again."

Evelyn led the way upstairs, stopping at the cardboard boxes piled high in the hallway. John lifted them down until there was a single layer of boxes laid out in a line before her. She opened the folded top of the nearest one and pulled out a heavy quilt. John watched her with a steady eye. Intricate scraps of fabric were meticulously stitched together. It looked like remnants of old clothing, patched together to make something useful. The materials didn't match, but in its entirety, the quilt was beautiful. "You could take this home with you, John. It would keep you warm." Evelyn draped it over his legs.

"Too many memories," he said. "I misses her too much. Some days it comes in waves until I feels like it's going to drown me."

Evelyn pulled out some of Annabel's clothes, and John turned away. She put a pretty cream shawl over her shoulders and buttoned up a leather-strap bracelet over her wrist.

"Look at this." Evelyn stuck out her wrist so James and John could see. "It's engraved with the initials A.T. and J. L."

John glanced at her. "I gave that to Annabel when we first started dating. She loved it."

"That's pretty amazing, Ev," James said.

"Anything you wants from here is all yours, Evelyn. Take it all if it's any use to you. It'll just sit here until I dies, and in that case, it'll be handed down to you anyway. So it's yours, either way."

Evelyn dug through each box.

"She's sure enjoying this," James said to John.

"As hard as it is, so am I."

Evelyn smiled and left the men to chit-chat while she explored every nook and cranny of the house, like a detective trying to uncover clues about the intimate details of her mother. Who she was, what she liked, how she did things. She went into a bedroom and opened the drawer of the night table. A pocket-sized leather book was inside with "Diary" inscribed on the front in faded gold stickers. A gold clasp held it closed, the type that needed a tiny key to open it.

"John! James! Come in here!"

Both men barged into the room.

"Did you know this was here?" Evelyn held up the book.

John squinted. "Oh my heavens. Now there's something you're gonna want to take with you. That thing would hold some lot of stories, let me tell you."

Evelyn passed him the book, and he broke the lock with a flick of his fingers. He flipped through the pages, and a tiny pressed flower fell to the floor. He picked it up and it crumbled to dust in his hands. "She loved to press wildflowers so she could smell them when the harbour was froze over." He put his nose into the crease and took a deep sniff. "Now that's Annabel."

Evelyn took the book and smelled the same page.

"Will you read a passage?" John asked. "I haven't read a word in twenty years, and I couldn't make out the letters anymore anyways."

Evelyn held the book like it was a fragile object worth a fortune. It was already a treasure, a gift her mother had unknowingly left for her. She couldn't help but sob when she saw the handwriting was the same as her own. "From the beginning?" she asked.

"That page you got opened is good."

John and James took a seat beside her on the bed.

"It's dated July 5, 1964." She traced the words with her fingers. "I swear, I could mistake this to be my diary." She could hardly believe that she was about to read the private words and thoughts of her mother.

> *Today was the first time me and Johnny ever got into a fight. He was mad as anything when I told him I wanted to move away. It's not that I don't love it here, it's just I wonders what it's like somewhere else. When I do think of all the people we love who had to leave, I feels just as mad as he does. I hates the government for forcing them all to leave, but now with nearly everyone gone, I feels left behind. I thinks they all must be so happy where they are. The situation here is pitiful, with everyone working their fingers right to the bone just to keep alive. I wonders what it's like to go places and see new things. I guess I'll wait and see. I hopes that he loves me as much as I loves him. I keep picturing my life with him, and it*

> *doesn't matter if I'm here or somewhere else. I just wants to be with him forever.*

Evelyn stopped reading. Her mother's writing packed an emotional punch for all in the room.

"I wasn't mad that she wanted to go," John whispered. "I just didn't want her to move without me. She would have written that just before I proposed to her that winter. I was afraid I'd end up losing her if we moved away."

Evelyn turned the page and continued.

> *Sometimes I can picture us leaving here, but I loves it here. I hopes we'll marry someday and have a family of our own. Lord knows, I can't wait to be called Mother.*

Tears overflowed from Evelyn's eyes. John sniffled, wiping his own tears away.

"I think we better get outta here," James said, looking up at the sagging ceiling when a strong gust of wind rattled the house. "A few stronger gales and I think the roof might collapse."

"Can we take this with us and read it on the way to St. John's?" she asked.

John nodded.

"Good, 'cause I'm starved," James said. "I could use a good feed right about now."

She offered the book to John, and he held it to his heart.

Evelyn sat between James and John on their way to St. John's. She couldn't resist the urge to read more from Annabel's diary. The three of them laughed over Annabel's recount of the time she shared a bite of her turkey sandwich with John, who was so hungry he took a big bite and crunched the tip of her finger.

"I remembers that like it was yesterday." John wiped his eyes again, but this time from laughing so hard. "That's enough now. I don't want to hear it all at once. Let's save some for later."

Evelyn dug through her pocket for a stick of gum, popped it in her mouth and tucked the gum wrapper in the book to mark her page. She slipped the book into her purse, though she longed to devour more of her mother's words. As soon as John closed his eyes, she pulled it out and continued reading. Annabel's fiery passion saturated each page describing a love so rare that Evelyn caught a glimmer of the man John used to be. She read as fast as she could, even knowing how the story would end. It was comforting to feel a connection to her mother, and Evelyn couldn't help but think that the diary was speaking to her. When James pulled into the parking lot of a gas station and chicken bar, Evelyn put the gum wrapped back in and closed the book, putting it back in her purse.

Evelyn gently nudged John till he stirred from his nap, then they all got out of the truck. Evelyn could tell from the stares of passersby that they saw John as an outsider, like someone who had come from the past and didn't belong in the modern world. Though physically fit, John walked with a hunched back, uncertain of his surroundings. He reminded her of a scraggy old moose with spindly legs, and a long dishevelled beard resembling a dewlap—a haggard solitary creature. Evelyn walked ahead of him and opened the gas station door. John looked around, mesmerized by the selection of snacks and toiletries. Evelyn tucked twenty dollars into his hand.

"I can't remember the last time I held a dollar bill in my hand, let alone a twenty-dollar bill," John said. "Not sure I ever have."

"Go on. Buy anything you like."

Like a child in a candy store, John bought a pack of cigarettes, a lighter, a box of chocolate-covered raisins, a can of birch beer and a pack of toilet paper. Evelyn smiled as he went to the check-out. He didn't wait for change or for his purchase to be bagged; he laid the twenty on the counter, wrapped his arms around the supplies, and headed straight to the truck. Evelyn collected the change without offering an explanation to the wide-eyed cashier.

She ran over to the chicken bar next door and ordered three individual portions of chicken and taters with sides of gravy and coleslaw. She grabbed three cans of pop from the cooler and paid for her order. Back in the truck, she watched John savour every morsel. He used his finger to wipe the gravy container clean, then licked up every last drop. After he ate, John remained quiet, looking out the window. The hum of the truck's engine and the rumble of the road made his head droop down until his chin touched his chest. Evelyn guided his head to her shoulder and let him sleep.

Teary eyed, Evelyn looked at James. "Thank you," she whispered.

James intertwined his fingers with hers.

She looked down at John and felt so sorry for him. He was so out of place in a civilized world. She was sorry for removing him from his comfort zone and wondered if the modernity would be too much for him.

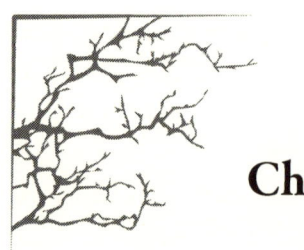

Chapter 24

EVELYN TOOK NOTE OF the ominous grey fog that crept over St. John's, such a stark contrast to James's colourful neighbourhood. Still, neither the weather nor the glum mood it cast over the city would damper John's homecoming. She couldn't wait to see Sarah and Charlie's reactions when they laid eyes on their long-lost friend. As James parked the truck in front of his parents' house, his mother was at the front door, her purse hanging from the crook of her elbow. She noticed them immediately, dropped the purse and ran over. She stopped in her tracks at the sight of John swinging his legs out of the truck.

"You looks like a lost boy, my son!" Sarah ran up to John and examined the sight of his raggedy hair and frayed clothes. "My good God, it's you. I can't believe you haven't withered away." Tears streaked down her face as she looked at James and Evelyn. "How in God's name did you get him to leave the harbour?"

"They're bringing me right back," John said in a monotone voice. "I needs some supplies to rebuild the church."

Evelyn noticed his eyes soften when they met Sarah's and held her gaze—a shared understanding that required no explanation, even twenty years on.

Sarah looked at him with concern then ran to the house and opened the front door. "Charlie! Charlie! You're never going to believe it! Hurry up, now! Come see this poor old bugger who finally came for a visit!"

Charlie came outside, eyes blinking, hair standing straight up on one side of his head. He looked like he'd just woken from a nap. "What's going on?" He gawked at John, and his eyes lit up. "Oh, John, me boy!" Charlie whooped and grabbed his friend in a bear hug. "Lord tunderin', my son, you're in rough shape." He placed his hands on John's shoulders to size him up.

"Come in, everyone!" Sarah said, picking up her purse. "I was going to the store for some stuff, but that can wait. We got lots of catching up to do."

Sarah and Evelyn got to work. Evelyn ran a hot bath, while Sarah laid out a pair of scissors, a razor, deodorant, towels and some of Charlie's clothes on the bathroom counter. John came in, hesitated, then sat down on a stool. Evelyn watched in awe as Sarah shaved years off his face with each snip of the scissors and stroke of the razor. As heaps of coarse hair fell to the floor, a handsome man with a chiselled face was revealed, though with cheeks sunken from malnourishment. The small bathroom was silent as Sarah finished the shave, only to have her hand slip and nick John's cheek.

"I'm so sorry!" She ripped off a small square of toilet paper.

"It didn't hurt, maid." John wiped the blood away with his forearm.

"No, you don't understand." She put the razor down. "For the last twenty years, I've wanted to tell you that I'm sorry and that I should have done more." Sarah reached out for Evelyn's and John's hands and clasped them together. "I knew all along that Thomas Slade took Evelyn."

Evelyn's heart lurched at the sound of her father's name.

"I was there when he took her from Lillian's arms," Sarah said. "She didn't want to give up the baby, but she was in shock when Annabel went missing."

John stared at Sarah in disbelief. "Took—"

"What are you talking about, Sarah?" Evelyn said. "I was adopted."

Sarah shook her head. "It was an adoption of sorts, I suppose, but not in the traditional or legal kind of way." She blotted her eyes with crumpled toilet paper. "In the beginning, John, I went along with not telling you because Bill and Lillian thought it best you didn't know. Thomas forgave your debt, forgave Bill and Lillian's too, in return for the baby. Lillian never could forgive herself for what she did that morning. But we told you Annabel had the baby, John. Right before we left."

"I thought it a trick to make me leave," John said to Evelyn, "but I only recalls it as a vague drunken memory."

"It was no trick, but I knows now I didn't try hard enough to convince you." Sarah nuzzled his head into her bosom. "We thought there'd be time for you to learn the truth once the grieving passed. But it never did."

John pounded his fist on the counter, and Sarah let him out of her embrace. His eyes were wild with a sudden fire that seared his soul. "Why the hell would they keep Evelyn from me? All these years!" His tone deepened when he spoke again. "All I did for them. I took care of Bill and Lillian; I took care of their daughter. I did it 'cause of the pride my father had for the island, but I did it for them too, for Annabel, for all of our futures. And they had the nerve to rip my future away from me? That should have been my decision to make, not theirs!"

"We all thought you'd leave the harbour after a while, and we decided we'd tell you all the details then." Sarah flashed an apologetic look at Evelyn.

"I should have believed you," John said with a faraway look in his eyes. A vein throbbed on the right side of his forehead and his face reddened. He slowly stood, and his eyes shifted from side to side, as though he were recounting a memory. He suddenly fell to his knees. "My sweet Lord, Jesus." As he fell forward, one hand propped him up off the floor as the other clutched his chest.

"What's gotten into you, John?" Sarah screeched. "My God, Evelyn, I think he's having a stroke!" She jumped forward and smoked her shin on the stool, toppling to the floor. "Charlie! Charlie! Get in here!"

Evelyn knelt on the other side of John and rested her head on his shoulder. "What's going on?"

John bowed his head and softly wept. "I knows now for sure what Annabel was trying to tell me before she drowned." He looked straight into Evelyn's eyes. "I can see your mudder's lips in my mind that night out on the water, the night she died. She was telling me about you. I thought she meant the baby still in her womb, but she meant you, Evelyn. That you were here. She said your name." John's chest heaved with a sudden sob.

The room spun around her. Her life as she knew it was a lie. She'd been ripped from a life she may have loved. No different from the stories Charlie shared about what Confederation had done to the outports. Evelyn couldn't believe it. Her adoption was actually a kidnapping. Her father had taken advantage of her grandparents, and John. She couldn't accept that her father was capable of such a travesty. Evelyn cried. Not for herself, but for the man who sat in front of her. She cried for the kind of love her parents had known and lost. For the love story that had lasted only a short time, and would take a lifetime to get over.

Once they all collected their composure, Evelyn embraced John. They held on to one another for a few minutes, like an act of forgiveness, until Sarah drained some water from the tub and then turned on the hot water until it was steaming, startling Evelyn and John from their reverie.

"Sorry," Sarah stammered. "It was getting cold."

"How's Bill and Lill doing?" John asked. "I'm still mad as hell at them, but after all these years, I'd sure love to see them before I leaves."

Sarah held out her hands to hold John's and shook her head. "They both died about ten years ago. Bill died first, and Lillian shortly after. Her heart was broken without her family. They were never the same afterward."

John looked as though he'd been hit hard in the stomach.

Sarah placed a small square of toilet paper on John's cut, which had started to bleed again. "Look at this man, Evelyn. He looks just as young as he ever was."

Evelyn watched her father's eyes scan his reflection in the mirror. She thought the skin on his cheeks and nose looked like the skin of a russet potato, while the newly exposed skin was fair and baby soft.

"What do you think, John?" Sarah asked.

"Well, I can't hardly see a thing, but it sure feels good." He smoothed his hands along his cheeks and chin.

Sarah rummaged through a bathroom drawer and pulled out a pair of glasses. "These are Charlie's spare set. Try them on. See if they works for you."

John put the glasses on in front of the mirror. "Sweet merciful . . . ." He leaned in close to the mirror. "I don't recognize myself." John turned to look at Evelyn, who stood beside him. "Well, look at that. You are every bit your mudder. I wasn't just imagining it." He stared at her like it was the first time he'd seen her.

"She sure is," Sarah said. "First time she came in the house, I fell right over. I thought she was Annabel's token come back again after all these years."

"Again?" Evelyn asked.

Sarah's eyes flicked over to John. "Yes," she said with hesitation. "She came to me the night she died, completely drenched."

"We saw her in the window," Evelyn said.

"Was the curtain drawn to the side?"

"Yes."

"I saw it too, the day after the storm. It's her, all right." Sarah sniffed into a crumpled wad of toilet paper. "Well, John, we got you looking the part. Let's get you smelling good too."

Sarah and Evelyn left so he could get in the still-warm bath.

JOHN WALKED INTO THE kitchen, hunched and awkward, Charlie's clothes hanging loosely on his frame, the glasses perched on the end of his nose. Evelyn, James and Charlie were seated at the table, Sarah was at the stove. Each turned in his direction. He didn't seem to know what to do next. His arms hung down in front of him, reminding Evelyn of a leafless tree in the fall. Barren and lifeless.

"Yes, b'y. You haven't changed a bit," Charlie said.

Evelyn patted the empty chair beside her, the one at the head of the table. John took a seat, spellbound by the beautiful but simple place settings and the mountain of food displayed before him. Sarah and Evelyn had been hard at work, preparing and cooking a feast for John. Sarah had to teach Evelyn along the way and Evelyn enjoyed the process, even with James snickering good-naturedly any time she made a mistake.

"Looks some good, Sarah." John licked his lips and propped up a fork and knife in each hand.

"Looks some good, Evelyn." James mimicked John and licked his lips.

They all laughed, which seemed to ease some of John's tension. He filled his plate with a dollop of potato salad, corn on the cob, and a homemade bun with a crust that glistened with melted butter. Evelyn could tell it was the small things, like salt and pepper, napkins and utensils, that were the greatest luxuries to him.

Sarah lifted a piece of battered codfish with a spatula from the frying pan and slid it onto John's plate. "Eat your heart out, my love."

He reared his head and looked at the fish as if it had been his heart battered, fried and served. "I haven't ate one of these sons of bitches since before that night." John laid down his fork and knife.

"Oh, John, I honestly never even thought," Sarah said. "Let me get you something else." She reached for his plate, but John was quick to hold it in place.

"It's not the fish, maid. Everything just reminds me that I have to live without her. Never knowing what could have been."

In the glow of the kitchen light, John confided all his trials over the years. He recounted all the times he came close to finding Annabel, his close encounters with death, the years he spent digging, and the perfect timing of Evelyn's visit to help rescue Annabel's soul from the clutches of the pirates.

"What happened after we left that night?" Evelyn asked, putting down her fork down and dabbing the corners of her mouth with a napkin.

"I can't tell you how hard it was waiting up to see if the pirates would come back after we buried the coin. I knew she was waiting too, 'cause the curtain was drawn. I expected them to come, so I sat on the bed and waited, and told her to stay in the room with me. Frightened to death, I was, to fall asleep in case they took her when I wasn't looking. But I played their game, and I didn't sleep a wink. The curtain was still drawn when the sun rose."

Evelyn put her hand on top of John's hand and squeezed. She looked to Charlie and Sarah, surprised to find not one hint of skepticism on their faces as they listened to John's tale.

"After so long, I fell asleep, but when I woke up, she was still there. The curtain only fell when I left the room. I think she followed me around like my own shadow."

"You want to know what I think?" Sarah asked. "I thinks this is all Annabel. An angel sent from heaven to make sure you two found each other. Nothing short of a miracle, if you asks me."

John cracked a wide smile. "That's what Evelyn said too."

"We've got to get you to the dentist, you poor soul," Sarah said at the sight of John's missing teeth.

John closed his lips. "I still got some good ones left."

"You poor bugger." Sarah laughed.

As the conversation changed to James's upbringing and other details of Charlie's and Sarah's lives, Evelyn tried to focus, but her attention was on John. He existed as two people: the person he was before Annabel died, and the person he was forced to become after her death. He was alive, but not living. Breathing, but dead inside.

Evelyn watched John carefully pick at the fish on his plate and put a small piece of it in his mouth. He reminded Evelyn of the way churchgoers ate the body of Christ, swallowing it whole without chewing first. He bowed his head as if praying a sinner's prayer. He didn't take another bite.

As the women cleared, washed and put away dishes, Charlie and John reminisced about their lives before the big move.

"I still remembers everything like it was yesterday," Charlie said.

Evelyn could barely understand their quick tongues as they spoke, heavy with Newfoundland dialect. It sounded to her like a foreign language. She loved to listen, though, and was amazed at how easily John and Charlie picked up from where they'd left off. They spoke to each other beyond words, with a look in their eyes and a tone to their voices. Their words and stories were full of inside jokes and secrets only they would understand. John became a new person as he warmed up to his environment. He seemed to feel like himself in the presence of old friends. Traces of the man he used to be surfaced like a ghost of his former self reincarnating, and Evelyn caught a glimpse of who John was through stories that lips couldn't move fast enough to share.

"Moving away brought no great opportunity." Charlie's voice faltered between resignation and anger when he spoke of resettlement. "Full of broken promises, they were. Makes my blood boil when I thinks about it. Even after one day, we knew we wouldn't be able to afford to survive—which wasn't much different from squaring up with the merchant each year, but there was no work. We moved out west for a couple of years, to get back on our feet, but soon realized we were better off back home, where there was family. The big city's not for someone who's been a fisherman his whole life. But, you know, no matter where I've lived, I still longs to be in Ireland's Eye."

"What's done is done, and what's happened can't be taken back," Sarah said. "There's no rewind button. Even if we could rewind, how do you know it wouldn't have been worse when we pressed play again?" Sarah put the kettle on the stove and took cherry cheesecake squares out of the fridge. She placed them on the table with a butter knife, a stack of plates and a pile of spoons. "Help yourselves, while I gets the tea ready."

Evelyn lifted a large slice of the dessert onto a plate and passed it to John. She sliced enough for everyone, then plated and served them around.

"Those sure were good days," John said.

"The joys sure matched all the torment, didn't they?" Charlie dug a spoon into the dessert Evelyn had laid in front of him.

"John, why don't you stay?" Sarah brought steaming mugs of water to the table and plopped a tea bag in each one. The clink of spoons was musical as everyone mixed in a little tin milk and sugar.

"Well, I can't imagine they're going to bring me back to the harbour tonight," John said.

"No, I mean, why don't you stay and live in town? You could stay here with us. We'd sure love your company."

Evelyn watched as Charlie perked up.

"That'd be good for Evelyn too," Charlie said. "Might help us convince her to stay if you were nearby."

"I don't feel Annabel here," John said. "The city suffocates my thoughts. Too many distractions to make me forget. I knows for a fact she doesn't want me forgetting her. She still comes in my dreams—well, more often than not nightmares—and I even dreams that I wakes up next to her. That dream is my favourite, and my worst. Sometimes weeks pass between the dreams, and the time sutures up my wounds, but

I think she enjoys picking at the scabs." He smirked. "I don't mind it, though, if it means I gets to see her, even briefly. I enjoyed the hot bath and the clean shave, but I don't need all this. I sure do miss home-cooked meals some lot, but I needs to get back to the salt water—where she is."

"Charlie!" Sarah almost spat out her tea. She ran to Evelyn and picked up her hand. "You told me James was up to something getting that ring sized! Look! Look! She said yes! I knew this day would come! I knew it!" She ran around the kitchen clapping her hands and slapping her thighs with excitement.

Evelyn looked at James and elbowed him. "Say something," she whispered in a sharp hiss.

"Why don't you?" James leaned into her and put his fist in front of his mouth to cover his sheepish grin. "You're the one who decided to wear the ring on your wedding finger."

Sarah was rummaging through her liquor cabinet. "We've wanted you as part of this family since you've been born. And now you're going to be!" She pulled out a bottle of screech rum. "I'm going to have myself a daughter-in-law! This calls for a good ol' celebration!"

Evelyn beseeched James with a distressed look on her face.

"I'm in love with you," he whispered. "And I'm not one to break my mudder's heart."

Evelyn blushed and looked to see John's reaction. She figured he'd tell her they were foolish, knowing each other for less than a week. She cleared her throat and was ready to speak, when John beat her to it.

"I told you, you can't escape what's meant to be," he said, rubbing his hands together. "I knew it all along. If your mudder was here, she'd be some happy, let me tell you."

Sarah poured the rum into little shot glasses and handed them around. "You're right about that. You know, it's not unheard of for the unrequited passion of youth to trickle down to the next generation. And if that's the case, you two are going to have some good marriage."

Charlie laughed. "You didn't waste any time, did you, James? Just like his old man, he is!" He let out hearty guffaws as he slapped his knee.

"Quiet, you." Sarah gave him a nudge and her best stink eye.

Evelyn laughed out loud at Charlie's candour.

"Should we play some of our ol' songs, John, me boy?" Charlie pulled out a fiddle and guitar. "What do you say to a good ol' kitchen party?"

John accepted the fiddle. It wasn't long before smoke rose, hovering like a cloud around the kitchen table as John and Charlie puffed pipes and cigarettes. They played fiddles, sang their favourite songs and stomped their feet while Sarah spun in circles and clapped her hands to the beat of the music. She pulled James up from his chair, and they danced until she had to catch her breath. James walked over to Evelyn and held out his hand. She shrunk a little at the invitation.

"I'm not a good dancer." Evelyn blushed when he didn't lower his hand.

"Neither am I. You've got no one to impress here, Ev. You already got us all falling for you." James grabbed her hands and twirled her off her chair as John and Charlie kept up their lively rhythm. James taught Evelyn how to dance a jig, never once letting go of her hand.

When the music stopped, Sarah let out a big yawn. "I hates for this night to end, but it's time for me to hit the hay. I'm not that old, but I'm not young like I used to be. Evelyn, you're more than welcome to stay here for the night, of course." She gave everyone a hug and made her way to the bedroom.

"James, will you bring me to the hotel?" Evelyn asked. "I can't stay." She'd been struck by a sudden urge to read her mother's diary. They said a quick goodnight to John and Charlie, once again deep in conversation about the government and the fishery. Evelyn and James slipped out the door.

"Why didn't you say something?" Evelyn squeezed James's hand.

"I guess I like the feeling of being engaged to you." He squeezed her hand back.

In her heart, she secretly liked the thought of being engaged to James, but she slipped the ring from her left hand to her right.

"What'd you do that for?" James asked.

"We have to tell them the truth."

"Not yet. Mudder's going to have my head when she finds out we gave her the wrong impression, and I'm not prepared for that. Just let her believe a little while longer, and I'll break it to her gently."

Evelyn rested her head on his shoulder as he drove to the hotel. The parking lot was full when they arrived, so James pulled up and parked alongside the front entrance. She felt him reach for her hand, watching as he switched the ring back to her left hand.

"Like I said, I likes the thought of being engaged to you." He pressed his lips to hers.

Evelyn could feel James's smile as he kissed her again.

"It's early still. Can I take you out?" He stroked her hair away from her face.

"It's not early; it's almost one in the morning!" Evelyn pointed to the clock on the dashboard. "I really want to read the rest of the diary." She pulled it from her purse.

James turned on the dome light. "I'd like to hear it too, if you don't mind."

"I don't have that much left to go. I've been reading it every chance I get. I want to read it all and then take my time and go through it again with John."

She opened the page with the gum wrapper between the two pages.

"This one's dated on my birthday." Evelyn looked at James. "This would have been the night she died, James." Evelyn hurried to read the passage.

I almost made Johnny stay.

James pulled Evelyn close to his side. "*Almost*," he repeated. "That has to be the saddest word in the entire world."

Evelyn continued to read.

A storm is on the way, and it's going to be a bad one. I never stopped Johnny because I knows we needs the money, but now I wish I had. Foolish to think we can start fresh with so much debt. But then I feels awful for not stopping him because I wanted him to be here for our baby girl's birth. He somehow knew it'd be a girl and told me we'd call her Evelyn. I love her so much.

Evelyn stopped and stared at the page. "That's how he knew my name." Her mouth hung open as she read on silently.

"Keep reading," James said.

I can't wait to share her with him. She's so perfect, and she has my eyes. Ruth thinks she's about eight pounds, give or take a few ounces. She's beautiful and came into this world without a peep. The storm's starting out there now, and it kills me to think of John and Charlie out there.

Evelyn stopped reading.

"What happened next?"

"That's it." Evelyn could see the haste in her mother's writing. There was one more word, but she couldn't make it out—must have been the moment Annabel decided to go after them. She wished the diary hadn't ended, wished her mother's story hadn't ended that night.

"I better go now," she said. Even with such a tragedy on their minds, Evelyn could sense that the chemistry between her and James would escalate the longer she stayed.

"You're right. You shouldn't invite me in either." James pushed his bottom lip out in a pout and gave her his sulkiest eyes.

"Why's that?" Evelyn played along.

"If I comes in, I may never want to leave," he said in a low voice and pulled her in close and kissed her.

"Good night, James." Evelyn stepped out of the truck. Her heart fluttered when she turned back and gave him a wistful look.

"All right! All right!" He put his hands up in the air. "I'm going, but call me before you goes to sleep." He slid over to the passenger side, reached for her hand and gave her another long kiss goodnight.

Chapter 25

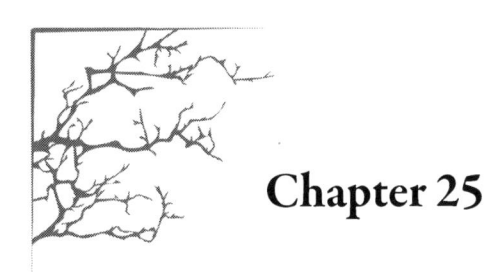

EVELYN WOKE UP AT SEVEN o'clock the next morning realizing she'd forgotten to call James before she drifted off. She picked up the phone, about to dial his number, when she heard a firm knock on the door. She ran across the room in her pajamas and flung open the door, expecting to see James with another tray of breakfast. To her surprise, Helen and Ethan stood in the doorway, looking windswept and tired.

Evelyn stepped forward and hugged tight to her sister. "What are you doing here?" She asked, letting go to give Ethan a hug. He was only a year younger than her, but nearly twice her size. "How were the football tryouts?"

He shrugged.

"I was talking to the lawyer after I talked to you yesterday," Helen said, "and he urged me to get here as soon as I could." She let out a huge yawn. "You better get ready. We've got our first meeting in an hour." She started walking away with her suitcase in tow.

"We're just down the hall," Ethan said, following his mom. "I'll come with you two later. Right now, I need a little shut-eye."

Evelyn remembered she was wearing her mother's ring. She took it off and put it in her purse.

THE MORNING WAS HECTIC, and Evelyn was feeling a little overwhelmed after the meetings with her father's lawyer, then with a real estate agent. Although Thomas Slade left everything to his daughters, he didn't have an actual lump sum of money in savings to divide between them. He did however own various properties all over St. John's, worth a fortune. Evelyn couldn't shake the discomfort that pressed in on her, intensifying her grief. Saddened by the news that this man had literally stolen her, she stubbornly didn't want anything from his will. At the same time, she missed her father fiercely and would exchange it all to have him back.

Evelyn's thoughts had been preoccupied with James during the meetings. He was all she could think about, and she wondered if he might have tried calling the hotel. In between appointments, she found a payphone but didn't have a quarter.

The realtor took Helen and Evelyn around to view the seven properties their father owned. They were to choose one each to keep their ties to Newfoundland, with the understanding they could sell the rest, which would be financially promising for both girls.

They drove up a narrow, steep road that crisscrossed up the slope of Signal Hill. Evelyn hoped they wouldn't approach an oncoming vehicle; the road wasn't wide enough to fit two cars side by side. Small, colourful wood houses, full of cultural personality, stood wedged together tight to the road, with no room for a grassy lawn, sidewalk or even a flower bed. The realtor called it the Battery, the city's own outport on the St. John's harbour. Backyards had stages and wharves situated between the rocks that jutted out from the base of the hill. Above the houses, the Cabot Tower overlooked the sheer rocky cliffs.

After a few hours, Evelyn and Helen were mentally exhausted as they faced the task of choosing a property to get the process moving. They returned to the hotel, where Helen immediately went to her room to shower. Ethan had left a note for them that he was at the hotel gym, so Evelyn went back to her room and called James.

"Ev, you're like trying to track a ghost through fog. I must've called that hotel a hundred times. I think the lady answering the phone thought I was crazy, or stalking you, even after I told her I was just worried about you. I even got them to check the room. When they said your things were still there, I thought you might have been kidnapped or run away or something. I was just about to call the police."

"I'm sorry, James. I had some errands to run. Would you like to meet for lunch?" She twirled her finger through the coiled telephone cord.

"Sure," James answered with enthusiasm. "Where do you want to go?"

"You name the place."

"What do you say we goes to a fish-and-chips restaurant on Freshwater Road for a good feed?"

"Sounds great. Can we meet in an hour, around one o'clock?" Evelyn thought of her sister and hoped she wouldn't be too tired. "Can you bring John with you?" She decided it best she didn't mention anything about Helen or Ethan; she feared John would be too stubborn to go.

"Yes. In fact, he's ready to go back to Ireland's Eye. He's got all the stuff Mudder gave him all packed in the truck. What do you say we leaves for Ireland's Eye right after we eats so we can make it back before dark?"

"That sounds great too. See you soon, James."

"And you knows my parents are going to want to come too!" James yelled before she hung up the phone.

Evelyn could tell James was repeating the words Sarah was telling him to say. "Yes, I want to see them too." She waited to hear the phone click before she hung up.

Evelyn went to Helen's room to wake her and met Ethan in the hallway, walking back to the hotel room from the gym. They found Helen dozing and gently roused her. Evelyn told them they were going to meet John for lunch.

"And we're also meeting a new friend of mine, James. Helen, you might know his parents, Charlie and Sarah Hodder?"

"Great," Ethan said. "Who's John?"

Helen dodged his question and went into the bathroom. She came out a couple minutes later, a little pale but prepared to face her past.

"John is a man I fell in love with a long time ago," Helen said to Ethan.

Ethan sunk into the nearest chair and didn't say a word.

"But my relationship with John was nothing more than a stupid girl thinking she could replace Annabel. When I brought Bill and Lillian out to see him for the last time, he looked straight through me as he spoke of Annabel. I was naïve enough to believe he could love me the same way. I know better now." She sat next to Evelyn and hugged her. "He also happens to be Evelyn's biological father."

"Did you know back then he was my father?" Evelyn asked.

"I didn't." Helen stretched to hold Evelyn.

Evelyn reciprocated her sister's embrace and noticed Ethan sitting across the room, eyeing his mother with suspicion.

"I'd like for John and I to reconcile our differences." Helen hurried to finish getting ready while Ethan showered.

Evelyn called a cab, and they made their way down to the lobby. Evelyn's eyes were on her sister through the entire cab ride. Helen looked out the window and stroked her hair, as if reciting in her mind what she would say and do when she saw John. When they walked into the restaurant together, Evelyn, in the lead, made eye contact with John, already seated with Charlie, Sarah and James.

Helen squeezed Evelyn's hand from behind. John was wearing Charlie's glasses, and Evelyn knew he could clearly see Helen, and she knew he recognized her. He lowered his head. It looked as though he expected Helen to seek revenge and spew her pent-up anger, like venom.

Helen let go of Evelyn's hand and rushed to John's side. "I honestly forgave you that morning," Helen whispered and crouched down beside him.

John tried to stand up but lost his footing and fell back into his chair. A quiet exchange of confused glances passed between Charlie, Sarah and James. Helen laid her hand on John's crossed arms.

"Don't leave, John, please. Hear me out." Helen stood up. "What I did was wrong. I knew you thought I was Annabel that night. You were drunk on moonshine, and I heard you call out her name. I knew you'd lash out when you found out it was me, that you'd want me to leave. I was terrified to face the cold, dark ocean that night, so I let you believe I was her until morning. I wanted to take the risk, in case there was some chance you could love me like you loved her."

"I'll never love no one like I loved her," John whispered.

Helen's cheeks reddened when she looked around the table and recognized Sarah and Charlie. She looked back to John. "I'm so sorry, John. I hope you can forgive me for that night."

John remained momentarily speechless. Uncrossing his arms, he propped his elbows on the table and held his head in his hands. "I've thought of you many times over the years." He lifted his chin and looked her in the eye. "I'm sorry too."

John accepted Helen's quick embrace. The reconciliation instantly cleared the air of the heightened emotion.

"Now who's this fine-looking gentleman?" Sarah asked.

"This is my nephew, Ethan. Though he's more like my brother," Evelyn said, as she introduced him around.

Ethan shook hands with the group. When he got to John, Helen broke down in tears, returning to her crouched position beside John. She tried to speak, but she made no sound. She shook her head and closed her eyes. "That night we spent together . . . that night left me with more than just heartache, John. I never knew how to tell anyone; in fact, I haven't told anyone. But this is my son, Ethan, and he's your son too." Helen dropped her head as if bracing herself to face John's wrath once again.

Evelyn's jaw dropped. Her face turned hot as the revelation sank in. She immediately turned to gauge Ethan's reaction. He stood motionless, staring at his mother, as if any movement would detonate an explosion of truth he wasn't prepared to face. No one said a word, though it looked as if Sarah was experiencing physical pain trying to contain her desire to say something. John took off his glasses, laid them on the table and began massaging his forehead. Before too long, he put his glasses back on and stood up.

"Well, for the love of God. Sure he's the spittin' image of me." John shook Ethan's hand again, this time hugging him with his other arm. "Well, sir, we got a lot of catching up to do now, don't we?" His eyes smiled, and he shrugged his shoulders. "This is some shock, let me tell you."

Ethan didn't respond. He glared at his mother without blinking. "You told me you didn't know where my father was."

"I didn't." She took a seat, then pulled him down to take the seat next to her. "You need to believe me. When Evelyn told me she met up with John, I knew I had to try to connect you. I thought if I told you, you might not come back to Newfoundland."

Ethan started to relax. "You're right. I probably wouldn't have."

Evelyn looked down on her sister with a blazing rage. "You're telling me that for my whole life you kept John and Ethan a secret from me? I've had a father and a brother, and you haven't so much as hinted that I have blood relatives?"

"I feared what our father would say, had he known. You have to believe that no one knew this. I'm so sorry."

"What did you tell our parents then? That you conceived immaculately?" Evelyn fumed.

"No. They didn't want to know, so I never had to tell them."

Evelyn knew there was truth in Helen's words, and she saw the pain in her sister's eyes. She knelt down and hugged her. "Well, if there are any other secrets, you better spill them now."

"I think that's it." Helen hugged Evelyn back, motioning for Ethan to join in.

"Didn't expect that when we walked in here," Charlie said. He gave a nervous chuckle and buried his head in the menu when the waitress came to take their orders.

Evelyn took a seat between John and James.

James cleared his throat. "Now that everything's out on the table, what have you fine ladies been up to this morning?" He squeezed Evelyn's thigh under the table, and she blushed.

"Well, according to the lawyer, it turns out our father owned a lot of properties here," Helen said. "Once they go on the market and sell, Evelyn and I will inherit the profit. And the properties he owned are worth a pretty penny." She couldn't contain her smile.

"Are you going to stay here, then, Helen?" Sarah asked.

"I'd like to move back someday. It's not the same in Calgary without Dad." Helen looked at Ethan. "But it depends on you, because if you want to stay in Calgary, I won't leave you."

"I'd consider it." He tilted his head into a shrugged shoulder, and smiled at John. "This place has a certain appeal."

John returned the smile. "A daughter and a son. B'ys, I tell you, this is unbelievable." He lightly rapped his fingers on the table, joy radiating from his face.

Evelyn had already thought long and hard about moving to Newfoundland, and at that moment, she decided to follow her heart. "I think I could live here too." She beamed at James.

Sarah smiled a huge smile. "That's great news! I knows a man who'd follow you wherever you go, so I'm happy you're both staying."

John looked at Evelyn. "Slade might have taken you away from me," he said, trying to sound stern but unable to restrain his giddiness, "but it seems now he's given you back. All them years of backbreaking labour and getting ripped off was like an investment, 'cause now it all goes to you."

"Where's your ring?" Sarah asked.

Evelyn glanced at her hand and shot a panicked look at James, who was also staring at her ringless finger. Before she could say a word, a couple of waitresses came with trays full of piping-hot plates of food. Evelyn dug in, blowing on a fork-full to cool down a bite of crispy deep-fried cod smothered in creamy tartar sauce. She hoped the food would deflect Sarah's further inquiry and Helen's questioning eyes.

Once the meal was devoured and Helen graciously insisted on paying the bill, they gathered in the parking lot. Sarah and Charlie offered Helen and Ethan a ride back to the hotel so James and Evelyn could take John to Ireland's Eye.

"What's all that, James?" Evelyn asked. Piles of boxes and stuffed black garbage bags were strapped down in his truck.

"That's all the stuff Mudder thought John might need in the harbour. At least a year's worth of toothbrushes and toothpaste, deodorant, razors, towels, bed sheets, blankets and pillows, a radio, a generator, propane tanks, a lifetime supply of canned food, and I think if you looks hard enough, you might find a kitchen sink—everything she could possibly think he'd need to keep comfortable."

"I don't need any of it, Sarah," John said.

"Well, I wants you to have it, especially if you wants me to ever come visit you," Sarah said. "Oh, I almost forgot. Charlie, grab me the tea bags I forgot to pack. They're in the front seat. Oh, and the bag that's in there too."

"Anything else, me love?"

It amused Evelyn that Charlie was always at Sarah's beck and call. He was never hesitant or annoyed with her small requests, and he seemed to expect nothing in return. Their marriage appeared very symbiotic; Evelyn couldn't imagine one without the other.

"Won't we sink with all that in the boat?" Evelyn looked worried.

"You'd think." James laughed. "We'll just throw the old man overboard and let him swim home if we goes to capsize."

"John, I wish we could have brought all this to you sooner," Sarah said. "We got so caught up in our daily lives. Always too busy or too poor to get back out to Ireland's Eye. Believe it or not, we're just getting back on our feet now. It's taken us twenty years to finally balance our books." John took off the glasses and tried to return them to Sarah. She stepped away.

"Oh no. You take those till you comes in again and sees the eye doctor."

John put them on and looked beyond the parking lot, taking in the details of St. John's exquisite architecture and colours.

When Charlie came back from fetching the items in the car, Sarah handed John the bag that contained a present wrapped in polka-dot paper.

"I dug through all our knickknack drawers in the house and gathered every single photo I could find of her last night." Sarah began to cry. "She was my best friend, and I misses her so much."

Evelyn watched John unwrap a photo album. His lips parted ever so slightly as he sifted through the pages, quickly at first, and then again with eyes that soaked up every memory in each photograph.

"Makes me cry, looking at you looking at her." Sarah tried to fan away her tears with her hand.

Charlie pinched Sarah's side. "How come you don't look at me like that anymore?"

"Go on, you old fool." Sarah slapped him away as she wiped the tears from her cheeks. "I hope it's all right, John, to see so many pictures of her at once. We sure had some good times together." Sarah peeked over to look at the page he stared at. "Remember this one? We were so young, weren't we? Remember when the black flies was so thick, we pretended we were frogs so they wouldn't bother us so much?"

John closed the book, and gave it to Evelyn.

"Take a look at these," he said. "You are the spittin' image of your mudder. I've no doubt about it now. My memory's all freshened up, just like these glasses freshened up my eyesight." He walked over to his friends and hugged them. "Thank you, Sarah and Charlie." John stepped back to look at them, with admiration and appreciation. "Now I best be getting back."

He stopped when he stood in front of Helen and gave her a nod. "Good to see you after all this time, Helen."

They faced each other awkwardly until Helen reached out and hugged his rigid body. She lingered in front of John as though she had something more to say. "Take care of yourself, John. I'm sure we'll see each other a little more often once we all move back home."

John nodded and patted Ethan on the back. "I hope to see lots of you, my son."

JOHN WAS SILENT THROUGH the entire drive to New Bonaventure. He didn't take his eyes off the photo album. Evelyn sensed his memory was reeling as it played a silent movie on the projector screen of his mind. She stared at the handsome man who had been hidden under twenty years of solitude.

Once docked at the wharf they reloaded the supplies from the truck to the boat, surprised it all fit, then set off for Ireland's Eye. As they approached the harbour, Evelyn noticed the curtain in the upstairs bedroom of John's house was drawn to the side.

"She's still here." A boyish grin spread across John's face. The lines around his eyes curved upward.

After they docked and carried the supplies into the house, Evelyn went back outside and took in a panoramic view of the harbour. For the first time, she saw past the desolation and felt what John felt: Annabel's presence. John and James stood on either side of her, overlooking the harbour.

"It's breathtaking," Evelyn said.

"We don't have any supplies to rebuild," John said.

"Don't worry, old man," James said. "I brought a measuring tape and some paper and a pencil to figure out exactly what you needs."

"I can't afford to buy anything, and I don't expect you to buy it."

"John, I have an idea," Evelyn said, before James could answer. "Would it be okay if I built a cabin on Ireland's Eye? I want to build a connection with you and to this place, and I'd like to start by planting some of my own roots here. We could fix up your house too so we can come visit you over the winter and spend Christmas together."

"That would be good," John said. "That would be real good for you to build a cabin and to have you here sometimes. Now, could I ask you a favour, Evelyn?"

"Sure."

"Could you call me Fadder?" John crooked his neck to look down at her.

Evelyn tucked a piece of hair behind her ear. An image of her father flashed in her mind. Her heart ached for the man who had taught her so much about life and who had protected her from the world. She wondered if it would be a betrayal to call another man her father. The desperate look in John's eyes told her it would be all right.

"Of course, I can." She almost leapt into his arms when she turned to hug him. "I love you . . . , Fadder." She knew the word sounded as awkward as she felt saying it. "How about I call you Dad?

"Good enough." He held her for the longest time.

"Oh, you two are too much," James said, wrapping his arms around the two of them. "Speaking of favours, I have one too."

"What is it? I don't have much to offer, b'y." John pulled his empty, hole-ridden pockets inside out.

The three of them laughed.

"I realize I never asked for your blessing to marry your daughter."

Evelyn's sense of humour came to a sudden halt as she feverishly tried to make eye contact with James.

"I gave you my blessing, the first time you left." John gave James a wink.

"Thanks, Skipper. Just making sure." James shrugged his shoulders and smiled at Evelyn.

"Well, if you two don't mind, I'm going to head in the house for a quick nap. I didn't sleep much last night. Come get me before you goes." John leaned over and kissed Evelyn on the forehead.

"What was that about?" she asked, chiding James as John walked away.

"What?" James feigned innocence.

"Asking John for his blessing."

"Don't you mean *Fadder*?" James poked her in the side.

"Answer my question." Evelyn tried to keep a straight face. "Why did you do that? Now it's going to be harder on me to break the news that we're not really engaged."

"What do you want to do for the rest of this afternoon?" James tried to deflect, interlacing his fingers with hers.

"You can't answer my question with a question." Evelyn could feel a strain on her heart as her blood pressure rose.

"How about tomorrow then?"

"Stop avoiding my question."

He raised his eyebrows and wrinkled his forehead. "How about the next hundred years?"

Evelyn gave him an inquisitive look. Something about his words made her heart race faster.

"I wants an answer for that one."

Evelyn shrugged her shoulders. "I guess we'll just do this: live day to day. We're not promised tomorrow or the day after that, let alone the next hundred years."

James knelt down on one knee in front of her. "None of us is promised any of those things, but just for a while, let's live like we are promised it. Marry me, Ev." James pulled a new diamond ring from his front shirt pocket. "I wants to show you I can cook more than just burnt toast."

"You can't be serious!" Evelyn's eyes shot up to the house to see if John was watching. He wasn't, but she noticed the curtain of Annabel's room was still drawn to the side.

"I am serious. I love you."

"But we barely know each other." Evelyn's rational mind overpowered her heart, making her doubt everything she had previously decided on. For a moment, she thought she was crazy for letting herself fall in love so fast, never mind deciding to move to Newfoundland.

"One look at you, m'lovey, and my heart stood still. It don't matter how long we've known each other 'cause I feels like I've known you my entire life. That's how I knows you've got to be the one. I can't explain it; I just knows it." His eyes bespoke the truth of his words. "You can still wear your mudder's ring, but I wanted to give you one with no superstition attached to it."

Evelyn opened her heart and let it decide for itself. She knew she was ready to take a chance.

"What would you think about getting married in Ireland's Eye so my father can walk me down the aisle? Maybe I could add it to my mother's diary?"

James picked her up and kissed her. "So that's a yes?"

So many thoughts plowed through Evelyn's mind, but she quieted them with a deep breath, letting her heart answer. "Yes, James."

"You'll have so many stories to add to that diary, Ev. I just knows it. I'd still love you if you would've said no. But I loves you even more now."

James swooped her off her feet and spun Evelyn around. The curtain in the window fell closed.

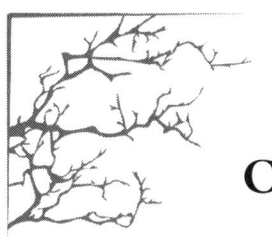

Chapter 26

June 1991

JUST BEFORE THE BREAK of dawn, John navigated his way down from his house to the shoreline of the harbour of Ireland's Eye. Summer had arrived, meaning he had survived another winter in the near-forgotten ghost town. He followed a path dimly illuminated by the semidarkness of first light, attuned to the sound of the surf in harmony with the brisk wind that shook the quivering trees. He patted the front pocket of his plaid coat and poked his fingers in to reach a cigarette and match. He flung the match against his trousers and turned against the wind to protect the dancing flame. Satisfaction rushed through his body with his first puff, calming his jittery nerves.

The search for Annabel no longer pirated his time. John had given up teasing death the way he used to tease the ocean waves as a child—as the ocean tide would recede, he'd get as close as he could to the retracted wave, then run as fast as he could back to shore when the tide let go and chased him like a bad dream. It was a dangerous game that made the ocean angry; it hungered to lick his feet, catch his leg, numb his senses, and swallow him whole. To find and bury Annabel's body was no longer feasible after twenty-five years. He drew a boundary between his mind and his heart to prevent himself from going insane. He surrendered himself to the joys and the pains of her memory, but he didn't think about it too much anymore.

He bowed his head as he walked past the rebuilt church. Though just a mini version of the building it once was, John was proud of his accomplishment; he had worked hard to piece it back together. With each board and nail, John had found redemption. He had taken responsibility for his destructive actions and, as a self-given penance, was determined to make things right. He often spoke to Annabel while he framed, assembled and repaired the pews. His desire to rebuild the church was also driven by Evelyn's wish to get married in Ireland's Eye. He couldn't believe five years had already passed since that blessed summer day.

Across the path, next to John's house, sat James and Evelyn's cabin. It didn't stick out or seem out of place, as he'd expected a contemporary building would. It was a humble, cozy summer home that looked like a descendant of John's old weather-beaten house. James and Evelyn made sure the cabin was built where no house previously stood, to ensure that it didn't stand on the ashes of resettlement, respecting the outport's deeply rooted legacy. It was the opposite of bittersweet, as it breathed new life to the island. In John's eyes, Evelyn had returned home. Sarah and Charlie also built a cabin beside the foundation where Charlie's parents' house once stood. Together they spent the summer months like the old days, fishing and berry picking, playing music and sharing delicious meals. John loved watching James and Evelyn's children, his grandchildren, four-year-old twins, Alex and Anna, play and grow.

John took one last long pull of the cigarette until the butt flamed red. He tossed it as he sat at the water's edge, and it sizzled in the salt water. He sat in the silence of the morning with a pensive look on his face. The sun crested above the horizon, its light reflecting on the rippling waves until it blazed a line of fire straight out to where he sat.

"It's been a while since I've come out to talk to you. A lot of time has kept us apart, but I feels nothing has or can change between us. I still feels you, Annabel." John closed his eyes as he spoke. "I knows now for sure why you wanted me to stay. It was you." His chin trembled when he tried to speak again.

The sun shone brilliantly, warming his body despite the shivering wind. He watched the seagulls overhead, thick as flies, admiring their ability to defy gravity. Whether Annabel was weightless in the Atlantic or ethereal as an angel in heaven, she had escaped the clutches of gravity that kept him here and pulled him down. Still, he had risen above his circumstances and kept at bay the madness that once clouded his eyes. In his transcendence, a renewed sense of vigor and purpose coursed through his veins, and his heart swelled in anticipation of the imminent arrival of his children and grandchildren.

"I never expected it, Annabel. Never." John paused, a thickness in his throat. "Not in my lifetime could I ever love another soul the way I loved you." He shook his head. He placed his palm over his lips to hold back a cry. "That moment I met Evelyn though, I felt it. I felt that same love. When I look at her, I see you in every ounce of everything she is. It shifted something in me, shifted the pain around and made a little room for something I haven't felt in a long, long time. A newfound love that gave this stubborn and heavy heart a reason to keep on pumping without you. And I hope to God you understands." He turned to peek up at Annabel's window and saw the curtain was still closed.

"I needs her to survive this life without you."

John dug for another cigarette and lit it, his hand trembling as he took a long drag. "Meeting Helen and seeing how important she is to Evelyn and finding out she was the mudder to my son...." He folded his hands between his knees as if in prayer, a private confession of the most intimate of sins. "I'll stay here forever with you, but I don't want you to go. Show me some sign you're here. I miss you so much."

He stopped and looked through the dense tree line and around the perimeter of the harbour. He looked for a stream of bubbles and listened for her soft voice on the breeze, but there was nothing. Just when he'd given up, the door of Bill's old fishing stage creaked. John ran to the wharf and approached the rickety building with caution. It was about to collapse at any moment, so he held his breath and gently pushed the door open. He let out a frightened gasp. From the light that trickled through the holes in the roof stood a figure he'd always recognize.

"Annabel."

She turned around, and John couldn't move or speak; he just stared. She was the same, but different. Older, but with the same fiery look in her eye. John could sense that she wanted to speak, but just like the night he lost her, her lips moved but made no sound. He didn't dare close his eyes, until the sting forced him to blink. In that split second, the room was empty. He clutched his chest as it heaved with longing and grief. Before he stepped out of the stage, he looked back, praying to see her again, but she wasn't there. He turned away, shoulders hunched, his hand on his chest.

He went back into the house for some breakfast, and when he burned a slice of toast, he opened the kitchen window that faced the harbour to let the smoke blow out. He delighted in the simplicity of tea and toast with a little partridgeberry jam. When the anticipated voices of his grandchildren rang out over the harbour, just the way the church bells used to, joy filled John's heart. They were a new generation that brought youth and life to Ireland's Eye. His children and grandchildren wholeheartedly embraced the culture of outport living and, in the process, without even realizing it, preserved its heritage.

John ran to the wharf and watched the boatful of family pull up. Warmth radiated through him at the sight of Evelyn, Ethan, James, Anna, Alex, Sarah and Charlie climbing out of the boat. Anna and Alex ran with bouncing blonde curls all the way to John, who was bent down with outstretched arms.

Wrapped in a blanket in Anna's arms was the doll. She offered it to John and he looked it over with astonishment. It had beautiful glass brown eyes with long eyelashes that fluttered open and closed as he moved it. A long brown braid came from a bonnet, and it was clothed in a matching dress. He hugged them tight before they scampered off to the hills to explore the nooks and crannies of the harbour. Helen was the last to exit the boat, and she flashed John a pensive look. A dog with a short blonde coat jumped out.

"What's this?" John said, accepting its slobbery kisses.

"Happy birthday, Dad." Evelyn hugged him and handed him a box with a ribbon tied around it. She took the doll from his hands. "Anna named the doll after Mom."

John smiled as he unwrapped the ribbon and opened the box. Inside was a red collar and a red leash.

"You probably won't be using a leash too much." James laughed. "More a symbolic gesture, according to Evelyn." He poked his wife in the side with his finger as he laughed again.

Ethan picked up the dog. "We called her Comet." The dog wriggled from his grasp and took off after the children, barking loudly, tail wagging. "Happy birthday, old man."

"Well ain't that great," John said. "I always wanted a dog, and a daughter, son, grandchildren and old friends." He counted his blessings, with a look at each of them as he spoke.

"There's one more thing." Sarah handed him a plastic grocery bag.

John looked inside and saw a tub of tobacco, a package of empty cigarette tubes, and a rolling machine. "I haven't seen one of these since my fadder rolled his own." An image of his childhood popped into his mind: a pyramid of rolled cigarettes at the kitchen table. John beamed. "I could use one of these, for sure."

"It's a gift from all of us." Evelyn hugged him again.

Charlie put his arm around John's shoulders. "Some good to see you, b'y!" He gave John a noogie on the head. "Just like it used to be."

SALTWATER JOYS

Staying on the island mustered a sense of contentment deep within John's soul. He was surrounded by an easy, peaceful quietude. As the family made their way up to the house, John's mind wandered to the solitary hurdles he had overcome to arrive at this moment. He realized Ireland's Eye was never an exile but an unwavering fight to persevere against the forces that sought to uproot him from a life he loved. The harbour looked like it used to, even with fewer houses standing. It was no longer a haunting reminder of what was lost in the tragedy of Confederation, and it no longer existed in the space between the death of a culture and a future of despair. The eeriness of the ghost town was replaced by the spirit of the island's living history. Each object in the harbour was imbued with the energy of those who came before. John continued to feel his mother and father's presence in the fallen relics of the past, as he sensed Annabel's presence in the objects and places special to her around the harbour, triggering memories, ones he loved to replay. The memories no longer hijacked his mind. He knew he'd always live with a heavy heart, but it was no longer anchored to guilt. He looked forward to keeping Annabel alive as he passed stories of her to their grandchildren.

As he watched his family enter his home, he was proud he had persisted. Now he had something to hand down to his son, daughter and grandchildren. After all the struggle and heartache, he felt like he had arrived in the future, where a new chapter of his life continued from the past—a newfound history that didn't replace the old way of life but grew alongside it. He was glad he had taken his chances, with those saltwater joys.

Don't miss out!

Click the button below and you can sign up to receive emails whenever Dianna Brown publishes a new book. There's no charge and no obligation.

https://books2read.com/r/B-A-MQWF-BJRS

BOOKS 2 READ

Connecting independent readers to independent writers.

About the Author

Dianna has a Bachelor of Arts degree in English from the University of Calgary and is currently a student at St. Mary's University, Calgary, to complete her Bachelor of Education degree in the spring of 2019. She has taken Advanced Fiction Writing courses through the University of Athabasca. She was born in Gander and raised in Kelligrews, Newfoundland. She currently resides in Calgary with her husband and two sons. She is currently writing the sequel to Saltwater Joys, as well as another literary fiction novel situated in the farthest remote community of the Canadian Artic. She is also working on a non-fiction book with her sister to help families who have a child with cancer, in hopes of sharing their family's experience to inspire and help others.

Read more at https://dianna-brown.wixsite.com/author.

Manufactured by Amazon.ca
Bolton, ON